PROJECT BARRIER

PROJECT BARRIER

Daniel F. Galouye

an imprint of

ARC
MANOR
Rockville, Maryland

ISBN 978-1-61242-252-7

www.PhoenixPick.com
Great Science Fiction & Fantasy
Free Ebook Every Month

Published by Phoenix Pick
an imprint of Arc Manor
P. O. Box 10339
Rockville, MD 20849 0339
www.ArcManor.com

CONTENTS

SHUFFLE BOARD

The frenzied bustle of Sector Headquarters hit Coordinator Vance McCune like a stifling blast as he stepped reluctantly into the arena-like control room.

He paused and wearily scanned the bulky correlator machines, the clerks and technicians scurrying about like distressed ants, the video-communication operators, the endless procession of control crewmen and survey-detection personnel.

A ripple of poised motionlessness swept across the room as they discovered his presence. The delayed reaction was somewhat like an assault wave.

"Old man's called a board meeting Thursday at the Secretariat."

"Crew Forty-Eight needs more shields south of Denver. Can I shift the plates from Flagstaff?"

"The Central Russian Sector wants us to run a high altitude current check."

"Commissioner Carmath wants a spot run down."

"Here's that oceanographic report..."

Before McCune reached his desk, he had taken in tow a scampering retinue of more than a dozen—all clamoring for preferential attention.

The Coordinator was a tall, rangy man with sagging, despondent lines in his face. If his hair seemed sparse and unkempt, it wasn't due as much to carelessness as to resignation to the inevitable.

He calmly held up his hands and quieted the restless mob. The job, he had learned, demanded a certain amount of forced detachment; otherwise it would be insufferable.

"One at a time," he admonished. "What's the latest on the tote board, Woolcut?"

The Detection Supervisor indicated the items with a stabbing finger. "Four new spots ranging from lukewarm to damned hot. One—an East Seattle area—might call for partial evacuation."

"All in our Sector?"

"Three are. One overlaps the Western Canadian area."

"What's the trouble?"

Woolcut made a demonstrative gesture of wiping his blunt brow. "A front's sweeping down the coast with a trace of warm rain. Not too much—it'll probably add only about a twentieth of a roentgen to the average exposure badge. But there'll be more if we don't cap the source."

McCune dropped into his chair and began thumbing through a sheaf of reports. "Where do you figure it's coming from?"

"Probably a mid-arctic disposal dump used by an early Alaskan reactor."

"One of those outfits with records that don't go back more than a hundred years, I suppose," the Coordinator offered dismally.

Woolcut's nod was commiserating. "When we track it down we'll probably find an exposed pile of light garbage. My guess would be selenium 79, with a half-life of six hundred thousand years."

"Send up all the crews we can spare."

McCune turned to the second in line. It was going to be another "just dandy" day—as they all had been in the eight years since he had taken over the Western US Sector.

Somehow it all struck him as being a paradox—a monotony of newness. The scores of detection and control problems that surged to the surface every day were all different. But the differences merely added up to the ennui of an eternal job that had to be done by the Radioactivity Control (or Shuffle Board, as it was facetiously known) if great-grandson was to be of the same genetic stock as great-grandpop.

But today, he reminded himself with a grim sense of desperation, *would* be different.... Beth had gone to the hospital. The thought and his inescapable reaction of self-abasement were like a cold sweat steaming deep under his tanned skin.

∝∝

The first avalanche of details attended to, McCune settled back in his chair and loosened his collar. He lit a cigarette and took a deep, exhilarating draught. But his respite was short-lived as the Detection Supervisor elbowed his way through the scurrying workers.

"Here's the latest on the Hawaiian Subsector," Woolcut offered in strained tones. "Geology's recorded another fault shift during the night. They're working out a probability table on whether Haleakala's going to blow."

"How much protactinium has been dumped in that crater to date?"

Woolcut gestured uncertainly. "We've only got a rough estimate from the eight reactor companies on the islands—something like seventy-two-thousand tons."

The Coordinator winced. "Damned fools! They were warned fifty years ago not to use that hole on Maui as a disposal site. Just because a volcano hasn't acted up since 1750 doesn't mean it won't ever bust loose again. What's three hundred and twenty-five years in the life of a volcano?"

The other shrugged noncommittally. "It'll sure raise hell if it starts blowing now. I have to think of evacuating five-hundred-thousand people on that island."

"Or maybe six million on the whole chain." McCune dismissed him and motioned for his Control Supervisor.

"What sort of standby complement do we have on Maui?" he asked.

"Three complete shuffle crews," Fordham disclosed.

"Any suggestions on what we can do with all that hot Pa^{231}?"

Fordham spread his hands helplessly. "The only safe place I could find was Diamondhead Crater on Oahu."

McCune looked up sharply. "But that's right in Honolulu—under the noses of over a million people!"

"I know. But it's the best we can arrange on a temporary basis. We'll line the crater and cap it, of course."

McCune leaned back in solicitous thought…. It was an endless game. After the emergency was over, public reaction would demand that the stuff be taken out of Diamondhead and dumped elsewhere. But the new disposal site would probably leak contamination into the environment and some harassed shuffle crew ten years hence would have to gather it up and find another place for it. And all the while the accumulation of reactor waste would continue inexorably.

"Who's in charge of the Maui operation?"

Fordham grimaced apologetically. "Nobody. We're fresh out of supervisory personnel, what with the Denver and Seattle deals and the new Mexico—"

McCune swore disgustedly. Then his blunt fingers drummed the desk meditatively.

"I know what you're thinking, Chief," the other broke in with concern, "Don't try it. If the Commissioner finds out he'll dump you off the board. It'll mean your job."

"It won't be the first time I had to supervise a UN shuffle detail."

"It won't even be the first time this month. But, hell—six years ago you were four times over your maximum allowable roentgen level. I'll bet you've absorbed eight hundred Rs in the fifteen years you've been with the Commission."

"Two or three more won't hurt," McCune offered laconically. "Won't even show up on my badge—*if I can arrange another switch.*"

He glanced down at the black square clipped to his lapel. Then he looked over at the rack where Miss Jarred's badge was visible against the light material of her coat. Someday his secretary would begin wondering where she was picking up so much radiation. Briefly, he considered how she might react when the inspectors told her she was rapidly moving out of the "genetically safe" range.

Fordham went off frowning disdainfully. "It might be all right for you, since you don't expect to raise a family," he mumbled over his shoulder. "But I'm keeping my level down. I've got two fine kids. And I'm going to make damned sure the third will be normal too."

This brought McCune's thoughts back to the inescapable and, hesitatingly, he dialed the hospital. He spoke low so the others wouldn't learn Beth *hadn't* been visiting her mother after all.

"No, Mr. McCune," the head maternity nurse assured. "Your wife hasn't left the labor room. We'll call you when she goes into delivery."

"No!" he shouted. Then, more softly, "No—I'll call back."

Numbly, he let the receiver dangle from his hand for a long while. He'd never intended having a baby. Beth, however, always had. And, after his carelessness, she had furtively kept her condition to herself until it was too late to do anything about it. Damn her!

It was mid-morning when Miss Jarred ushered in the reporter from the wire service. The Coordinator recognized Neil Lancer, one of the top-spot news men, even before she announced him.

McCune regarded him with a half-venomous look of resignation and reluctantly offered a chair.

Diffidently, the other eased his hat up off his forehead and lit a cigarette. "Office wants me to get your views on those statements by Dr. Puang."

"Who's Dr. Puang?"

"The Pakistani geneticist." Lancer leaned forward. "Maybe you haven't run across the articles, so I'll brief you. The boys back in the LA bureau are anxious for your reaction."

Like hell they were, McCune decided. Lancer wasn't the kind of man they'd send out on a feature assignment…. They'd got wind of the Hawaiian situation.

"Puang," the newsman said, crossing his legs, "has come out with a treatise on adaptive evolution. He seems to think the human race is inherently equipped to take care of any reasonable change in its environment."

If there was a Puang, McCune felt sure, he would have heard of him. Furthermore, it was obvious from the way the reporter was glancing alertly around the room that he was trying to pick up answers to questions he wasn't going to ask.

"Make it short," the Coordinator snapped. "I'm busy."

"Well, Puang believes humanity will eventually adjust itself to living in a radioactive environment." Lancer abstractedly fingered his radiation-tabulator badge. "He sees adaptive evolution producing a strain that'll withstand increasingly higher levels of radiation without going off the deep end with runaway mutations."

Woolcut pushed up to the desk. "We've located that garbage heap in the arctic!"

The Detection Supervisor nodded anxiously. "Just as I guessed—selenium. They had it capped under the edge of a glacier on Victoria

Island. But erosion exposed the dump and arctic winds are beginning to pick up contamination."

"Good work. Give your data to Fordham. Tell him to set up liaison with the Western Canadian Sector and get the stuff recapped until we figure out what to do with it."

McCune faced the reporter again. "All right, Lancer. Let's bury this Puang guy and call off the play acting. But first I'm going to read you the riot act.... Section Twenty-One of the Public Panic Law deputizes—"

Lancer moaned dismally, took up the chant, "—deputizes all Shuffle Board members to classify certain data as restricted in the interest of public safety. But hell, McCune, give me a break!"

"Under the protective provisions of Section Twenty-One," the Coordinator continued dispassionately, "I'm charging you with the information that a critical situation is making up in the Hawaiian Islands. A dead volcano crater that has been used as a dump for reactor waste is now showing signs of erupting."

One of Woolcut's assistants called over from a desk halfway across the room, "Another R-level increase in the coastal waters off Oregon!"

McCune's shoulders fell dejectedly. Punch the ball in on one side and it bulges out the other. You couldn't win; couldn't even get ahead long enough to relax.

The assistant came over. "You suppose it's the Portland reactor cluster?"

"What else? They've been sluicing off Fe^{55} solute through the Columbia River into the Pacific. But hunt it down to make sure before we get them on the carpet."

The assistant hesitated.

"Yes?" McCune asked.

"Just wondering what they'll do with the stuff now."

"That's our problem. They'll probably still be able to sluice off half of their garbage. We'll just have to find a place for the other half."

Watching the man return to his desk, McCune let his thoughts drift back through the years to his uncle's farm.... They'd had a hound dog that used to make a ritual out of burying a bone. It would dig first here; decide it didn't like the spot after all; pick up the bone from the half-excavated hole, and try another location. After four or five false starts, it would finally shuffle the morsel to what it considered an adequate cache.

The RCC was confronted with much the same problem as the hound dog. Only, the adequate place seemed eternally elusive and the shuffling endless.

He remembered the reporter. "All right, Lancer. You're charged with top confidential information. If it gets into print, you and your bureau chief could get up to twenty years."

Disgusted, Lancer strode towards the door, brushing past Woolcut who was on his way to McCune's desk.

The Detection Supervisor's face was drawn and haggard. "Volcanology has confirmed the subterranean rumblings in the vicinity of the Haleakala Crater."

McCune sprang up. "Send out Crews Four, Seven, Thirty-Three, Thirty-Four and Forty-One."

He cupped his hands and shouted over to the communications section, "Get Volcanology and find out when we can take our men into the crater.

"Miss Jarred," he tossed at his secretary, "call Supply and have them ship all available shielding material to the Hawaiian Subsector.

"Woolcut—tell Flight Operations to service my ship."

With each shouted order, Coordination Headquarters had seemed to shift into a more agitated temp of scurrying activity—until now the huge room was a blur of erratic motion.

But, for McCune, there was nothing to do but await the "go ahead" from Volcanology. He couldn't shrug off the sensation of denial and thwarted purpose brought on by the delay. Impatiently, he clawed at the armrests of his chair.

Remembering Beth, however, he jolted erect and grabbed the phone.

"Yes Mr. McCune," the nurse said indulgently, "she's in delivery now. But it'll be another hour—"

He dropped the receiver back in its cradle. He'd been a damned fool too. He should have ensured against anything like this happening. Then he would have avoided the months of worry—months during which they couldn't see a doctor for fear their identity would become known and they'd be turned into objects of public curiosity.

The papers would have liked that. Even now he could visualize the headlines: "Sector Coordinator, Four Times Over Safe Genetic Level, To Have Baby."

Not seeing a doctor until the last minute had been a source of constant apprehension. He was sure Beth had worried as much as he had over the fifty pounds she had gained.

Blaring rockets crescendoed to an ear-splitting roar and died off abruptly, like a reverberating peal of thunder. The craft, a mile over Los Angeles Headquarters of the Western RCC Sector, shifted to its rotor and McCune listened to the fluttering grumble of the blades as it cushioned to a landing on the apron outside.

Commissioner Carmath, formidably stocky and bristling with a bearing of intense purpose, pushed his way towards the main building.

McCune met him at the entrance and was promptly brushed aside as the Chief of the UN Radioactivity Control Commission ploughed a furrow through the scampering workers and drew up before the main tote board.

"This Hawaiian thing—that the only emergency situation you got working?" he demanded.

"The only one of any consequence. We've got twenty-six other operations—"

The Commissioner silenced him with an indignant stare. "This thing had better be worked out, McCune," he threatened. "I'm holding you responsible for the whole affair!"

"But they've been dumping in that crater for a whole generation!"

"If you had the merest suspicion something like this might develop," Carmath went on uncompromisingly, "you should have taken preventive steps."

McCune stiffened with resentment. "Is that the way the Commission feels?"

"That is the considered opinion of every single member of the board except yourself!"

The Coordinator smiled bitterly. They hadn't wasted any time in tagging their scapegoat. Well—to hell with the job. Let somebody else shuffle the stuff around for a change. Anyway, if they had run a total on his *actual* accumulated exposure, he would have been pensioned off years ago.

"Let's be reasonable about this, Commissioner," he began nevertheless. "In the past week this Sector has had to control environmental radiation increases in more than a hundred—"

Carmath threw up his hands impulsively and moved towards the door. "I've no time to listen to you complain about routine control measures. A ten-thousand-square-mile patch of Japanese fishing waters was declared contaminated today because some crackpot Coordinator picked the wrong spot in the Pacific to dump niobium[94] fifteen years ago.

"In France, an entire dairy farming section has to be moved, lock, stock and barrel. Why? Because the pastures are picking up radiation from God-knows-where—probably in rain from some hidden dump in the Alps."

He stopped and propped his hands on his hips. "You'd think shuffling americium[241] a hundred miles into the Everglades would be a safe proposition for Miami, wouldn't you? But what happens? Hot insect life crops up in the area and now we've got one hell of a capping job, if not an all-out shuffling operation!"

Carmath scowled. "And *you* try to tell me about *your* petty problems!"

McCune wished to hell he'd get out. If the okay on the Haleakala Crater shuffle came through while the Commissioner was still around, he might learn there was nobody but McCune to supervise the operation.

Fortunately, the Commission Chief turned and stormed out.

McCune headed for his desk, almost colliding with the Detection Supervisor.

Woolcut flashed a smug smile of satisfaction. "We've finally licked that hot artesian water problem in the Clovis-Tucumcari area."

"Well, don't bother me with it!" McCune rudely waved him off. "Take it to Fordham."

Immediately contrite, though, he gripped the other's arm. "Sorry. The Commissioner crawled all over me…. What's the deal in New Mexico?"

Woolcut grinned. "An oil well ran dry about seventy-five years ago and someone pumped it full of promethium[145]. That stuff has a short half-life, but not short enough. It finally worked its way into the subterranean water supply."

McCune shrugged hopelessly. "Then there isn't too much we can do, except padlock the artesian wells and pipe in water from a clear area."

Disconsolately, he returned to his desk. Was the world radiation level increasing astronomically? Or did it just seem that way because he was thoroughly tired of working out the day-to-day challenges?

Real or imaginary, he conceded, everything was in one hell of a mess. Civilized humanity had been reduced to four billion radiation-exposure badges with one person attached to each...at least, that was the burlesque impression he carried around.

Four billion badges that had to be replaced monthly so the radiation they had absorbed could be measured and the figures entered on a million ledgers. That was the only way tabs could be kept to see that the natural mutation frequency wasn't being knocked out of kilter.

When he looked up, Fordham was standing in front of his desk.

"Volcanology says we'd better start the Haleakala shuffle," the Control Supervisor announced tensely. "They figure we got ten or eleven hours to move the Pa^{231} from the crater."

McCune nodded resignedly and glanced over at Miss Jarred's coat. Whistling abstractedly, he rose and strolled to the rack.

His back towards the secretary, he clipped her badge and pinned it to his lapel, replacing it with his own. With the designation on the reverse side, it was hardly likely she'd notice that the one on her coat wasn't hers.

Before he left the building, he called the hospital again.... No, Mrs. McCune hadn't come down from the delivery room yet.

Five minutes later, the Sector Headquarters apron fell away as the blades of his shuffle craft churned the air with a muffled roar. A mile up, he hit the power-shift stud. The rotor retracted and the tubes took over with a furious grip of acceleration.

Within the hour, Coordinator McCune stood on the jagged rim of the crater, zippering up his plastic envelope and sealing off the seams. The Haleakala shuffle, he wearily acknowledged as he broke open the compressed air valve, was going to be one of the damnedest operations he'd ever seen.

Already the emergency crews had set up their equipment along the bowl of the crater. Their positions, behind mobile shields, were as he had assigned them over videocom while en route.

Across the bowl, a steam shovel and half-dozen bulldozers started down the slope, heading for the piles of Pa^{231} that glistened like blue-steel hills in the early morning sun. Beyond, the sky was dense with hovering shuffle craft, waiting to be called for loading.

The crater itself was like a dismal plain of hell, with everything there but the heat. No, McCune corrected himself—the heat was there, too. Only it was a kind the traditional hell had never seen. But curlers of grey smoke streaming from crevices in the bowl's floor were a derisive indication that even fiery heat would soon make the illusion of Hades complete.

"Attention all crews," he directed over the radio as he started down the slope. "Keep the hot stuff in front of your shields. Take the outermost piles first and work in."

The ground rumbled as tractors lumbered in from the rim, hauling empty packing crates. Then there was a softer but more ominous rumble and denser smoke curled from the fissures.

Two bulldozers joined forces with one of the mobile shields and advanced on the nearest piles. The steam shovel and three tractors with packing cases took the cue and clumsily charged in.

"That crew on the left!" McCune shouted, squinting to discern the number on its shield. "Crew Forty-One—your flank's exposed! Either square around or back up."

He started forward again, drawn hypnotically towards the intense activity. But a special instinct of fear and danger held him back. Trapped between the two impulses that were like magnets, he was painfully strained with indecision.

"You there—in Crew Seven," he ordered. "Get back behind your shield. Outpost, send in two more shovels. Crews Thirty-Three, Sixteen and Two—take the third pile on the left. Shuffle Craft Number One—stand by to load."

Apprehensively, he fanned his radiation detector ahead of him. Its clatter rose to a steady, alarming whine.

It was going to be a disastrous job for the men in the Haleakala shuffle. No longer would it be a matter of fighting for genetic safety. Such a petty consideration, McCune realized, had long been exceeded. For, when you spoke of genetic purity, you were speaking in terms of only forty or fifty roentgens. These men would sop up radiation in the *hundreds* of roentgens. Now it was a fight for physical survival.

Shuffle Craft One plummeted down, drew up sharply and hovered above the crane that was shoveling Pa^{231} into the cases.

A thousand frantic voices suddenly shouted a hoarse alarm.

McCune swore desperately as he watched the blast from the craft's rotor buffet the blue-steel hills and scatter pulverized protactinium like dust.

The swirling cloud of grey powder spread over the crater like a pall of death.

"Get that copter out!" the Coordinator bellowed, retreating before the deadly dust. "All crews fall back!"

But the men had already broken and were fleeing in frenzied disorder up the slope.

He drew up as the copter skittered beyond the rim. "Outpost! Call in all shuffle crafts and lay dolly tracks down into the crater. We'll have to cart the stuff out."

Volcanology came in. "We expect a major eruption within eight hours, Coordinator. You'd better rush it up."

McCune forgot about his plastic encasement and tried to wipe his forehead. He only succeeded in smearing perspiration over the transparent surface so that he could hardly see through it.

"Communications!" he called urgently. "Get out a general alarm. Have all Sectors send Class I emergency crews and equipment.

"Supply—break out the double-shielded manipulator suits and mobile platforms; we're going to have to wallow in this damned stuff.

"Civil Control—evacuate Maui and have your forces on the other islands stand by."

He took another reading from his R-detector and estimated the amount of radiation being absorbed by Miss Jarred's badge, on his lapel. There was *bound* to be an investigation at the end of the month!

A civilian turning up with a hundred and nine Rs in thirty days' time would raise a stink anywhere. His years of badge switching were sure to be discovered.

The last crews to leave the bowl were straggling past him. Watching them clamber up the slope, pale and haggard, he was thankful now that he had ordered a full Medical Standby complement assigned to the Outpost.

Making doubly sure that the crater was unmanned, he climbed up to the ridge.

A huge red and white shuffle craft roared in from the east, kicking over from rocket power at only a thousand feet above the crater. The blast of its rotor further agitated the hot dust and the Coordinator swore volubly.

"McCune!" came the enraged response. "Is that you down there?"

He winced as he recognized the heavy voice of Commissioner Carmath and noticed the UN-RCC symbol on the craft.

Watching the ship land he numbly peeled off his plastic envelope and, holding it by an inside fold, dropped the thing into a disposal bin.

Carmath stormed over, sweeping the area before him with counter. "McCune, you're cashiered as of now! I'll take over until another operation supervisor gets here."

The Coordinator shrugged indifferently and started back towards his shuffle craft.

Doggedly, Carmath followed. "I told the Chief Correlator you were pulling something like this. But Ronson said no. He said he investigated and found nothing.

McCune paid no attention. Instead, he grinned as he realized suddenly that the magnets he had fought for nearly half his life— the alternate poles of duty and self-consideration—were no longer pulling. It was like a great burst of freedom. He would never again have to worry about operational radiation.

She was asleep. Beneath the white sheet, McCune's wife looked strangely small and helpless. Her face was wan and the lingering scent of the anesthetic was heavy in the room.

For months he had feared this moment. But now that it was here, he felt hardly any emotion at all.... The baby had been born, as it inevitably would have been come hell or high water or fifty shuffle emergencies. And now that it was over, all the anxiety was gone, even though he hadn't seen his daughter yet.

Instead, there was the calming realization that Beth had been right all along; that they had desperately needed a child. And if the baby were something less than human, they would only love it all the more.

His shoulders were squarer than they had ever been in all his thirty-eight years as he kissed his wife on the forehead.

"Dr. Logan says you may see your daughter now, Mr. McCune."

He turned towards the nurse in the doorway. "Is—is the baby all right?"

"There's—" the nurse hesitated awkwardly. "Dr. Logan is waiting."

She led the way down the corridor and he followed.... So there *was* something wrong. Still, he felt no dejection. After all, hadn't he sincerely expected some sort of deformity?

She motioned him to a halt in front of the glass partition of the nursery and went inside. He watched her cross to a doctor who was bending over one of the cribs. Then she spoke against the back of her hand and the physician looked up sharply and started anxiously towards McCune.

But he paused and gestured for the nurse to follow with the baby. Her eyes widened apprehensively and she shook her head.

Tensing, McCune strained to see over the side of the crib. He was suddenly sick inside at the portentous pantomime he was witnessing. Why, he wanted to shout, was she afraid to pick up the baby?

She was spared the apparently repulsive task, though, as five men wearing the arm bands of the UN Medical Research Commission swept down the corridor and barged into the nursery. Three of them crowded around the crib while two held X-ray plates up to the light. Astonished, they pointed with shaky fingers at details on the negatives.

Good God!

He hurled the door open and charged in. But his presence went unnoticed in the din of excited voices.

"...compensative muscular development..."

"...completely enclosing the stoma and replacing the serous membrane..."

"...might be mistaken for splenomegaly, if it weren't for the other decisive evidence..."

Nudging two of the medical men out of the way, McCune gripped the side of the crib and stared down.

Dr. Logan came over and grasped his shoulder. "This isn't the first case. There was one in Germany eleven years ago. But that one died. Oh, it wasn't because of this," he added hastily, waving his hand over the child. "It was a perfectly normal infant mortality. Then five years ago there was another case," Logan continued. "Two more cropped up three years ago and five in 2074. This is the fourteenth this year.... Of course, the UN has classified all information on the cases as restricted until they can be thoroughly studied."

"But what is it?" McCune demanded, exasperated.

"Pick up your child, Mr. McCune," one of the Medical Research men suggested.

McCune slipped his hands under the infant's back and thighs and lifted, gently at first. Surprise streaked his face and he hastily lowered the child.

"Why," he began, dumbfounded, "she—she must weigh . . ."

"Twenty-three and a quarter pounds, to be exact," Logan said.

Someone shoved one of the X-ray plates in his hand. "This is the child's spleen and here is part of the reproductive system—the ovaries."

All McCune could see, though, were intensely white patches on the negative where the doctor indicated.

"Our highest X-ray voltage," Logan explained, "couldn't penetrate those areas. We haven't yet analyzed the substance or determined what sort of biological miracle the hypertissue represents. But one thing's certain—as far as blood composition and genetic tolerance are concerned, your daughter will be able to accommodate a radiation level several thousand times as high as you or I without any ill effect."

⤙RECOVERY AREA⤚

Mounting the booming fury of the thunder, Zu-Bach's anxious voice bellowed from the forest:

"K'Tawa! Where are you? There's great danger!"

K'Tawa jolted from Meditative Withdrawal. Sighing, he shook his maned head in weary resignation. Always, for Zu-Bach, there was something compelling his attention. But never was it Spiritual—only Material.

The Old One disengaged his lean limbs from the cramping convulsions of Cogitative Posture. Then, with a rasping intake of breath, he resumed respiration.

"K'Tawa, answer! Remember the Thing That Trapped? I've quazed more of them—in the Upper Endlessness!"

Zu-Bach's more specific identification of the danger impressed the Old One but negligibly. It only verified his suspicion that the other's concern was trivial, Materialistic.

But Zu-Bach was young. Why, his quazehorn was still puny in its immaturity. Many sleeps had yet to transpire, no doubt, before he would be ready to enter Phase One in his Ascetic Ascendancy. With that realization, K'Tawa felt tolerably disposed towards his youthful kin. But being tolerant certainly didn't mean he would have to indulge the other's minor whims. The better course—much better— would be to remain quiet and hope that Zu-Bach would go away.

Which was what he seemed to be doing. At least, the sound of his thrashing about in the forest was growing more remote.

The Sorrowing Sea, restless with anger and racing before the lash of the wind, was hurling itself against the rock upon which the

Old One sat. While he had Meditated, warm rain had plastered his beard against his chest. Above, the Perpetual Clouds writhed as they roared at one another and hurled fierce bolts down upon the inland forest.

Things That Trapped, in the Upper Endlessness—indeed! K'Tawa smiled at his young kin's imagination. But, just to be sure, he quazed up into the Clouds. There was nothing there, of course.

Yet, there was some hope for Zu-Bach. For, at least, his interest *did* extend in an encouraging direction. Throughout the First Phase of Ascendancy he would have to concern himself solely with the Upper Endlessness.

The Old One folded his arms, drew in a final breath and, thanks to the suggestive effects of Zu-Bach's words, was soon pondering the Dichotomy of Endlessnesses.

Of things without limit there were but two—the Upper and Lower. The former, of course, could be dismissed with a meditative flick of the wrist. Above the clear air there were Clouds, and Clouds, and Clouds—as far as one chose to conceive. The Lower Endlessness, on the other hand, was an infinite downward continuity of stone-impregnated mud and water—little of the former, but much of the latter. And between the Endlessnesses—

"K'Tawa! K'Tawa!"

He wrapped himself resolutely in his thoughts. Between the Endlessnesses, he resumed annoyed, was the Day—the *Eternal* Day. Then he puzzled over his conceptual concoction: an Eternal Day squeezed in between two Endlessnesses. Why an Eternal Day? Did that suggest there might somewhere, somehow be *another kind* of Day?

Troubled, he tried to envision a non-Eternal Day. Without luck, he cast about for a rational concept that would embrace a non-Day, or even an un-Day, but it was all beyond grasp. Moreover, not even in all the ancestral memory at his disposal, as far back as he could reach, from the vantage point of Phase Seven, was there anything relevant to the enigma he had posed for himself.

"*There* you are, K'Tawa! Wake up!"

The Old One shook off the grip of strong hands on his shoulders and sprang to his feet. "Never," he rebuked, "never arouse anyone from Meditation in the Upper Phases! It might be fatal!"

The rain had stopped. But its final drops were clinging to the incipient quazehorn that rose from Zu-Bach's matted white hair.

"There are many Presences in the Upper Endlessness!" he announced. "I counted them. Forty small ones and one large one!"

"Where are they now? *I* don't quaze them."

Zu-Bach pointed off to where the Sorrowing Sea met the Perpetual Clouds. "They're gone—into the Horizontal Endlessness."

K'Tawa dug a finger into his beard and scratched his chin. The *Horizontal* Endlessness—hm-m-m. Interesting concept. At least the boy did appear to have a worthwhile imagination. "About your Ascetic Ascendancy—have you decided—"

"The Presences, K'Tawa!" Zu-Bach seized his shoulders again. "What about the Presences?"

"You said they were gone."

"But they'll be back! They went straight that way." He pointed with his spear. "They won't turn. But soon they'll reappear—from *that* direction." He indicated the opposite horizon.

The Old One laughed. "With Endlessnesses in all directions, how can they come back without turning?"

Zu-Bach spat in the sea. "They *did*—four times since I started looking for you."

The Old One, without realizing it, had closed his eyes and opened his mind to the intriguing possibilities of a Horizontal Endlessness and Presences that could go off in one direction and return from another. If that concept were valid, he reasoned, then one was to believe that Endlessnesses might be bent back upon themselves. Which meant that—

"K'Tawa!" the other shouted. "The Presences are *dangerous*! I quazed that much. They're just like the Thing That Trapped. Remember?"

Indeed he did remember. But the Old One had never quite believed that preposterous account. Oh, he could quaze that Zu-Bach had encountered *something*. But the encounter may well have been with nothing more real than his prolific imagination.

"I wouldn't worry," he advised. "If there are Presences up there and if they *are* menacing, we can at least be thankful they're not down here."

"But the Thing That Trapped was up there before it came down!"

K'Tawa was becoming quite impatient. His thoughts were at a most productive peak at the moment. And he should be directing all their energy into the Spiritual Development of Phase Seven, into his Search for Origin and Meaning, his Total Communion with the Fundamental Endlessnesses. But this non-Ascetic, this Prephase supplier of food was seemingly intent upon complication his Withdrawal from the Material. "What do you want me to do?" he asked finally.

"Help me quaze them next time they go by. If they *are* like the Thing That Trapped, we'll warn the village."

K'Tawa drew back. Warn the village indeed! And jar scores of Meditators from their Pursuit of the Spiritual Significances? What insolence!

Lowering himself on his haunches, the Old One said, "I must ponder it a moment."

After attaining the Upper Phases, one never lied. And the fact of the matter was that K'Tawa *had* intended to explore the feasibility of disturbing the Ascetics. But hardly had he seated himself when he found his thoughts drifting to the concept of an Endlessness folded back upon itself.

How fascinating! For instance, one might imagine a trip (by tunnel or cavern-like passage) through the Lower Endlessness, only to find himself breaking through another surface and gazing overhead at the same Upper Endlessness!

No. It wouldn't be *another* surface. It would be the *same one* bent back upon itself—just like the outside of the clay he used to play with in his pre-Prephase days!

It was astonishing. Yet—it *was* true! From a thousand sources now, all buried deep in ancestral memory, came irrefutable verification.

A Lower Endlessness complete within itself and limited by its surface—its unbroken, spherical surface!

He leaped up, shouting exultantly. There was no doubt about it— he was mastering Phase Seven! No one else before him had done it. Could he dare hope to push on, perhaps to an *Eighth* Spiritual Level?

Zu-Bach, he was aware, was only staring uncertainly at him. "The Presences," he asked. "What about the Presences?"

K'Tawa glowered—then restrained himself with the realization that Kinship must be respected, even the most distant. How else could anyone hope for Total Communion? "What Presences?"

"There!" the other shouted, pointing his spear towards the Clouds. "Those!"

The Old One tilted his horn in the indicated direction. There were Presences, all right. Many small ones, all in a line—followed by one huge something that seemed to defy quazing. And he puzzled over the fact that the invisible things, too far away to be seen even if there were no Perpetual Clouds, were travelling incredibly fast. Yet they *appeared* to be moving extremely slowly.

He quazed strength and power, hardness and intricate design and durability—purpose and determination.

Many Presences from a distant—a distant what? K'Tawa couldn't quaze the concept. It was too alien, too awful.

Leaning forward in his inertial couch, Colonel Scott O'Brien squinted through the forward port at the logistic train as it orbited ahead of the Argo into blazing sunrise.

One by one, the supply capsules—the resurrected Mercuries, modified Geminis, converted Apollos—streaked from the obscurity of night and flashed into scintillating brilliance. Forty vivid diamonds in a sparkling tiara around the cloud-veiled head of Venus.

O'Brien, alert and lean, sagged back in the couch and shifted his attention to the microwave radiometer screen. The Van Horstein scanner was penetrating both the ionosphere and the cloud layer at full glare, etching the grid with fine detail.

Venus' solitary strip of land, almost two thousand miles long but only a tenth as wide, snaked across the scope. He adjusted the transverse reference control and watched the red line leap into luminescence on the screen.

"TR locked in phase," he called out to Commander Green in the adjacent couch. "We'll hit the sequencer in fifteen seconds."

Green's characteristic grin was rampant on his blunt face now that the two-hundred-million-mile journey was at an end. "Ready on the SQB."

O'Brien stared at the grid until the red line drifted to the central crosshairs, carrying with it the surface features it was tracking. "Mark!" he shouted.

"Mark," Green echoed.

"Phased landing sequencer set for Recovery Area, Southwest Quadrant. Countdown under way. Ten minutes to Zero. Everything positive."

After an impatient moment, O'Brien prompted, "Wastrom?"

There was no answer from the couch directly behind him.

Green leaned over. "He's probably praying again. Somebody sure slipped up when they psyched him out for this junket."

The Colonel reared back. "*Wastrom!*"

There was abrupt movement aft. "Yes?"

"The train—how about it?"

"Oh. Retro systems positive."

"All forty?"

"I don't see any red lights."

"How about the 'chute packs?"

"All green. Everything's ready. Think we'll make it okay?"

O'Brien didn't answer. He was tired of reassuring the electronicist. What made the situation all the more ridiculous was the fact that Wastrom, youngest of the four-man crew, was also the most rugged and competent-looking. But it was clear now that he had left most of his guts somewhere between Earth and Venus.

"Nine-thirty and counting," Green announced.

And a vigilant voice responded from the right rear couch, "All Argo systems positive."

O'Brien glanced back and nodded in unconscious approval of the contrast between Frank Yardley and the other civilian member of the crew. As the Argo's nuclear technician, Yardley was almost fifteen years Wastrom's senior and, seemingly, half the latter's size. But O'Brien wouldn't have swapped half a Yardley for all the Wastroms he could find.

"Nine minutes to Zero," Green said.

O'Brien watched Yardley's hand dart to a toggle switch. A shudder ran through the ship as coupling bolts exploded.

"Capella stage separated," the nuclear tech said.

Colonel O'Brien relaxed, passing a hand back over the bristles of his closely-cropped, blond hair. That left the Argo clean for entry. All that remained now, of what had once been a massive configuration, was the III-D 'chute assembly, Jason capsule, Procyon IV-B solid fuel stage for blast-off and the Spica fin-and-retro pack.

One-hundred-and-fifty-five feet of precision engineering and intricate instrumentation that would soon be plunging planetwards. Meanwhile, the Capella II, with its oxygen difluoride-diobrane fuel load, would be dutifully waiting for orbital reunion.

Commander Green's voice broke the silence. Eight-ten and counting. Ready, Scott?"

"Ready." O'Brien reached for the attitude sequencer lever.

Green intoned, "Eight even."

Throwing the control, O'Brien settled back while the ship lazied about. The forty supply caps, all arow and aglitter against the fiercely white cloud mantle, drifted from view as the Argo turned her back on them and steadied in braking attitude.

"You—you suppose it's hot down there?" Wastrom asked.

O'Brien concealed his annoyance. "A dozen flyby probes showed that the "severe heat" isn't connected with the surface at all.

"The preprobe boys were led astray by a high electrondensity in the ionosphere," Yardley added. "Our soft-landed probes proved it rarely gets over a hundred planetside."

"But how can we be sure?" Wastrom demanded.

"Well, it goes like this," Green offered without the trace of a smile. "The last instrumented probe broke an egg on a Venusian sidewalk. It didn't fry. Seven minutes. All systems positive at Post One."

O'Brien adjusted the phased entry system oscillator and coaxed out a higher-pitched whine. If Wastrom was prepared to trot out his fear that the soft-landed probes had not detected lurking, hostile lifeforms, he might decide on complaining about his eardrums instead.

Thus far, it had been a remarkably uncomplicated trip. And O'Brien could only hope the two other deep-space trains following at one-week intervals would have it half as good. They probably would— if they had no Wastroms aboard.

In all, it was a fairly impressive effort—as well it should be, what with a price tag of forty billion. But you didn't quibble about costs when the Reds, in effect, held the moon as a protectorate with the sanction of every noncommitted—and trembling—nation on Earth.

A score of lunar bases, all secretly armed but with the Kremlin "guaranteeing" their military neutrality (without inspection, of course), comprised a formidable ace-in-the-hole and an insurmountable diplomatic club. Earthside armament systems neutralized each other. But the Soviet lunar development, begun five years before the US had acquired the capability of landing a man on the moon, was the margin of difference.

Unless Uncle balanced the scale by developing his own reserve extraterrestrial backstop, he might as well dig his hole.

O'Brien shrugged unconsciously. So Venus gets tabbed and trains of supplies and personnel, followed by a caboose of inter-planetary armament, are in deep space in a one shot arsenal-build-ing project.

"What if there's life down there?" Wastrom's voice quaked above the oscillator's whine. "Hostile life, I mean. Intelligent enough to stay away from scanners."

Before O'Brien could dig up one of his well-worn rejoinders, Commander Green declared, "Three minutes, thirty seconds to Zero."

"I said," Wastrom persisted, straining forward, "what if there's hostile life? The scanners spotted only two four-legged things and one small biped—nothing else. Where're the lesser forms? What if—"

"Three minutes, thirty seconds!" Green repeated irately. "That was *your* cue, Wastrom!"

Pulling against his harness, the Commander leaned back towards Wastrom's couch. His hand darted between tubular braces and flicked a switch on the electronicist's console.

There was another shudder of distant concussion and Green said, "ComPac ejected."

"Sorry," Wastrom offered.

O'Brien checked the separation on his scope. The orbital radio relay station, a bright blip close to the center of the screen, was pull-ing away steadily. With its signal-sensing antennae, it would be a necessary link in Earthside-Venus Base communications.

Still scowling, Green removed his earphone. "ComPac signal strong and clear." Somewhat more softly, but still loud enough for the Colonel to hear, he added, "They'll know we got this far at least."

O'Brien chuckled. "Oh, we'll get you back safely to the wife and kids."

Wastrom raised a hand. "I *said* I was sorry."

Two action-filled minutes of final check-off operations passed in silence as the Colonel sketched his imaginary diagram of an entry trajectory for the Argo that would plop it down in the center of the target, with forty supply caps spaced at half-mile intervals westward through the Recovery Area.

Then Green warned, "Ten seconds to Entry Zero."

At the count of five, O'Brien punched in the stud to activate the landing sequencer.

Now there was nothing to do but hang on and wait.

II

Grudgingly, K'Tawa followed his young kin towards the village. This imposition on his Contemplation was most inconsiderate. But there was little he could do except respect Zu-Bach's urgent plea. The Code of Kinship required no less.

Still, his own interests were impelling at the moment. So he compromised. With eyelids lowered in Visual Withdrawal, he relied on the perceptual faculty of his quazehorn to guide his footsteps through the forest. Meanwhile, he consigned full Meditative attention to his Seventh-Phase pursuits.

Progressive Ascendancy came quickly, encouraging the hope that his recent results had not been spurious. There was, for instance, a remote forebear (whose name appeared to have been something like "Y-Lem'Ah") who had managed to pass on to ancestral memory-searches of the future a vivid impression of his features. He had done that by spending endless periods gazing into the shining surfaces of ancient objects his people had found on their tiny "island?"

Then K'Tawa's brow wrinkled, even despite his semi-withdrawal. Y-Lem'Ah had had *no* quazehorn—none whatsoever! Nor had any of his people—at least not until the time their "island" had sunk in a Minor Debacle and he and some of his kin had floated on rafts to Onlyland.

The recollection faded and K'Tawa was left with a hollow, searching loneliness. Yet he was exuberant in his accomplishment.

Nobody had yet reached back to the time when Onlyland had evidently been "Mainland!"

Up ahead, Zu-Bach paused and waited. "You'll tell the Meditators how important the Presences are? They respect *your* opinion."

"Why shouldn't they? Am I not the most advanced Contemplator?"

"Then you will help me convince them."

"I can do no more than attest to the presence of the Presences."

"But they'll be able to quaze as much for themselves!"

"Of course they will. And what you should be concerned over is the possibility that they'll also quaze your obstinate rejection of Spiritual Ascendancy."

Suddenly intolerant, Zu-Bach turned and stomped ahead. The Old One followed, resenting the demanding Responsibility of Kinship.

The village was a confusion of stone-thatch huts that grew from the soft mud and, like a mangy nakedness, laid bare in its spot the rain-washed sweep of forest.

K'Tawa, with Zu-Bach beside him, paused at the edge of the clearing and watched the Pre-Meditation Ceremony of the Summoning of the Hot Tongues.

Exemplar L'Jork stood solemnly before the Drying Hut, elevating to the Upper Endlessness a bundle of crisp leaves. His ample quazehorn was rigid in its upthrust orientation with the Perpetual Clouds. His drawn face, lined with the humbling evidence of self-sacrifice and frustrated Spiritual ambition, was both sober and serene. K'Tawa reorganized the inappropriateness of the title Exemplar. But it wasn't because of any shortcoming on L'Jork's part. Rather, the demands of leadership in the provision of communal necessities severely limited his own Ascetic Ascendancy—to the extent that he had never progressed beyond Fourth-Phase Contemplation.

The Exemplar came forward and the other Meditators closed ranks behind him. He placed the leaves on the Central Slab and knelt before taking up the Starting Stones. Then, with all the others crowding around and blowing rapidly at the leaves, he began striking the rocks together.

Soon the first Hot Tongues materialized and the Meditators blew even more eagerly. Additional Hot Tongues appeared among

31

the leaves and the dark Vaporous Offering began lifting itself gracefully to join the Perpetual Clouds.

Unable to constrain himself any longer, Zu-Bach surged forward.

"Meditators!" he shouted, waving his spear. "Your attention!"

Exemplar L'Jork glanced up and scowled. The Elder Contemplators broke their compact circle around the Slab and faced the source of disrespectful interruption. With a final issue of Vaporous Offering, the Hot Tongues vanished from the leaves.

Behind his young kin's back, K'Tawa spread his hands apologetically. "Your indulgence, Exemplar. Zu-Bach would be heard."

"In view of your sponsorship," L'Jork said solemnly, "we shall hear him then."

With another helpless gesture, K'Tawa signified that he was, as yet, certifying nothing.

Several women poked their heads out of the huts to see what was going on. One, departing with her yet unborn child for the Retreat for Delivery and Training, paused curiously.

"We have quazed forty-one Presences in the Upper Endlessness!" Zu-Bach blurted out. "*Evil* Presences! And they will come down!"

L'Jork glanced at K'Tawa and the Old One nodded confirmation.

Several of the Elders, disinterested and intent on getting started with their Meditation, began drifting off. After all, the Materialistic was Zu-Bach's responsibility, not theirs.

"But this is important!" K'Tawa's young relative pleaded. "They may turn out to be Things That Trap!"

L'Jork regarded the Old One for further verification.

"I didn't quaze *that* likelihood," K'Tawa said. "But if they are, as Zu-Bach says, Things That Trap, I should imagine all we would have to do is stay out of their way."

The Exemplar thoughtfully combed his beard with long, curving fingernails. "This Thing That Trapped—what was it like?"

"It was broad and round at the bottom and narrow and round at the top—all shining and hard, determined and cunning." Zu-Bach directed his words at the remaining Elders, who even now were beginning to turn their backs. "I found it on the beach and watched it through many periods."

Only L'Jork and K'Tawa remained to listen—the former but perfunctorily. All the Elders had seated themselves on their individual Thinking Slabs in front of their huts and had assumed Cogitative Posture, heads bowed under the weight of burdensome quazehorns.

"Nevertheless," Zu-Bach went on, addressing his appeal directly to the Exemplar. "It had an eye that wasn't an eye at all but that kept looking around. I quazed that it was searching and I stayed hidden all the while. It breathed in the air and lapped up the water and caught the rain. It scooped up sand and mud and spoke in a continuous chatter that—"

"Spoke?" L'Jork repeated. "To whom?"

"I don't know. I couldn't quaze that. I couldn't even quaze what it was saying in its silent, humming voice. But I was watching from the bushes when a herola came trotting up and paused to sniff the Thing. Suddenly there was an opening in the side and—"

"And the herola went in?" the Exemplar asked cagily.

"Of course not. Herolas are too cautious to do anything like that. A puff of green air floated out and the herola fell still. An arm, thin like the shaft of a spear, appeared through the opening and pulled the animal in. Three sleeps later I found the herola outside again—dead. The Thing That Trapped had finally quit chattering. I could quaze it was lifeless. I hurled it into the Sorrowing Sea."

"It was small enough for you to hurl?"

"Yes, Exemplar."

"Then it couldn't have trapped you. How about the forty-one Presences in the Upper Endlessness—could *they* trap one of us?"

"One is large enough to trap many of us."

K'Tawa, who had been considering snatching a few moments of Contemplation, straightened alertly and looked around. All the Meditators were stirring on their Thinking Slab. They had quazed *something*. And now L'Jork and K'Tawa themselves were quazing it—a lynko.

The small, friendly animal had entered the village clearing. Sauntering in its upright attitude, the furry creature dragged its tail behind as it foraged about the huts. And each Meditator rose and touched his quazehorn respectfully as it passed.

33

K'Tawa quazed Zu-Bach's feeling of insignificance. The animal had received the consideration from the Meditators that he had been denied. But, the Old One realized, Zu-Bach would eventually learn that the Code of Kinship extended sympathetically to the presumptuous lynko because, unlike the other creatures, it walked upright.

The Exemplar bestowed his respectful gesture on the lynko and turned his back to Zu-Bach. "Very interesting," he said, heading for his hut, "—your Thing That Traps and the soaring Presences. I'm sure they will provide me with subject matter for Contemplation through many Withdrawals."

Frustrated, Zu-Bach gripped his spear and stormed off.

L'Jork paused, turned and nodded understandingly at the Old One. "Keep your quazehorn on the boy, K'Tawa. He's impulsive. Needs guidance if we ever expect to get him started on Ascendancy."

The Old One indicated his agreement, then trailed after Zu-Bach. He overtook his lesser kin at the edge of the forest.

"For all they care," Zu-Bach said, sulking, "one of the Presences could come down and trap the entire village!"

"The first step towards Withdrawal," K'Tawa began soothingly, "is to learn Forced Dissociation with the Material. Next—"

"Oh, lynko dung!" the other exclaimed.

Then, above the swish of softly-falling rain, above the Ceaseless Thunder's roar, a great howling rent the sky somewhere near the sea. And a queer, hazelike glow of prolonged Lightning limned the bellies of the Perpetual Clouds with an angry, pink cast.

"They're coming down!"

"There!" Zu-Bach shouted. "They're coming down!"

He started to race off towards the coast. But K'Tawa exercised the Prerogative of Undeniable Seniority.

"Stay!" he ordered. "It is almost sleep period. We will have nothing more to do with the Presences 'til after first meal."

Shoulders sagging submissively, Zu-Bach followed him back towards their hut. And the Old One foretasted the pleasant period of Meditation he would enjoy before sleep came.

Colonel O'Brien stood before the still-closed outer hatch, slipped the plastic respirahood over his head and secured its wrap-around oxygen cylinder to his waist. Then he reached under the transparent bag to reposition his throat mike and earphone.

"Testing," he said softly.

And the comsystem grated with Commander Green's instant acknowledgement from the other side of the air lock.

Beside the Colonel, Wastrom raised his own hood towards his flushed, tense face, then paused. "What if all that carbon dioxide comes up under this bag?"

The Colonel constrained himself from complaining that O'Briens weren't ordinarily *that* lucky. ""Venus" atmosphere is eighty-five percent carbon dioxide," he recited tonelessly. "CO_2 is heavier than the stuff we breathe. It'll stay down. The oxygen, being lighter, will stay up in the hood."

"I see," Wastrom said, as though he hadn't often been reassured during training.

O'Brien reached for the hatch handle. "Ready?"

"Can't we wear space suits—for protection against infection?"

O'Brien closed his eyes in momentary pursuit of fortitude. "One: It wasn't planned that way. We have no portable air-conditioning units. You'd swear you were in an oven. Two: Tymaroff showed conclusively just a couple of years back that a specific relationship has to exist between pathogen and host. That relationship has to be developed through thousands of years of evolution, not just during a few hours exposure. In short, the chance of infection from a Venusian bug is nil. Ready?"

Reluctantly, Wastrom positioned his mike, introducing his voice into the comsystem. "You think twelve hours was long enough for the ground to cool off from the Spica's braking—"

"Look, Wastrom—we've got thirty-six supply capsules out there that survived entry. They're waiting to be assembled into US Venus Base. We have only one week before Train Beta arrives. Either—"

"I'm ready," Wastrom broke in, shrugging his adequate shoulders.

Green's voice sifted through the Colonel's earphone. "How about me helping you on pickup, Scott?"

"No. We'll stick to the planned procedure. You and Yardley will monitor the scope and match our blips with the capsule blips."

O'Brien jerked on the handle and the hatch swung open on a dismal panorama of shadows and deeper shadows. The hot, humid stuff that passed for atmosphere enfolded him like a wet blanket just taken out of the oven.

Outside, it was twilight of the stormiest day he had ever seen on Earth. The drenched ground and, in the distance, the rain-slicked forest still bore evidence of the torrential downpour that had just turned the Jason capsule into a deafening drumhead. Concussion-like thunder roared from the cloud-packed megaphone of the sky and O'Brien counted a half-dozen bolts lashing the ground simultaneously.

He swung out the boom, fastened the nylon line's harness around his chest and stepped out of the hatch. Down he went alongside one-hundred-and-fifty towering feet of the Argo, past the Procyon IV-B stage, past the Spica fin-and-braking assembly.

He landed on the slippery but surprisingly firm ground, squirmed out of the harness and gave it a tug to start it on its way up. Then he went around the Argo and checked the lightning arrester for proper grounding where it had harpooned into the soil—insurance against having the Procyon's load of solid fuel ignited by a bolt.

"Coming, Wastrom?" he asked. When there was no answer, he called out again, then looked up.

The electronicist was on his way down. But he was out of contact. His earphone could readily be seen dangling by his waist.

"Trouble?" Yardley inquired over the radio.

"Nothing unusual. Wastrom just lost his earphone."

Yardley continued: "I'm sorry about all this, Colonel. And I feel guilty since—well, he and I represent the civilian side of this outfit."

"I understand how you feel, Frank. And thanks."

"No," the nuclear tech insisted. "I want to make up for it. I'm checked out on most of his chores. If you'd like to shift any of them on my shoulder—well, it's sturdier than it looks."

"We'll see. When it sinks in that we made it over safely and nothing's going to happen, he may come around."

O'Brien lifted his hood, cupped his hands around his mouth and shouted, "Wastrom damn it! Fix your earphone!"

Green didn't have to direct them to the first supply cap in the Recovery Area. Clinging to a hillside, its orange 'chute vividly contrasted the olive-grey grass ('moss' would have been a better word, as far as O'Brien was concerned) on which it lay.

Explosive bolts popped and the conical capsule flared open on a six-legged Bondley Terrain Walker, top speed twenty mph with its three hundred kilowatt-hour Reinhold battery.

That, together with coaching from the Jason's observation-command gallery, brought them swiftly if not smoothly to the next two capsules. There they acquired a Mark VI Modified Electrical Crane-Tractor and a train of "cat-tread dollies."

Within several hours O'Brien, having counted upon but received little help from Wastrom, had loaded the train with the contents of twelve supply caps.

Securing the last load to the final dolly, he leaned back against one of the Terrain Walker's legs. He held his breath while he removed the respirahood and sleeved perspiration off his face.

Miserly, he inventoried his acquisitions. They included such indispensable items as a Collard Mark IV nuclear power plant with accessory battery chargers, Del Rouad transmitter-receiver keyed in with the orbiting ComPac relay station, inflatable Mannerheim Home Environment Igloo and a Westinghouse Oxyaccumulator-Compressor.

Those—together with the field laboratory equipment, the main consignment of CO_2 cylinders, Spica stage fuel containers, non-concentrated food supply and other useful if not essential articles—were beginning to make the place seem more like home by the minute.

Let's go back," Wastrom urged, fidgeting with the Terrain Walker's tiller.

But Yardley's voice vibrated in the earphones. "Your next cap is only a couple of hundred yards off—beyond that hill."

"We're loaded," the Colonel explained, heading for his tractor. "Anyway, the rest of the stuff'll keep. Five more capsules and we'll have one complete set of everything."

"We've come out a lot better than I hoped we would," Green said. "I'm sold on this system—a supply train in two sections, one half a duplicate of the other."

"Every piece of equipment has its backup."

"We were lucky, too. Of the four caps lost in entry, no two were alike. So we're not completely out of anything."

O'Brien started up the tractor but paused to reach under his hood and wipe more perspiration from his forehead. Actually, there was nothing to worry about. Train Beta was due in another week. It was a duplicate of Train Alpha. If the first mission had succeeded, Beta would establish a second base. If not, the backup train would contribute its resources to the Alpha effort.

Then in another week Train Gamma would arrive, bringing its missile crews and the first consignment of interplanetary weapons with their ace-in-the-hole warheads. Indeed, there was nothing leisurely or stinting about the operation.

"Scott—Green again. Our scope just lost the signal from the farthest capsule down the line."

"Which one is that? What's its cargo?"

There was a pause while Green checked the master sheet. "Power tools, medical supplies. You figure something happened to the cap?"

"No. It's about time at least one minor piece of equipment failed. I'm thankful it was just a Here-I-Am transmitted."

Falling in behind the Terrain Walker, O'Brien sent the tractor crawling towards the Argo. Then he noticed Wastrom was nervously securing his belt around his neck, pinching in folds of the hood.

"What's that supposed to be for?" the Colonel asked.

"That damned carbon dioxide—I can smell it!" the electronicist cried. "It's poisoning me!"

O'Brien had no comment. What could he say when he was beginning to suspect the other was just indulging his eagerness to grumble? Wastrom had certainly been sufficiently filled in on the nonpoisonous nature of Venus' carbon dioxide and nitrogen. He couldn't have forgotten that the only danger the atmosphere posed was one of suffocation as a result of oxygen starvation.

"Colonel, this is Yardley," the earphone hummed. "Those caps we haven't recovered yet—a little water won't hurt them, will it?"

"Of course not. Why?"

"We just lost our screen blip from the *second* farthest capsule—the one with the standby long-range radio gear."

O'Brien frowned. "I won't buy another Here-I-Am failure."

"I don't think you have to. You see, the scope shows the far end of the capsule line stretching out across the beach of a bay. There the capsules almost missed land."

Green came in. "So we figure transmission is being grounded out by a rising tide."

"Sounds logical. We'll check it out tomorrow. Our first concern is blowing up the Mannerheim Igloo and hooking up the Del Rouad. Then we'll be able to contact EarthOrb Station next time the Com-Pac relay swings into position."

The Terrain Walker and tractor crested a hill and O'Brien felt somewhat more at ease at the sight of the Argo five miles off—proud and competent as it reared cloudwards and fitfully reflected the brilliance of distant lightning.

Then his brow furrowed in belated consideration of the lost capsule signals. Venus wasn't *supposed* to have any tidal action! But then, that didn't rule out the possibility that persistent winds might occasionally pile up water upon the beaches.

III

His limbs protesting at unaccustomed travel, K'Tawa lowered himself on his haunches but resisted lapsing into Meditation. Instead he watched Zu-Bach cautiously approach the next descended Presence.

Laying down his spear, the latter knelt beside the shining object and directed his quazehorn at its various portions. Then he paused and glanced back at the Old One.

"*I* don't quaze any danger," K'Tawa assured. "And it certainly isn't intended for Trapping."

Zu-Bach pounced upon the Presence, raised its glistening hulk over his head and hurled it to the ground. He retrieved it and smashed it against a boulder. Then he dunked it in the restless sea, hauled it out again and began beating on it with his spear.

K'Tawa smiled his approval. The youngster appeared to be enjoying himself immensely. To say the least, he *was* working off a goodly amount of energy. Maybe he was getting all the Materialistic inclination out of his system at one time.

Zu-Bach pushed eagerly on to the next hated Presence and K'Tawa trailed along. Then, as the other reached in cautiously down for the thing, the Old One shouted a warning.

He went over, closed his eyes to avail himself of the concentration that Visual Withdrawal would provide, and carefully quazed the object with a meticulous circular motion of his horn.

"There's much danger here," he disclosed. "Tremendous force and power—something like the Hot Tongues in the Pre-Meditation Ceremony. I quaze, perhaps, a fierce and deadly noise."

It was all in the realm of only extreme possibility. But he had decided to put it on a bit thick and see if he couldn't humble Zu-Bach with an appreciation of the inadequacy of his own quazehorn.

"Also," he went on, "I see maybe a great angry cloud billowing into the Upper Endlessness, taking with it part of Onlyland and leaving another bay to embrace the Sorrowing Sea."

Warily, Zu-Bach retreated from the Presence. But, on second thought, he reached out and snapped off its long, thin horn. The thing's silent voice went dead and he grunted in satisfaction.

K'Tawa regarded the Presence. It *was* dangerous. So he decided not to move it into the cave where he had hidden the other two. One he had saved because he had quazed its ability to talk with other remote Presences in the Upper Endlessness. The other he had rescued on impulse from Zu-Bach's avid grip. Its contents had been queer and useless—only stale air, all pressed together. But he had vaguely quazed that a beneficial purpose might be found for it.

The next fallen Presence was quite harmless and the Old One watched Zu-Bach attack it with keen enthusiasm. The boy had accepted it as a challenge, since it was twice the size of the last one and since he could lift it only with great effort.

K'Tawa quazed ahead to the distant great Presence that stood upright and conveyed its impression of lurking power and clever ability. And he puzzled again over the four little, living Presences. There, too, he detected treachery and cunning, hate and possessiveness. Zu-Bach had not yet quazed the minor, soft Presences that moved around.

When he did, though, there was no doubt that he would be furious. K'Tawa knew him that well.

Thinking next about the concept of more things in the Upper Endlessness, the Old One, without realizing it, surrendered to the welling urge for Cogitative Withdrawal.

Was it normal, he wondered, for Presences to exist up there? If there were many more, as suggested by the total impression he got from the landed things, they must be coming from *somewhere*. But how could there be a *somewhere* in the Endlessness of Perpetual Clouds?

Then, from the depth of his mind, an obscure ancestral recollection incidentally offered the suggestion that the Clouds might not be Perpetual. Nor might they extend throughout the Endlessness.

Perplexed, K'Tawa asked himself the inescapable question: If the Clouds were not everywhere up there, then *what* existed in the Cloudlessness?

The answer came like a whispered voice from the long-dead past: Blackness. And in that Blackness—

"K'Tawa, let's move on. I've exhausted all the possibilities of destruction with *this* Presence."

The Old One snapped from Withdrawal and stared irately at his relative. At times, he reflected, it required no small degree of fortitude and restraint to pay due respect to the Code of Kinship. There he had been—on the threshold of Phase Eight, perhaps even hopeful of glimpsing the Great Debacle. But now—well, he felt like exclaiming, as Zu-Bach would have done under comparably disappointing circumstances, "Oh, lynko dung!"

The time eventually came, as K'Tawa had quazed it soon would, when Zu-Bach had run out of Presences to destroy. But, by then, he had got a quazescent of the four minor, living Presences.

Amused, the Old One had watched him drop the shattered remains of the last provocative thing and turn towards the towering, glistening object in the distance. Now, tense and alert, he was sweeping his horn imperceptibly from side to side, finely sorting out details of what lay ahead. Wedged around the tip of his upthrust spear was a battered remnant of the last Presence he had destroyed. But it was obvious that he didn't intend to dislodge it. Rather, he was displaying it proudly as a symbol of triumph, as he was the other piece of the Presence he had wrapped around his wrist.

"K'Tawa—"

"I know. Four *living* Presences."

"Queer things—like the lynko. But without tails."

"What else do you quaze about them?"

"Hate—plenty of hate. Scorn, too. And treachery and greed and watchfulness."

K'Tawa nodded commandingly. Zu-Bach seemed to be developing his talents a bit more now. "Can you quaze what must be done?"

"Yes." The other's grip tightened on his spear. "They must be destroyed. They will do more than Trap. If they get the chance, they will—kill?"

"I'm afraid so. At first I was confused. There are obviously similarities of a sort between them and us—such as the fact that they breathe, even though it *is* only stale air. But the similarities are only Physical. Spiritually, we have no common ground—as far as I can see. They are totally Materialistic."

"There is no relationship then?"

"None whatever. When you stop to think about it, how could there be when they come from the Endlessness?"

K'Tawa rose from his haunches, ignoring the complaints from his tired muscles. "Onlyland will be much the better when they are removed, together with all their lifeless Presences."

"They shall be removed," Zu-Bach vowed.

"But you must be careful. There *is* danger of a sort. However, I'll come along and quaze it out for you."

Rather than approach directly, Zu-Bach swung over to the forest. And the Old One smiled in satisfaction over the other's prudence. It perhaps signified the proximity of long-awaited maturity.

"They *are* evil Presences, aren't they, K'Tawa?"

"Yes. I can quaze anxious fear and wariness, distrust and malice. Feel no compunction about destroying them, boy. Not when one of them wouldn't hesitate to destroy another, if it meant personal gain. One is particularly like that."

"And the other three?"

"I'd say they too are of the same nature—by extension.

Let's look at it this way: The Meditators Meditate while we let you and the other Prephasers do all the routine work. It must be the same with the four intruding Presences. Three of them have more important jobs to do. The fourth we quaze as particularly evil, I suppose, because he will do whatever killing must be done."

Directing his horn at the back of Zu-Bach's head while they walked, K'Tawa sensed surging anticipation. As a matter of fact, he was inclined to interpret it as a lust for the fascinating excitement that lay ahead.

Ordinarily, the Old One would have been somewhat concerned over Zu-Bach's purely Materialistic preoccupation. But expediency had to be served. And his young kin would only be doing what *must* be done if Spiritual Ascendancy was to be preserved as a way of life.

That much he could quaze clearly.

A hundred feet in diameter, compartmented by flexible partitions and rising twenty feet above the Venusian surface, the Mannerheim Igloo rustled its plastic shell. Ironing out the final wrinkles, it strove for rigidity. Electrical energy for its oxyaccumulator-compressor and air-conditioners flowed smoothly from the Collard nuclear power plant Yardley had set up in a conveniently located coastal cave.

Outside, the tail end of a brisk shower drummed against the transparent dome. Inside, O'Brien and Green, each with an arm wrapped around Yardley's neck, tried a second chorus of "Home Sweet Home." The song ended on a sour but exuberant note and Yardley went over to where Wastrom stood staring out at the bleak landscape.

"Come on, get with it, Calvin!" Yardley slapped him on the back. "We've got our toe-hold!"

Wastrom's stare was unresponsive as he moved several feet away along the inner curvature of the plastic wall.

Disconcerted, Yardley returned to the two officers.

"Let him sulk," Commander Green advised.

"We're well over the hump," O'Brien added. "Even if he doesn't lift a finger, we've got it made."

"As long as we don't run into any complications with the gear," Yardley reminded. "Some of that stuff would be pretty complicated to anybody but Wastrom."

"It's preset," Green said. "All we have to do is uncrate it."

O'Brien glanced around, smugly surveying the now stiffly partitioned interior of the Igloo. Being inside—without a respirahood, with eighty-degree air bringing relief from the humid hothouse out there, with the reassuring *chug-swish* of the oxyaccumulator pulsing in his ears—brought an unanticipated pleasantness.

Within a few days, he reminded himself, the Igloo wouldn't be so starkly bare. There would be bunks, the soft lights of a humming communications command section seeping through transparent partitions, a galley redolent with the odors of familiar foods—even shower stalls. And it would make little difference that the water being sucked out of the ocean would be carbonated.

The colonel cast a solicitous glance at Wastrom, then went over. "What's the trouble, Calvin? Anything I can do?"

"No." The other surveyed his hands. "I don't suppose so."

But when O'Brien started to walk away, Wastrom added hastily, "It's just that—I don't know. Maybe sometimes you expect too much of yourself. I guess it's like Green said: They must have done a lousy job psyching me out."

O'Brien half turned from the pathetic sight of a robust man capitulating to unreasonable fear. "You'll be okay," he said, but not with conviction.

"But it isn't right to go streaking off across God's universe!" Wastrom's voice rose abruptly. "We're challenging—"

He paused, forcibly restored his composure and exposed his hands once more to his gaze. "Colonel, I'm the youngest man in this crew. Yardley's almost forty-five. But I don't suppose I have half his guts."

"None of us is as calm as he appears."

"But I ought to be the one least concerned. I don't even have a family, like Yardley and Green do."

"Look at it this way: We're here. Everything's working out. No complications. And getting back Earthside is going to be a lot easier."

"*If* we get back."

"All right, Calvin—why do you imagine we might not?"

Wastrom motioned outside the transparent shell. In the distance, O'Brien recognized what the probe data processors had dubbed a "venusow" sloshing through a swamp.

"That's why," Wastrom went on softly. "That's life—Venusian life. It's a lot like ours. It exists and moves around and breathes. But it *can't* do those things because there's no oxygen in the air. It—"

"Animal life on Venus," O'Brien recited, his patience extended, "is adapted to a bio-chemistry in which nitrogen replaces oxygen in the energy relations of the organism. Carbon dioxide comes into the picture too. The nitrogen is oxidized to nitrate and carbon-nitrogen bonds are formed."

"That's just the point! Life *is* possible. Animals *can* live here—not only the ones we know about, but perhaps ones of a higher order, too!" Wastrom's eyes were restless again and his voice unsteady.

Green shouted from across the large compartment, "Time to get to work." He brought over respirahoods and oxygen tanks.

Yardley covered the stacks of supplies with plastic tarps while Commander Green completed the network of protective lightning arresters. "O'Brien, with Wastrom close by so he could keep an eye on him, had the Del Rouad transceiver cabinet slung under the tractor's crane and was moving it into position beside the Igloo.

He paused and adjusted his throat microphone. "Yardley, you'd better start staking down our dome before the next storm comes up."

He sent the tractor creeping forward with its load, but paused again and called directly down to Wastrom, "Move that Walker out of the way so I can get this thing in place."

Wastrom mounted the Terrain Walker and started it up, setting the drive for reverse motion.

"Watch it!" O'Brien shouted. "You're backing into the Igloo!"

Wastrom brought the Walker to a halt and stared down over its rear legs. A footpad had become entangled in one of the Igloo's tie-down grommets.

"Well, don't just sit there!" Green admonished, coming over. Then, "Never mind, I'll free it myself."

But Wastrom had already leaped from the cab.

Instantly, Green shouted and dived out of the way as the immobilized machine clanked back to life and lurched forward.

Wastrom fell sitting in the soft mud and scurried as far from the runaway Walker as he could get. "My sleeve! It—it caught in the switch as I jumped!"

The Walker attained full speed, plopping one footpad down in front of the other. When the entangled tie-down line pulled taut, the entire Igloo fell in behind the machine in an inexorable march across the beach.

Green helplessly seized a fold of the plastic as it went by and tried to hold the inflated dome back.

Yardley raced after the Terrain Walker. But it was obvious he would never overtake it.

O'Brien swore, started up the tractor, then lost half a minute lowering the encumbering Del Rouad cabinet from the crane.

When he finally backed around, however, he could only sit there and watch the Walker splashing out into deeper water. A gust of wind caught the Igloo and sent it scudding ahead of the legged contraption until its tie-down line finally snapped free.

Ten minutes later it was swallowed up by a rainstorm several miles out at sea.

Commander Green finally broke the silence. "Thank God for little girls and backup supply capsules."

O'Brien said, "We've got our work cut out for us now."

"What's first on the program?" Yardley asked.

Green glanced at Wastrom, who was standing sullenly off by himself. "I suppose lynching's out. In which case we can hide ourselves into the Recovery Area and retrieve the backup Igloo."

"Unless," Yardley suggested, "Colonel O'Brien wants to try to set up the Del Rouad gear *without* the Igloo so we can get a message back to EarthOrb Station."

"That's what we *should* do," the Colonel admitted, "since we've already been here twenty-four hours. But we'll try to get the standby Igloo set up first."

Wastrom came over finally, his hands spread out characteristically. "I couldn't help it. You see, the Walker's pad got—"

Green reached for the electronicist, but O'Brien caught his arm.

"Just find some place to sit down," the Commander snapped, "—and stay out of our way!"

Wastrom retreated a step, his puzzled expression half obscured by the wrinkled plastic of his respirahood. "I'm trying to be helpful, if you'll let me. I was going to suggest that we just suspend operations until we get our balance again. It's been thirty hours since we've had any sleep."

This time O'Brien had to place himself tactfully in front of Yardley, who showed indications of imminent explosion.

"I'm going after the backup Igloo," the Colonel said hastily.

"Yardley, you get on the Jason's scope and guide me."

He turned to Commander Green. "Ken, I've got an idea: we might be able to raise the ComPac relay station next time it orbits by if we retune the Jason's transmitter and step it up. See what you can do. Wastrom, that's in your line. Give him a hand."

Yardley and Green struck off for the Argo.

O'Brien paused to stare along the shore. Disappearance from the scope of two Here-I-Am supply capsule signals had suggested an unstable water level. But now, as he surveyed the huge outcropping of rock a hundred yards down the beach, he could see no evidence of tidal action. The mouth of the cave in which they had set up the Collard nuclear power plant was still several feet above the water line.

He headed for the tractor, watching first Yardley, then Green ride the constant-tension lift up to the Jason capsule's hatch. Yardley and Green—but not Wastrom.

Puzzled, he spun around. Following along, the electronicist was carrying a brick-size rock. When O'Brien stared questioningly at him, he tossed it in the air and caught it.

"I think you ought to let me retrieve the backup Igloo, Colonel," he proposed as they continued back towards the Alpha Base site. "After all, I'm the one responsible for this complication. We'll operate more efficiently," O'Brien pointed out, "if we stay within our assigned capacities."

They had reached the tractor when Green came in over the com-system. "Wastrom, come on up here and—"

"Colonel!" Yardley's anxious voice broke through. "The supply cap signals! They've *all* disappeared from the scope!"

Perplexed, O'Brien stared first at the towering Argo, then out into the Recovery Area. Thunder rolled angrily overhead and a bolt of lightning crashed into the swamp beyond the ship. Another speared directly down at the Jason capsule. But the Argo's arrester took the full charge with no arcing.

"Check your gear, Frank," O'Brien suggested. "Maybe it's a matter of gain adjustment."

"No, it's not the gain. I'm picking up *your* blips clearly."

Then Wastrom's face froze behind its plastic hood as he stared off towards the nearby trees.

"Good God!" he shouted, his hand whitening in its grip on the stone. *"Look at that!"*

O'Brien whirled around, then fell back astonished.

Men! Naked giants! Two of them—stepping out of the forest. Great brown bodies with immense shocks of coarse, white hair and leering, grotesque faces both horrible and primitive.

The foremost, carrying a long pole with something shining and terribly familiar around its tip, loosed a roar that was finally drowned out only by a somehow mightier blast of thunder.

"They look *human!*" Wastrom exclaimed. "And that thing on the stick—it's part of a supply capsule!"

The comsystem was overwhelmed with the startled voices of Yardley and Green, who had evidently bolted back to the outer hatch.

Covering the ground in immense strides, the nearer giant reached the first mound of supplies. He dropped his staff and scooped up a half-buried boulder. Raising the rock again and again above his head, he pounded the pile of equipment into rubble.

Wastrom, crouching with O'Brien behind the tractor, hurled the stone he had been holding. It glanced off the creature's back with no apparent effect.

"What *is* it?" Yardley rasped over the comsystem.

"It's twenty-feet tall if it's an inch!" Wastrom observed. "And look—it's got a *horn* growing out of its head! They both have!"

O'Brien tugged at the other's sleeve. "Let's work our way back to the Argo!"

The creature paused before a pile of neatly stacked oxygen-difluoride cylinders and an adjacent mound of diobrane tanks. He barked at his companion, who had drawn up calmly beside him. The latter barked back and they moved on from the Spica stage's reserve fuel to the Del Rouad transceiver. In three blows, the metal cabinet was shattered, its electronic viscera spilled out upon the ground.

Half concealed behind a ridge, O'Brien and Wastrom scurried for the Argo.

The more restrained giant seized the obviously enraged one's arm and pointed at the fleeing figures. But the other shook him off, hefting a still unopened supply capsule. Grunting, he heaved the modified Mercury into the sea.

"There goes our oxygen!" Green moaned.

Wastrom reached the constant-tension line and secured the harness under his armpits. Before he could activate the hoist with the pull of his weight, though, O'Brien grabbed on to the nylon rope. Together they started up—but at a painfully slow rate.

The bellowing creature raced forward, but paused to lift the crate of field laboratory equipment and hurl it to the ground. Then he skirted a Gemini capsule containing construction tools and explosive charges and headed once more for the Argo.

O'Brien almost lost his purchase on the line but resecured it by hooking his arm over part of Wastrom's harness.

Abruptly there was a startling explosion next to his ear and the crisp smell of gunpowder drifted in under his hood. Wastrom had a revolver in his hand and was aiming down at the lunging giant.

The electronicist fired twice more before he lost his grip on the gun. O'Brien was certain he had scored at least one hit. At any rate, the thing's roaring was now at a frenzied pitch.

But that didn't discourage the creature. He beat his fists against the Procyon stage of the ship until it seemed the hundred-and-fifty-foot-long configuration was rocking under the impact of the blows.

O'Brien and the electronicist reached the hatch and were pulled in as the boom retracted automatically.

"Good God in Heaven!" Green swore. "This *can't* be happening!"

"What'll we do?" Yardley asked, staring down at the ravaged Alpha Base site. "Blast off?"

"Not with the Spica's fuel still down there." Wastrom knelt and peered below. "It's incredible! Humanoid life on Venus!"

The two giants met amid the devastation and barked at each other until the larger discovered a crate of supplies he had overlooked. Infuriated, he hurled it at the ship, missed, then rubbed his shoulder where a trickle of dark fluid appeared to be erupting from the skin.

Kicking the tractor over on its side, he rejoined his companion and they headed for the forest as thunder boomed accompaniment to their footfalls and rain obscured their withdrawal.

Green eventually recovered his voice. "Let's get *out* of here! The lift can take us all at one time!" He reached frantically for the boom. "Help me, Scott! It's hung up!"

The others only stared at him as a jagged streak of lightning lanced down a quarter of a mile away.

"The lightning arrester!" the Commander explained. "That giant tore it loose! If the Procyon's fuel load takes a bolt, I don't want to be within a mile of the Argo!"

IV

When Zu-Bach finally snored himself awake and rolled over on the shelfbed, K'Tawa swam up out of Meditative Withdrawal.

The Old One rose, uncoiled from Cogitative Posture, ran briefly through the Stretching Exercises and glanced over at his kinsman.

Zu-Bach sat up and massaged his shoulder. "The sting is gone."

K'Tawa quazed the flesh around the wound and learned that the small foreign object had worked itself out. Moreover, the pierced skin had almost healed.

Kneeling beside the shelfbed, Zu-Bach directed his horn in a methodical scanning motion back and forth across the mud floor of the hut. Then, "*Here* it is—the stinger."

He rose holding a tiny piece of hard substance between his thumb and forefinger.

K'Tawa shied from the thing. "A hate pellet. Get rid of it."

Zu-Bach went over to the wall, swung the rain shield open and tossed it out.

"Leave it open," the Old One said. "The air is so stale that I wouldn't be surprised if L'Jork could conduct his Ceremony of the Hot Tongues in here without even the help of the Meditators."

The other turned, silhouetted by the weak light coming in through the rain shield opening, and hesitated. K'Tawa could almost guess the question before Zu-Bach asked it. Eagerness was that plain among his features.

"The Presences, the living ones—what are they doing now?"

"I'm not too certain there *are* any living Presences remaining. Soon after you fell asleep there was a tremendous noise. When I quazed in their direction, I encountered a heat and light that were stronger than thousands of Hot Tongues."

"And the Presences?"

"As I said, I'm not at all sure you need concern yourself with them any longer."

"But more will come. We both quazed that much."

K'Tawa drew in a deep, disappointed breath. His lesser kin had not sated himself on the Material. His purpose was still, oh, so singular. It was clear that even now he had no appreciation whatsoever of the Spiritual Values.

"When the time comes," the Old One said heavily, "I'm sure you'll be equal to the situation—and perhaps without out my help."

"Oh, you don't think I can quaze the dangers of the lifeless Presences on my own."

"Now, now, boy," K'Tawa chided. "I'm not belittling you. I'm just trying to make you understand that you've been taking up my time during a period when I should be fervently trying to accomplish *Eighth*-Phase Contemplation."

Zu-Bach bristled, with no apparent appreciation at all of the significance of Meditative Ascendancy. "I don't need your help any longer. You think I didn't quaze the danger in the cave by the sea, don't you? Well, I did! And I'm going to do something about all the dangers we left behind!"

"Suit yourself, boy." K'Tawa wondered whether he shouldn't feel guilty about not discouraging the other. But, on second thought, he had certainly discharged all his responsibilities under the Code of Kinship.

The hut's main shield swung open and Exemplar L'Jork entered. "I quazed crosspurposes. Is anything wrong?"

"Zu-Bach," the Old One explained, "has still not had enough. He wants to destroy more of the remaining Presences."

"Oh come now, boy," L'Jork scolded. "Materialism has its place. But—"

"K'Tawa will tell you that more Presences are on their way through the Upper Endlessness."

"On their way—from where?"

"I don't know. But when they get here, there will be *more* dangers to cope with. And perhaps more after that. All while you and the others sit around and Meditate!"

He spun on his heel and strode for the main opening. "Be careful, Zu-Bach," K'Tawa called after him. "Don't underestimate the danger in the cave."

After he had gone, L'Jork asked, "Will he be all right?"

"I think so. The main reason he's going back, as I quaze it, is that he left his spear behind."

"Maybe you *should* go, too."

"The Code of Kinship is not without its limitations. Besides, L'Jork, I'm on the threshold of Phase *Eight* Meditation!"

"Phase *Eight*," the Exemplar repeated, visibly impressed. "You don't say!" Then, with unconcealed envy, "Do you suppose you might actually glimpse Origin and Meaning in their fullness?"

"Possibly."

"Then you *have* no responsibility under the Code of Kinship. Indeed not. Your first obligation now is Meditation."

On that K'Tawa agreed, and with but few reservations.

"I'll let you alone," L'Jork said respectfully, "so you can get on with your work."

Deep Cogitative Withdrawal came quickly for K'Tawa this time, as it had on every recent occasion of Meditative Introspection. It was as though he were becoming marvelously efficient in achieving the Ascendant Attitude. Why, it wasn't even necessary for him to engage in the Preliminary Mental Exercise any longer.

Through the fragmented experiences of scores of remote ancestors, he pursued the elusive concept of the Upper Endlessness, searching almost desperately for reference to the Blackness that had already been suggested by the long-gone past.

This Blackness that shared the Endlessness with the Perpetual Clouds, he wondered—what was its nature? How widespread was it?

Thousands of disembodied memories swam up at him. But they only lapped at the fringe of his curiosity—until—

Once there had been a woman named "Vir-Ela." She had been young and attractive and Intolerant, K'Tawa shunted aside the welter of irrelevant, personal information that would swamp him with trivia if he let it. And he guided his question concentration down to the very core of the matter.

Once Vir-Ela had looked up into the Blackness of the "Night?" (The latter was a concept he couldn't grasp, but he passed it over in fear that the rest would elude him, too.) And in that Blackness were myriads…(the word escaped him, but he had at least trapped its meaning) myriads of tiny, shimmering motes of light, similar to the Hot Tongues but pin-point and precise in definition and brilliant, unmoving in their—"Celestial?"—positions.

The motes inhabited the Blackness and *it was the Blackness that was Endless, not the Perpetual Clouds*! Actually, he learned in astonishment, the Clouds were neither Endless nor perpetual. Their existence had been short indeed, as measured against the great time cycles observed by the brilliant, dancing motes. And the full reach of the Clouds was unbelievably insignificant compared with the vast scheme of things beyond them.

Inexorably, the word-visions that came from Vir-Ela faded and K'Tawa, bereft, cried out in despair. But the ancestral memory bridge spanning the Vir-Ela generation had only gone a step further, he saw suddenly. It had been drawn to the more remote anchorage by the close bond that had existed between the woman and her mother.

The latter, whose name appeared to have been "Cel-Aroa," had vividly recorded for posterity's sake magnificent, sweeping scenes of Onlyland.

But it *wasn't* Onlyland! For the Old One knew that, compared with the Sorrowing Sea, Onlyland was but a spit of mud and stone. And the land Cel-Aroa had thought about had been vast and almost unbroken, with only small bodies of water here and there.

Now he was getting down to Origins, perhaps. It might even be that he had penetrated so deeply into Phase Eight Ascendancy that he was reaching back to *before* the mysterious Great Debacle!

The concepts he was receiving were no less than amazing! Cel-Aroa's people had been as great in number as the very land on which they lived was vast in area. And on that Vastland were—what?

He intercepted the concept of huge, shining huts. Only, they weren't huts because they all served inconceivably more complicated functions than the dwelling places to which the people were presently accustomed. And these glittering structures had been piled up beside one another at many locations on Vastland, all reaching for the sky and all full of and surrounded by swarming people.

Oh, but all the people were different then—*so different*! Not a quazehorn among them! ("That came later," the voice of Y-Lem'Ah, from the more recent "island" generation. seemed to mock.) And there was *something* about their size and their convictions, their manner of life. But what?

Now he had it! Those illustrious ancestors, those incomparable intellects with whom all the Meditators sought to Commune—they, themselves, were not Spiritually Inclined! Not in the least.

Was he to conclude that Ascetic Ascendancy was a way of life that took shape *after* the Great Debacle?

What, he wondered intensely, *was* the Great Debacle? But no responsive thread of memory arose to satisfy his poignant curiosity.

He had gone *so* far, he realized as he swam exhaustedly up out of Withdrawal. But he had so much *further* to go if he expected to fathom True Origin and Full Meaning.

Nevertheless, K'Tawa found himself yearning for the power and wisdom, the might of those quazehornless ancestors of the remote past, even if all those attributes *were* only Materialistic.

Twenty feet back from the cave entrance, Colonel O'Brien tossed restlessly in half sleep. His boot thudded against an oxygen cylinder and instantly he was awake.

He sat up groggily, his need for rest after thirty hours' work still not fully satisfied. The dim, everlasting light of Venus' murky sky seeped into the chamber, etching somber shadows on dank walls. In the distance, inside a second entrance to the cave, the Mark IV Collard reactor hummed in wasteful production of electrical energy that would never be used, that was even now discharging itself wantonly to ground.

O'Brien untied the cord that was pinching the respirahood securely about his neck. Now that he was upright, there would be no danger of the oxygen being displaced by Venus' carbon dioxide. Quietly, so as not to disturb the others, he returned the misplaced O_2 cylinder to the stack from which it had rolled.

"Not many left, are there, Scott?"

He started at the suddenness of Green's whispered voice, further muffled by his respirahood. The Commander came over and knelt by the sparse supply of oxygen containers.

"For the few we do have we can thank Yardley," O'Brien reminded after making certain his transmitter was turned off, too. "When that creature got through with Alpha Base, Frank was the one who realized we were wearing the only O_2 we had left. If he hadn't risked his life to toss those cylinders out of the Argo, we wouldn't be around to talk about it now."

As it was, the Colonel added under his breath, the remaining supply of oxygen was no less than fatally inadequate. And Train Beta wasn't due to arrive for another *five* days.

Squatting, Green slapped his knee. "Well, what do we do now—go back over the Recovery Area and see what we can salvage?"

"There won't be *anything* to pick up."

"You think that unicorn thing smashed *all* our other caps?"

"You saw what he had wrapped around his staff. Those Here-I-Am capsule blips didn't just *disappear* from the scope."

Yardley had awakened. He came over and joined them, sitting silently on his haunches and appearing to O'Brien like some prehistoric savage brooding in the dismal confines of his cave.

"Good God!" Green lurched up. "Train Beta—I'd forgotten about them!"

"I hadn't," O'Brien said gloomily.

"What'll we do?" Yardley asked. "There's no way of warning them! That creature smashed both our Del Rouad transmitters!"

"I don't know," the Colonel admitted. "Unless—yes, there *is* a chance of getting through to them—at the last moment."

Yardley stared expectantly at him.

"If they don't hear from us," he went on, "they'll be guarding our field comsystem frequency on the way down."

"We can warn them then!" the nuclear tech exclaimed.

"Yes. But there are two drawbacks. One: It'll be too late to stop their landing—and they won't be able to get off again until after they pick up their Spica fuel capsules."

"And the other objection?" Green asked.

"You won't like it. I don't. The oxygen we have left will last the four of us only two days. If we're going to get any warning at all off to Train Beta, we'll have to arrange it, somehow, that *one* of us will be around for *five* days."

Nobody said anything.

O'Brien turned and faced an arm of the sea that ran along the far wall of the cave. "It isn't a decision we have to make immediately."

"When *do* we have to make it?" the Commander wanted to know.

"If four of us use up oxygen for twenty-four hours, there'll still be just about enough left to carry one from that point up to Beta's estimated time of arrival."

Green paced to the subterranean river and back. "I'm glad Wastrom isn't awake to hear this."

"Oh, Wastrom's all right now," Yardley assured. "It took those giants to snap him out of it. But did you see how he reacted? He even attacked one with a rock and wounded it with his gun."

Green and O'Brien exchanged awkward glances and the latter said, "Sorry to disappoint you, Frank. He apparently did come around for a while. But it didn't last long. You'd have seen for yourself if you could have stayed awake a while longer."

"He went to pieces," the Commander verified, "—screaming about violating God's laws and getting the giants as a punishment. Finally whimpered himself to sleep."

Yardley appeared thoroughly disappointed.

"What puzzles me," O'Brien went on, "was his gun—what prompted him to bring it along in the first place, how he hid it."

"I suppose if you were as terrified of space and Venus," Yardley offered, "you might have smuggled a weapon along, too, even though you were assured you wouldn't need one."

"Right. But the point is that he didn't appear to be terrified when he sneaked the revolver aboard. He didn't show any neurotic tendencies at all until a week ago."

56

Green stared at O'Brien. "Where's the gun now?"

"I've got it. You didn't think I was going to give it back."

Yardley tensed. "Listen!"

O'Brien heard it, too—a clatter of metal on metal coming from the direction of the demolished Alpha Base. It sounded like someone walking through a field of tin cans.

"Those giants are back!" Yardley shouted.

"Quiet!" O'Brien cautioned. "They don't know we're in here."

Green crossed fingers on both hands and displayed them high in the air. "Maybe that thing'll go to work on the reserve Spica fuel this time!"

Yardley grinned expectantly. "Colonel, if the Irish have the luck market cornered, you'd better cash in your share right now. Our troubles may be over if that Venutian starts banging those oxygen-difluoride and diobrane containers together!"

"It'll be just like another Argo going up!" Green assured.

"That makes for nice wishing," the Colonel commented. "But I find it more than coincidental that he purposely passed up the Spica fuel first time around—the Gemini with the explosive charges, too."

Green protested, "You're not suggesting the thing *knew*—"

From the subterranean stream behind them came an abrupt splash.

When O'Brien spun around, Wastrom was standing by the oxygen cylinders, reaching down for another.

"It's coming back!" he shouted. "Can't you hear it out there? It won't let us alone until it's destroyed everything we've got!"

Wastrom faced the stream and lifted the cylinder over his head. But before he could hurl it, Green drove his shoulder into the electronicist's midsection and sent him flailing back.

"We've got to destroy everything!" Wastrom screamed. "We've got to do what it wants!"

"Shut him up!" Yardley urged. "Before he has a dozen giants breathing down our necks!"

Green followed through and smashed a fist into the electronicist's face, even as the latter filled his lungs for another outburst.

Then the Commander knelt beside the unconscious Wastrom to make certain his respirahood had not been damaged.

"Back!" Yardley cautioned. "Get back! That thing's right outside!"

O'Brien could hear the giant's labored breathing, like the measured hiss of a safety valve on a steam engine. He drew Wastrom's revolver from his pocket.

There was an enraged growl and a great, leering head poked into the cave entrance. But when the shoulders couldn't make it through, the creature drew back and roared. Then a massive arm rammed in and a clawing hand swept back and forth from wall to wall.

The revolver barked three times as O'Brien emptied it at the thing's biceps. One of the slugs grazed flesh.

Bellowing, the giant lunged back. And O'Brien, tracing his retreat by the dwindling sounds of his breathing, went cautiously ahead.

"Careful, Scott!" Green urged.

Hesitating, O'Brien stepped outside and watched the massive creature withdrawing back through the base site.

"It's leaving."

"But it'll be back," Yardley guessed. "I'm sure of that."

"It wouldn't if we had a few weapons," Green said.

"Our Venutian *does* seem to hurt and scare easily," the Colonel agreed. "If we could manage to kill one of them, I'll bet the others—if there's a whole settlement of them—would promptly turn tail."

Green ventured farther from the cave. Pensively, he walked a short distance along the beach, then turned towards the base site.

"Ken," O'Brien called after him. "Where are you going?"

The other paused. "There may be just two of those things. Or there may be a whole nest. We've got to know what the odds are. I'm going to find out."

"Ken, come back here!"

It was apparent, however, that he wouldn't be stopped.

O'Brien started to follow.

But Yardley trapped his arm. "Would you really like to kill one of them, Colonel? I think I know how it can be done."

O'Brien, staring anxiously after the Commander, was restrained by the realization that the information Green sought *should* be passed on to Train Beta. "How would you do it, Frank?"

"Set a trap." The nuclear technician indicated the heavily insulated cable that snaked across the beach from the Mark IV Collard reactor. "Our tractor's not damaged—just knocked over on its side. I checked it while Green was salvaging those tins of food. We can right the tractor with its own winch, assuming that if the Venutian comes back he'll want to kick it over again. But this time it'll be parked on several insulating layers of plastic tarps. And this high-voltage cable will be bolted to the tractor's frame."

V

K'Tawa bestirred himself from Meditation, reluctantly yielding his grip on the inherent, sometimes incomprehensible impressions that had been seeping into his conscious. That these impressions were being dredged from the very bottom-most depths of genetic recall left no doubt that he was well into Phase Eight Ascendancy.

At the moment, however, he was concerned over Zu-Bach. Even now he could quaze his youthful kin as he left the coastal plain and entered the forest. Zu-Bach, it appeared, was fuming over—something.

The Old One steadied his horn in that direction. Why, it seemed the boy had been stung again by the little Presences, who evidently were still somewhere near the beach!

Then K'Tawa tensed. Not all the living Presences were on the coast. One, he could plainly quaze now, was following furtively behind Zu-Bach, advancing from tree to tree. Only, Zu-Bach's thoughts were so full of rage and vengeful plans that he hadn't noticed the small one at all.

K'Tawa considered going out to meet his kin and making an issue of his utter lack of vigilance. But Zu-Bach would only be resentful of that Exercise of Seniority. Anyway, the Old One saw now, there was no evidence of harmful intent on the part of the trailing Presence. Curiosity, perhaps. And a tinge of bitter frustration. But certainly he harbored no immediate aggressive plans.

Still quazing, K'Tawa watched Zu-Bach lumber up over a hill. After he had started down the other side, the Presence clambered up the elevation and dropped on his chest to peer over the crest. He remained there a long while, staring down into the valley and studying the village. Then he rose and headed back for the coastal plain.

Zu-Bach, meanwhile, had reached the village.

And K'Tawa delayed his return to Contemplation while he listened to his relative trying to interest several of the Meditators in an account of what had happened to him. But Zu-Bach had forgotten that this was the Feast of Introspection and that the entire period, from sleep to sleep, was set aside for Ascetic Ascendancy.

Thwarted in his quest for attention, Zu-Bach impetuously strode for the nearest hut. He brushed disrespectfully past its Meditating owner and lowered himself on to the shelfbed within.

K'Tawa continued with his own Introspective Quest. And, as a stepping-off point, he concerned himself with an unrestrainable flow of questions that phrased themselves spontaneously in his mind:

Why was the Horizontal Endlessness (correction: the curved-back-upon-itself surface) almost all water now, whereas once it had been practically all land?

This concept "night" that he had got from Vir-Ela—could he reasonably assume that its corollary was "day?"

And what had the wet-dry, night-day dichotomies to do with the Great Debacle?

Then, from a distant ancestral source, so close to the Great Debacle that it conveyed all the terror and confusion associated with that event, came a momentous suggestion.

There was a *third* dichotomy directly involved in the exclusive interrelationships: "stale-poisonous," as they applied to the air.

Even in his rigid Posture, K'Tawa squirmed in protest. It was an incredible pairing! Dichotomies were made up of opposites. But here was one with parts that were almost compatible. "Pure-poisonous," for instance, would have been logical, as would have "pure-stale." But—"stale-poisonous?"

He turned from the incongruous matter as another link abruptly established itself in the ancestral recall chain. This time he had reached back for a handful of perceptions from one who had called himself "Dis'Pauz." And the memories were all the more welcome because they had obviously been acquired just before the Great Debacle—when knowledge and ability were at a peak.

From that source the Old One received the illuminating impression that the surface-bent-back-upon-itself had once had another name—"The World."

Moreover, The World was *not* alone in the Upper Endlessness. There were other The Worlds—shining deep in the Blackness's vastness!

K'Tawa almost bolted from Withdrawal. *That* explained the origin of the little Presences! They had come from another The World! And the one nearest his ancestors' Vastland enjoyed a day-night dichotomy, just as Vastland itself once had before the Debacle!

Then, as though caught up in a raging vortex of the Sorrowing Sea, the Old One found himself dizzily fighting a relentless, confusing assault of concepts and impressions.

Night-day. Wet-dry. Stale-poisonous. Still another polar pair: Blackness-Light, in its more than ordinary implications. Shimmering motes and The Worlds. Quazehornless ancestors. Vastland—Mainland—Island—Onlyland—

Night was doubtless the corollary of day, just as wet was so obviously the opposite of dry. And Blackness of Light. But did "little ancestor" have any opposite? Was Blackness synonymous with daylessness. And did—

Then into his foundering Meditation was thrust a quite rational and almost calming recollection bequeathed by Dis'Pauz:

There was the Endless Blackness with its shimmering The Worlds and with its...("lightgivers" was the closest word K'Tawa could find for the concept), which also cast brilliance about them.

And suddenly, deep within the Blackness the Old One saw a huge, white, sparkling cloud—odd-shaped and wispy. And shy, too, for it always hid its long, thin—"tail?"—from the Lightgiver with which it was associated. K'Tawa saw, too, that Dis'Pauz was terrified by the Cloud from the Blackness. And his terror was shared by all the billions of quazehornless people.

Did the Cloud have anything to do, the Old One wondered, with the Great Debacle?

At this point K'Tawa's Meditations, though compelling, were becoming quite burdensome and exhausting. Consequently, he did not know when Contemplation trailed off into sleep.

When he awoke from prolonged Posture, he quazed that Zu-Bach had gone from the other hut. He was in the forest now, returning to the coastal plain. And his scorn and wrath had renewed themselves.

K'Tawa stretched and quazed ahead to the beach. Now that he definitely knew the little Presences were there, he had no difficulty discerning them. They were in the cave, not too far from the Greatest-of-All-Perils. In order to save their stale air, they were resting, having just finished—having just finished—

The Old One rose trembling. Just as Zu-Bach had originally feared, they had turned out after all to be Things That Trap! They had just devised a most ingenious snare—not one that would simply take its victim, but one that would *kill instantly*!

And the victim, K'Tawa saw plainly, would be Zu-Bach.

The Old One rushed from his hut, trying to quell his inner anxiety so that the other Meditators wouldn't quaze it and be disturbed. He struck out through the forest.

How malicious were the small Presences! Until now, he had hoped they might not all be as evil as the one had seemed to be. But, whereas before only the one had wanted to kill treacherously, now that one hardly appeared interested in slaying. The other three, however, were lustful in their eagerness to take Zu-Bach's life. What a queer reversal of quazable attributes among the Presences!

Pushing as swiftly as he could through the forest, K'Tawa focused his attention on the Trap. Most clever indeed. And it involved a peril that was quite obscure and original—so much so that he felt certain Zu-Bach would never quaze it for himself.

It seemed that the Presences had taken their Thing That Crawls and put it in full sight on the beach near their cave. They had attached to it a hidden something that would leap like the very Lightning itself into Zu-Bach's body.

K'Tawa, his aged lungs burning with unaccustomed exertion, burst out of the forest. Across the coastal plain, his young kin stood uncertainly on the beach, letting the Sorrowing Sea lap at his feet.

Immediately before him was the Trap!

K'Tawa raced across the plain, quazing the four Presences as they watched expectantly from the mouth of their cave. He shouted:

"Zu-Bach! Watch out for the Thing That Traps!"

But the other, hearing, only cast a disdainful look at his senior kinsman and started forward.

Then there was a quazable commotion at the mouth of cave as one of the living Presences—the one who had first impressed K'Tawa as being wholly evil—came running out and waving his arms.

The Old One had almost reached Zu-Bach. But it was too late. For the latter, lurching forward at the sight of the hated Presence, swung an arm in front of him to push the Trap out of his way.

An odd sort of Lightning played all around his hand where it had come into contact with the thing and he toppled forward.

The excited Presence, terrified now, tried to scurry out of the way. But he failed utterly. Zu-Bach's quite ample chest fell full upon the minor creature.

And K'Tawa, pausing in midstride to ponder his complete failure at saving his kin, quazed that two living beings, Zu-Bach and one of his tormentors, had both achieved instant and final Spiritual Withdrawal.

The Old One sat on the sand, head lowered and thoughts saddened. For a long while he had proudly committed himself to personal direction of Zu-Bach's Ascendancy. But now his junior kin would taste not even the pleasures of *First* Phase Contemplation.

He glanced at the cave. The three remaining Presences had drawn back inside. And the concept of intelligent beings hiding in a cave touched off almost instant Meditation.

All the evidence now being offered by genetic recall pointed to the fact that his ancestors, too, had once lived underground.

But why? Because, came the explanation from a vague source in the far past, if they ventured outside the air would choke them.

The very sky itself, it seemed, had almost—"overnight?"—been filled with suffocating stuff. And there had been other things too—wetness to subdue the dryness, great convulsions of Vastland, total destruction of the day-night dichotomy.

Henceforth, came the unwitting information from his remote forbear, there would be the—Eternal Day.

K'Tawa stirred troublously on the beach. Was that, then, the Great Debacle? Had he had a glimpse of the Awful Disaster?

Despite his fervent search for the answers to those questions, however, his Meditations struck out in their own direction, still drawing from genetic recall:

Quazehornless people in caves. Caves that provided breathable air because their vast underground passages and chambers had been filled with it. Caves that would sustain the handful of people and some of the animals. The air was still fresh there, but would not be for very long—only a few generations. For it was being forced out of the upper openings by water seeping into the lower passages.

Part of the Debacle?

Yes (came confirmation from the impressions of an "Edu'Aken," who had lived during one of the cave generations), part of the Debacle—an after part.

Was it related to the Vast Cloud that had come from the Outer Blackness?

But nowhere in K'Tawa's genetic recall heritage was there a ready answer to that question.

Then he dragged himself suddenly up out of Withdrawal. He had quazed return of the minor Presences to the mouth of their cave.

Damned little things! But, then again, perhaps he shouldn't be too intolerably disposed towards them. He saw now that their presence had not been all harmful. It had, by association, suggested new channels for his Quest for Origin and Meaning.

They were much like his remote ancestors must have been, he conceded. But, oh, so different! So malevolent! Even now these three in the cave wanted to destroy, trap, kill, possess.

Still confused, the Old One headed wearily back towards the village. The others would have to learn Zu-Bach's fate, if they hadn't already quazed it.

Green ventured uncertainly from the cave, stared back over the plain, then returned. "He's gone!"

O'Brien shrugged. "Which leaves us exactly nowhere unless we managed to buy a little respect for Train Beta when it drops down."

"Poor Wastrom," Yardley said, staring at the fallen giant. "But at least he went out with honor."

"Or," O'Brien added on second thought, "*did* he?"

"What do you mean?"

"Nothing. Just trying to put a few pieces together."

"Well, when it looked like the giant wasn't going to fall for the trap, Wastrom raced out to lure him on."

Green and O'Brien stared at each other.

"Well, didn't he?" Yardley persisted. "Wasn't that what he *said* he was going to do when I tried to stop him?"

"Yes, he did," Commander Green admitted. "But—well, he went out there waving his arms, didn't he?"

"And," O'Brien put in, "I got the impression he was trying to work his way around the tractor, rather than keep the tractor between him and that creature."

"That's what I thought, too," Green agreed.

Yardley looked from one to the other. "What do you mean?"

O'Brien frowned. "I'm just wondering: Can you turn a neurosis on and off? Here we had a man obsessed with the fear of death, frightened, whimpering. Can that sort of person go out and destroy himself heroically for a cause?"

"You've got a point," Green observed. "Wastrom could turn it on and off, all right. He wasn't at all neurotic when the Venutians first attacked. He was more rational than any of us."

Again, the Commander and O'Brien traded glances. The latter asked, "You thinking what I'm thinking?"

"Possibly. Let's kick it around a bit. Let's go back to the gun. Why did he conceal it from us—unless he had a good, logical reason for us not to know he had it?"

"Preposterous!" Yardley protested. "Are you suggesting he might have wanted to use it on us? If so, why didn't he do it out in space?"

"Because," O'Brien said impulsively, "he didn't *have* it out there! It would have shown up in deviation in our instruments if he had!"

Green snapped his fingers. "That's right!"

"Then where *did* he get it?" Yardley asked densely.

"It must have been concealed in one of the pieces of equipment we picked up in the Recovery Area."

"But he was never anywhere near any of that equipment Earth-side!" Yardley reminded. "It was prepared, assembled and launched hundreds of miles from Kennedy!"

O'Brien nodded. "Which indicates that Wastrom was far from being alone in his enterprise."

Yardley only shook his head incredulously.

"No," Green said. "It wasn't the psych boys who slipped up. It was the security boys."

"His neurosis was all an act then?" the nuclear tech asked.

"A very good one," O'Brien said, impressed. "He knew this operation would be most vulnerable in its earliest stage. Yet, his stake in it was something he had to play by ear. Pretending to be terrified ensured tolerance for his 'mistakes.' Until the giants came along, he wasn't at all sure of success, but he was trying."

Green looked up sharply. "The runaway Terrain Walker!"

"There would have been more accidents like that."

"I don't think so. He would have used the gun to simplify matters. But he had probably just got it before the oversized Venutians showed up."

"And when that happened, he lost his gun. But in the Venutians he saw his opportunity to let them accomplish his purpose for him—not against Alpha, but against Beta and Gamma and anything else we would send over."

Yardley straightened. "But he *shot* the first giant!"

"On impulse. He realized later that the last thing he wanted to do was scare them off. That's why he dropped his neurotic act again and turned hero at the end—so he could save the Venutian while pretending to lead him into the trap."

Green went and got three fresh oxygen cylinders and passed them around. "Well, we know how this operation stacks up in the Kremlin's book. Think of the effort they took to plant Wastrom."

O'Brien discarded his empty cylinder and snapped the new one around his waist. He stared down at a serpentine length of high-tension cable that stretched across the dank floor. "I think our final reflection on Wastrom can be one of thanks."

"How so?" Green asked.

"He suggested our logical next step. He was probably right in his idea that we might strike fear into the Venutians and discourage them from attacking Train Beta."

"I don't think the boys in that village will play follow the leader to that rigged tractor—not with one of them bringing the message back."

"No, of course not. So, the thing to do is take the attack to them—before they gang up on us. Frank, that Collard reactor—what's its alternate function?"

Yardley paused. "The plan was that if all the power plants came through and we needed a nuclear blast for construction purposes, all we'd have to do is goose a Collard up to chain reaction."

"And this one we *will* goose up—after I sling it on the tractor and haul it over to that Venusian village."

Green loosed an exuberant shout. Whooping too, Yardley slapped him on the back.

But then the nuclear technician turned sharply towards O'Brien. "We don't have the radio gear to trigger it off."

"Then it'll have to be done manually."

Yardley was silent a moment. "Right," he said crisply, not broaching the ominous ramifications of the Colonel's statement. "But *I'm* hauling it over. That's in my department."

"No," Green put in determinedly. "*I'm* taking it."

O'Brien hesitated, realizing he would only have a more vigorous argument on his hands if he tried to eliminate them on the basis of their obligations.

"Nobody's playing hero here," he said. "Things are going to be even tougher for you two. You'll have to decide—and within the next twelve hours—who'll be around when Train Beta arrives."

When K'Tawa reached the village he encountered a scene of agitation such as he had not witnessed before. Exemplar L'Jork and five—he counted them twice—five Meditators were awake and active, despite the fact it was sleeptime. Two of them paced beside the Central Slab while the Exemplar and three others held court, with much gesticulation, in front of the Drying Hut.

Rarely had the Old One seen *that* much disquiet. It was evident they had quazed Zu-Bach's tragic death.

L'Jork hurried over to meet him. "I'm afraid we have concerned ourselves excessively with the Spiritual. We should have listened to the boy, shouldn't we?"

"It was a most regrettable Spiritualization," said the Old One. "Poor Zu-Bach."

"Could it have been avoided?" asked Lank-Tro.

"I tried. Perhaps the Exemplar is right. Maybe we should have given Zu-Bach a more receptive ear. But, still—"

"Yes?" L'Jork prompted.

"I don't know. I'm a bit confused."

"Well, *we* aren't." L'Jork faced the others. "Rin'Au, arouse the Prephasers."

"What do you intend doing?" the Old One asked.

"We're going to deal with the living Presences. But first we'll have to send for Prephase help from the other villages."

"And," Lank-Tro added, "we'll also be prepared when the other Presences drop down from the Endlessness."

K'Tawa only stared at the ground, somewhat befuddled.

"You don't approve of the plan?" the Exemplar asked.

"I don't know. L'Jork, I'm fully into Phase Eight Meditation now. And I can't be certain the flow of impressions doesn't point to some sort of deep significance."

"Involving the intruding Presences?"

"Perhaps. But then, again, perhaps not. I'd like to Contemplate more—much more."

L'Jork stared critically at him. "K'Tawa, we respect your Eighth Phase achievements. But sometimes we wonder whether you aren't becoming senile in your Meditations. Do you actually expect us to believe that at the very moment you start discovering Meaning concerning small, quazehornless people of the past—at that very moment and by a great coincidence, quazehornless Presences begin making their appearance here?"

"Oh, no. The coincidence would be too far-fetched. But it could be the other way around. Maybe the appearance of the Presences merely suggested fruitful channels of Contemplation that hadn't occurred to anyone before."

Rin'Au asked, "What do you advise—about the Presences?"

"I advise nothing. All I'd like to do is Meditate some more."

"You can Meditate all you want," the Exemplar said stiffly. "But I've already decided what has to be done."

K'Tawa quazed that the decision involved precipitous action against the Presences as soon as the Prephasers could be assembled. Nevertheless, he returned to his hut and anxiously distorted his complaining limbs into Cogitative Posture.

Sadly, he realized that all the evidence, fragmentary though it might be, pointed urgently to the Great Debacle as the paramount modifier of Meaning. But for recall after recall, now, he had thrust only along the fringe of the Calamity. He had indeed thrown much illumination on his Quest for Significance. But whatever he had recalled had been so confusing that he was unable to wring any comprehension from it.

Perhaps a period of Meditative review was in order. From the reassessment of inherent memories might come understanding, or at least a more Meaningful order.

There had been day and night, of that he was certain. Night spawned out of the Endless Blackness. And quazehornless people who were incredibly knowledgeable, who had lived in huge collections of shining structures on Vastland and had known about other The Worlds.

And out there in the Upper Endlessness had been a huge, shimmering Cloud, turning back part of the Blackness. Only, it *hadn't* been a Cloud, as he normally entertained the concept. It had been composed of—(he coaxed himself) composed of—

The source from which the answer came was as obscure as the information itself was Meaningless. At any rate, it appeared that the vast, wispy Cloud had been made up of hard-like stone pieces of water, countless numbers of them. And something else—"solid?"—poisonous air. No, not quite. But it *had* been hard and, when warmed, it would turn into first choking, then non-choking air.

K'Tawa paused in Contemplation. Why "choking" then "non-choking?" How could the air quit being of the one nature and start being of the other? It was beyond comprehension, unless—unless the change had been in the *breather* rather than in the *breathed!*

He tried to pursue the recollection. But, somehow, he sensed he had gone up a blind channel. Then, from a wholly new direction came—*something*. Straining, he forced an element of identity from the impression that was trying to break through.

69

There had been a—"Fos-Batl?"—who had lived during one of the early cave generations, just after the Great Debacle.

And from that observant individual came fascinating mind-images. Of frightened people massed at the very mouth of a cavern, the gentle flow of fresh air, trapped for generations, passing reassuringly around their bodies. And, in front of them, so close that they could step easily across it, was the line-of-farthest-advance-without-suffocation.

Outside was the poisonous air, it seemed. And inside was the—"fresh?"—air. There was much confusion here. And K'Tawa was certain that somewhere along the way Meanings had been swapped. What had once been "stale" or "poisonous" was now "fresh." But he sloughed off the temptation to become involved in semantics. And he sought a closer togetherness with Fos-Batl and the bequeathed memories.

The Old One watched, entranced, as some of the people gathered huge see-through lenthral bags that grew underground. Inflating them, they tied the openings securely about their necks. (The living Presences too, he realized suddenly, used see-through bags of a sort!) This apparently provided portable fresh air and made it possible for the people to stay out of the cave long enough to gather food from the plants for themselves and the animals.

Fos-Batl's contribution to Meaning faded before yet another identity that seemed to tug for K'Tawa's attention. Now he opened his mind to Bel-Uri, of a later cave generation. He noted the young woman's sadness and loneliness as she watched her toddling son play just beyond the line-of-farthest-advance-without-suffocation.

She was heavy-hearted because she knew her progeny was a poisonous air-breather. And he would live on the invisible boundary line only until he had gone through sufficient Physical Ascendancy to strike out on his own. Then he would join the handful of people and animals that had already crossed over.

The point of Meaning here seemed evident: With infinite mercy, Providence had gradually given the people the ability to breathe the new kind of air that the Cloud from the Blackness had brought. Just as, later, that same Providence had provided quazehorns.

He tried to penetrate even deeper into the mainstream of ancestral memory. But the impressions came too rapidly to be orderly, and they were too vague for useful comprehension.

"K'Tawa, wake up and quaze towards the coastal plain!"

The Old One reluctantly returned from Withdrawal and opened his eyes to see L'Jork standing anxiously above him.

The Exemplar pointed. "Quaze out that way, quickly!"

And K'Tawa took in the approach of the living Presence on the Thing That Crawled. Too, he sensed the Awful Danger the little one was bringing.

Steering the tractor through a field of strewn boulders, Colonel O'Brien finally left the coastal plain and headed into the forest. Suspended on the crane ahead of him, the Mark IV Collard reactor, damped into silence, swung ponderously with the lurching motions of the vehicle.

"All right, Scott—I can't see you any longer," came Commander Green's voice over the comsystem. "You're on your own."

"Straight into the woods?"

"As straight as you can go. Soon you'll see a small stream—"

"Crossing it now."

"And then, on the other side, a lot of short, thin trees with leaves that look like black cobwebs."

"Roger. I'm in them." O'Brien used a dripping hand to wipe an accumulation of raindrops off his respirahood. "There's a channel through them that looks pretty well trampled."

"That's it. Just follow it on. And Scott—keep in touch."

"Right."

The tractor's right tread dropped into a depression and the Collard reactor jerked over in that direction, coming down hard on its suspension cable. O'Brien couldn't understand why the line hadn't snapped. He decreased speed markedly.

He glanced up at the black rolling sky and watched several bolts crash down into the forest. But soon the torrential rain was obscuring even the lightning.

That, however, was to his advantage, he assured himself. In an Earthside environment, this sort of operation would be carried out under the cover of blackest night. But with Venus's eternal day, the next best thing was a severe rainstorm to add to the murkiness. That the chance of taking a bolt broadside had also increased was, of course, an added complication.

"Frank?" he called.

"Yes?" Yardley's answer was instant.

"You sure you've got this thing rigged up right? It's our only shot. I wouldn't want to blow it."

"She'll go," the nuclear tech promised. "All you have to do is touch the free wire to the negative pole of your battery. Everything else'll take care of itself."

O'Brien squinted through the rain, checking the twin leads that rose along the suspension cable, curved in and out of the boom's bracework and dangled down beside the seat. One lead was already grounded on the steering column. The other, well wrapped in makeshift insulation, lay beside the open battery box, anchored there with a piece of plastic cord.

Again his hood had become almost opaque from perspiration within and the pelting rain without. He removed it and pulled out his shirttail. While he gave the hood a thorough wiping, he breathed slowly at first, then gaspingly. Venus' air went in and out without any difficulty. But the "trace" of oxygen was too pitifully inadequate for starved capillaries.

Swiping the tepid rain from his face, he lowered the hood once more. He imagined he was a bit more comfortable—but only immeasurably so, what with carbonated water and sweat pasting his clothes against his body.

"Getting anywhere, Scott?" Green asked.

"I've left the saplings—if that's what they were—behind now. Going into some pretty stout timber."

"Just push on straight ahead."

"Which way is straight ahead?"

"You should see a swamp off to your right."

"Roger."

"Beyond that and bit off to the left there should be a hill."

O'Brien peered past the swinging Collard reactor. "I can just make it out. The rain's letting up. A hill with no trees on top?"

"That's right. From the crest you'll see the village."

"Good enough."

The Colonel took his attention momentarily off the swinging power plant and glanced up at the trees—crazy, grotesque things that reared somberly into the Venusian twilight for perhaps fifty feet or so, then broke out into a ridiculous pattern of twisted branches and impossible foliage.

Only vegetation like *that*, he reflected, could be expected to exist on this kind of a world. It was undoubtedly efficient in separating what little oxygen there was from the Venusian atmosphere. But when it got through taking care of its bio-chemical needs, there was none left to discharge into the air.

Suddenly Yardley was back on the comsystem. "Scott, I can't let you go through with this—not when there's a way out!"

O'Brien sighed. "I was hoping you wouldn't discover the way out for at least another fifteen or twenty minutes."

"You *know?*"

"Yes, I thought of it. But getting this job done is more important. If we're talking about the same solution, you'll know it was a matter of 'either-or.'"

"Yes, I see that now," Yardley acknowledged listlessly. "And I suppose you're right. Getting rid of that nest of Venutians as quickly as possible is more important."

Commander Green's puzzled voice erupted. "How's about letting *me* in on this?"

"Well, we could have blocked off a small section of the cave," O'Brien explained. "With all the juice this Collard puts out, it wouldn't have been too hard to set up some sort of electrolytic process. It probably wouldn't have given off a *lot* of oxygen—but maybe enough to keep us going."

"Sounds great! We could hibernate here until just before Train Beta's ETA, *then* rig up the attack deal you've got going now." But exuberance faded from the Commander's voice as he spoke.

"Yes?" O'Brien encouraged.

"Oh, I see. That would give the Venutians four days to figure out some way of smoking us into the open. And then we might not have a shot at their nest before Beta arrives."

The Colonel crested the hill and pulled the tractor to a halt. Ahead, the forest thinned out on the downslope. And perhaps half a mile off was the village—a disarray of huge, clumsy huts of no apparent standard shade or formal design.

Then he tensed. Four huge Venutians, all carrying stone-tipped spears, were lumbering up the hill. A fifth, lean and slower in his stride, followed. O'Brien recognized him as the one who had twice been to the Alpha Base site.

He started the tractor forward at full speed. "This is it," he said calmly into his throat microphone. "There's a counterattack shaping up below. But I'm going to try and crash through to their nest."

"What if you get hemmed in before you reach the village?" Yardley asked.

"I'll let it blow right here. We'll get at least five of them. And the blast should have some effect on the village."

He skirted around a tree, half skidded into a ravine and lumbered out again, then broke into an open stretch.

The four giants had mounted a violent charge. But the fifth was acting as oddly as he had after the death of his companion on the beach. He had seated himself, crossed his arms and legs and bowed his head until touching the ground.

O'Brien unsheathed the negative lead to the Collard reactor and held it in readiness above the battery box.

But while he had taken his eyes off the Venutians, he hadn't noticed that the branch of a scrub tree had got caught in the crane's suspension cable.

The tractor's forward momentum had bent the bough like a bow by the time he saw what had happened. Desperately, he tried to brake his speed. But it was too late.

The branch slipped free and lashed back, catching him full in the chest and catapulting him from the seat.

Stunned, he struggled up and staggered after the vehicle. But he hesitated, realizing that many things were horribly wrong.

The tractor, trailing the negative lead that was to have set off the Collard's chain reaction, was going too fast for him to overtake it.

Furiously, the giants were bearing down on him.

And his lungs were convulsing from lack of oxygen.

74

As he slumped, suffocating, to the ground, he saw the reason for the latter complication.

His respirahood—oxygen cylinder and all—had been hurled into the tree and was caught on a branch twenty feet over his head.

VI

Commander Green paced the beach near the cave while Yardley sat staring at the forest.

"It's no use," the latter said dejectedly. "It's been over three hours. He would have set it off by now."

"What do you suppose happened?"

"With him out of radio contact, we can only assume the worst."

Green leaned against a boulder and glanced down at the gauge on his oxygen cylinder. It showed only a couple of hours' supply left. He wondered if the nuclear technician, too, was aware that their cut off point was only two hours away. At that time, there would be fresh oxygen—but only for the one who would hang on to warn Train Beta.

Nervously, Yardley scooped up a handful of wet sand, tossed it into the air, caught it and hurled it seaward. Then he disappeared into the cave.

Green stared at the entrance, shifting his gaze alternately to the forest. He knelt on the beach. With a stiff finger, he inscribed in large letters on the moist sand:

"I won't be back. Carry on. Tell Beta hello for me."

Purposely, he snapped off his personal transceiver so he wouldn't have to put up with any argument. Then he struck off inland.

Exemplar L'Jork and Meditators Rin'Au and Lank-Tro sat around staring uncertainly at one another in the overcrowded confines of K'Tawa's hut. Occasionally they cast impatient glances at the Old One, who was coiled up in Cogitative Posture against the wall—motionless, un-breathing, deep in Withdrawal.

"I must admit," Lank-Tro complained, "that I don't know what's going on."

"K'Tawa's Meditating," the Exemplar said evenly.

"Yes, I know. But why did he want us all in here with him? And why was he so explicit in his insistence that we should *not* Meditate ?"

"Because he wanted us to stay awake."

"But if we were Withdrawn, it wouldn't be so stuffy in here."

"He tried to explain, but I didn't understand. He was in such a hurry to return to Contemplation."

Rin'Au betrayed his own confusion. "What's he Meditating on?"

"Ultimate Meaning, I believe he said."

Rin'Au glanced unappreciatively around him. "I don't like it—catering to the whim of an old one. I—"

Lank-Tro sat up sharply and aimed his horn in the direction of the hut's south wall.

"I quaze it, too," L'Jork spoke out, "—another little Presence making his way through the forest."

"I don't quaze any danger."

"No, but he must be attended to nevertheless."

"I'll get some of the Prephasers to take care of him in the same manner K'Tawa took care of the other intruder."

The Exemplar went out of the hut and returned—all in the space of but a short while.

"Can we be sure there is no longer any danger from the Thing That Crawls?" Rin'Au asked after L'Jork had again seated himself.

"Absolutely. K'Tawa personally gave it a good quazing. Then he did what had to be done to deprive it of its hazardous potential. Anyway, he had it removed from the immediate area."

Silence claimed the hut as the three Meditators quazed clearly that the bold living Presence who had been advancing on the village was properly taken care of by the Prephasers.

There was much shrill shouting for a while, of course. But what could the little one do against the grip of hands that were so huge, relative to his own?

Later, when the see-through Covering was snatched from his head, there was such a commotion that the Meditators were led to declare they had never quazed such fright.

Then K'Tawa stirred and all eyes turned expectantly on him. He disengaged himself from cogitative Posture and took his time going through the Prescribed Exercises.

Finally L'Jork could wait no longer. "Was your Contemplative Quest as successful as you thought it would be?"

"Even more so." The Old One's eyes were full of wonder and respect, as though they had beheld nothing less than Total Revelation. "Did you dispatch the Prephasers?"

"They are on their way and should be nearing the cave by now."

Lank-Tro added, "But only one of the Presences is still there. The other—"

"Yes, I quazed what happened."

"Your Meditations, K'Tawa," the Exemplar begged, "—*what* did you learn?"

"I might not have learned anything if the direct sight of the little Presence gasping for stale air out there on the hillside hadn't suggested the final direction of Meditation."

"But what *did* you learn?"

"The Meanings of a vast Cloud in the Blackness, of another The World, of air that suffocates, of the Great Debacle, of a distant quazehornless one—not an ancestor, because he established a divergent, independent lineage—one who built a huge ship, of—"

"Get to the point, Old One," L'Jork urged. "If you *have* achieved full Eighth-Phase Ascendancy, I should imagine that Origin and Meaning would come through much more coherently."

"The incoherence is in the relating, not in the understanding."

"Who was this quazehornless ship builder?" Rin'Au asked.

But the Old One had decided upon his approach. "Imagine a great Cloud coming out of the Darkness far from Onlyland—rather, Vastland. The Cloud is shaped like a spearhead. The people *see* it and are afraid, for there are no Perpetual Clouds in the way.

"This thing from the Outer Blackness passes close to The World. It leaves part of itself to settle down into the air. It dumps much water into and through the air—enough to cover practically everything except what we now know as Onlyland. The influence of the Cloud itself, followed by the almost instant grip of water on land, makes the Day Eternal."

K'Tawa pinched the bridge of his nose, as though to coax out more of the things he had recalled.

"Even before the vast Cloud arrives, though," he went on thoughtfully, "the builder of the ship—I have yet to remember his name—gathers about him a handful of frightened people and loads them aboard his great vessel."

"Where did they go?" L'Jork asked, interested.

"To another The World—the one that was, rather is closest to what our ancestors called their The World. In that way, the builder established his independent lineage."

"And *our own* lineage?"

"It derives from the remnants of those who stayed behind—stayed behind and acquired quazehorns and grew in size and learned to avail themselves of ancestral impressions and—oh, yes, I almost forgot: You see, this vast Cloud from the Outer Blackness also brought with it practically all the air that exists today. But it was air that our ancestors couldn't breathe."

Lank-Tro frowned dubiously. "If *they* couldn't breathe it, how is it that *we* can?"

"Somewhere along the way we *learned* to breathe it. Rather, we underwent changes that *enabled* us to breathe it."

L'Jork stared across the hut. "But you said all this had something to do with the little intruding Presences."

"It does. Those Presences descended from the ship builder."

"You mean they are covered by the Code of Kinship?"

K'Tawa nodded soberly.

"I won't believe that, although I know you couldn't consciously falsify. If they are Kin, then why did they kill Zu-Bach?"

"We overlook one thing. Zu-Bach tried to kill them first. Anyway, they must have lost their knowledge of Origin and Meaning, just as we did—although they seem to have climbed back closer to the level of our common ancestors than we have."

K'Tawa bowed his head, only now beginning to appreciate the significance and impact of the Revelations. Kinship had, in a manner of speaking, been actively re-established. And, even from the constricted vantage of the present, the Old One could quaze that life would soon be unrecognizably different for the Onlylanders.

There would perhaps be not as much stress on the Spiritual, much more on the Material. And there would come the time when the Onlylanders, too, would use the great, shining instruments of the intruders and themselves wander into the Outer Blackness.

L'Jork broke the silence. "What *about* the stale-fresh air?"

"That was the most difficult of all to comprehend. And, when it finally came as I Meditated briefly on the hillside, it didn't all come from ancestral impressions. Part of it I quazed from the sight of the little Presence gasping for breath beneath the tree."

"What about the stale-fresh air?" the Exemplar prodded, trying to guide him more directly to the point.

"It's simple now. We learned to breathe the new air that the vast Cloud from the Upper Blackness brought. When we did, we also started breathing *out* the kind of air that the little Presences must breathe *in*."

K'Tawa glanced sympathetically, almost affectionately at the small Presence who still slept on the floor of the hut. He hadn't moved since he had been placed there.

The Old One quazed L'Jork and the two other Meditators. Now they understood. And they didn't mind that they had to sit around in a stuffy hut so that the little one might not suffocate.

With the distant booming of thunder still fresh in his ears, awareness gradually returned to Colonel O'Brien. Sensing an underlying inconsistency, he lay there without moving.

Then he tensed with the suspicion that it might not have been thunder at all. It had been too regular, modulated by a cadence that was all too suggestive of—

Abruptly his mind was aswirl with vivid, harrowing recollections of gigantic Venutians bearing down on him, of his respiragear caught irretrievably in the tree, of himself suffocating in the Venusian sea of carbon dioxide and nitrogen.

Confounded, he lay still and cautiously flicked an eyelid open.

Right there in his immediate field of vision was a naked foot fully the length of his arm!

With the motion of but a single eye, he traced the ankle to the massive calf and followed the limb on up to its ponderous kneecap.

The leg moved slightly and, instantly, O'Brien snapped his eyelid shut. Thank God, he reflected, that he had had the presence of mind to remain absolutely motionless! At least, he might hope for the advantage of surprise.

Something that felt like a log came out and prodded his shoulder—but not roughly. The giant *knew* he was awake! Nevertheless, he stayed rigid—until—

He lurched into a sitting position and his hands shot up to explore his face.

No hood! Here—in this Venusian hut, apparently—he was breathing normally, comfortably without *respiragear*!

His astonishment retreated before burgeoning fear as the nearest Venutian—there were four of them, he saw now—dropped anxiously to his hands and knees and advanced.

The creature was the one who had been on the beach. And he was smiling. But O'Brien couldn't tell whether it was an expression of malicious anticipation or amusement or something else entirely.

He cowered against the wall and dodged the great sharp horn when he found it poised above him. Then the huge head came within inches of his own, pulling in a mighty lungful of air and—*blew it out gently into his face!*

It was pure, fresh—like the exhilarating afterbreath of an Earthside thunderstorm!

O'Brien only sat there paralyzed with astonishment. But perhaps it *wasn't* so incredible after all. In a metabolism based on the formation of carbon-nitrogen bonds, the carbon dioxide would have to be reduced—in a process analogous to photosynthesis, perhaps—so that carbon would be available for molecular combination. As a result, the left-over oxygen might be discharged from the system!

He was suddenly aware of the pressure of the microphone against his throat when he heard the earphone's diaphragm vibrating tinnily in the silence. Retrieving the latter instrument as it dangled from his waistband, he positioned it in place.

Yardley was shouting, "Green, where are you? Come back! Something's happened!"

O'Brien answered, "Yardley, what is it? Where are you?"

"Scott! Good God, but you *can't* be alive!"

"I'm here in the village—with the Venutians."

"*What*?" There was utter disbelief in the nuclear tech's response. "But your oxygen gave out hours ago!"

"Apparently I don't need any—not here, at least. What—"

A third voice broke in on the comsystem. "Scott! Is that you— *here in the village*?" Green demanded.

"Yes, you see, I—what do you mean—*here* in the village?"

"That's where I am. I got jumped in the forest and they took me into one of their huts and relieved me of my hood and—"

"And you aren't having any trouble breathing."

"No, of course not. You aren't either. Why?"

"There're a few Venutians in there with you?"

"Three."

"As I thought," O'Brien disclosed.

One of the Venutians, the same one, had come forward again— but still not threateningly. He looked up occasionally and smiled as he traced designs on the hut's soft-mud floor.

Yardley finally broke in. "Well I wish somebody would explain it to *me*. About half an hour ago three Venutians showed up on the beach. One was dragging the tractor-crane and the Mark IV reactor. Another had our standby Del Rouad transceiver capsule. The third brought the backup cap with all the reserve O_2 cylinders. I don't know where they got them, but the stuff is all in front of the cave now."

"In which case," O'Brien said smugly, "You might mount the tractor, drop the Collard power plant and come pick us up. And, oh yes, you'll find some spare respirahoods packed in within with the O_2 cylinders. Bring a couple along."

The now obviously friendly Venutian had finished his sketch. He stepped back and proudly gestured towards it.

He had thumbed a large depression in the floor and drawn three concentric circles around it. In each circle he had thumbed another indentation. He touched the second largest circle and spread his arm all-inclusively around him. Then he touched the largest and pointed to O'Brien.

It was evident that these Venutians, their gaze forever obscured by an eternally unbroken cloud cover, somehow had access to knowledge beyond their apparent reach.

"How," O'Brien decided, would have to be explained later—as would their humanoid forms and their sudden reversal in temperament.

"Scott," Green said, "there's a lot we have to learn about these natives."

"An awful lot. And I think we're going to run into a few surprises along the way."

"What about Train Beta?" Yardley wanted to know.

"Come and pick us up and we'll set up the Del Rouad so we can contact them. We ought to let them know that everything's positive in the Recovery Area."

RUB-A-DUB

The Tub was surly and fretful. And, as if that weren't enough, Bruce Craig could also sense vague undercurrents of despair, resentment and self-pity in the mainstream of her conscious.

Ordinarily he wouldn't be that mindful of her inner emotions. But the bond of direct communication had become stronger over the years.

Vivien? he called tentatively.

But The Tub wasn't answering. He could almost feel the disdaining pressure of her indifference.

Outside (he had come more and more to think of the vast, objective world as something "outside" his realm of experience) the solarium was warm and serene, its broad windows opening on an undulant, sun-washed countryside.

Vivien!

Leave me alone.

Look, Tub. We don't have to be at each other's throat.

They say the less I have to do with you the easier it'll be. And don't call me Tub!

We've called you that for eight years.

Things are different. The flight's over. I'm no longer a naive twelve-year-old, like I was when it started. And I don't want to be called Tub. It's stupid and vulgar.

A new thought-stream intruded: *Rub-a-dub-dub! Rub-a-dub-dub!* Craig recognized the sardonic timbre. It was Gottweld, the nucleonist. *Three men in a tub. Tip the tub and what've you got? A sub, bub! Rub-a-dub-dub!*

Gottweld was cracking up fast. But that was as it should be. He was the oldest (forty-six by now, Craig calculated, thinking back over the impossible eight years). And the institution was concentrating on him first.

The derisive taunts had faded for a moment, but now they were coming back strong in the communal thought stream—strong and depraved:

Rub-a-dub-dub! Sink the sub. Free the three from the central hub. Rub-a-dub-dub! Rub—

Damn you, shut up! It was a new identity—Paulson, the pilot—who exploded. *I've had all I can stand!*

All you can stand, man? We'll all be nothing in the flick of a hand!

Gottweld and Paulson faded out, withdrawing into their shells.

Vivien, Craig was suddenly aware, was sobbing. Her hands came up to cover her face and draw a curtain of darkness over his vision. Momentarily he felt a pang of compassion. And he wished that he were a real person of fleshy substance so he could sit beside her and comfort her.

But he rejected the maudlin thought. Such sentiment was only hypocritical. He couldn't escape the basic premise that only by subduing the personality that was Vivien Walters, The Tub, could he continue to exist.

Vivien, he tried softly, forcing her hands away from her face and letting the warm light flood into her eyes.

What do you want?

You think there'll be another session?

We're scheduled for one a day, aren't we?

One a day—inevitably, inexorably, inescapably.

Tell them you don't feel up to it, he pleaded.

Why should I?

He bristled. *Because they're going to destroy three men! And you're helping them!*

He sensed it—a brief surge of doubt and solicitude. But she shrugged it off instantly.

Can't you understand, Bruce, that you've got to be erased? You've served a purpose, but it's over now. And I've a right to a free, normal life.

Haven't I as much a right? Hasn't Gottweld? Paulson?

No. You're just impresses—bundles of thoughts and motives and desires. But you aren't real. You're only reflections of real persons, created for specific jobs. The jobs are over. The impresses have to be removed.

"Miss Walters."

Vivien looked up and Craig shared her glance at the nurse who stood before them in the doorway.

"Dr. Dorfman's ready now," she announced.

Dorfman was a slim, anxious man whose hollow habit of sliding a hand up and back from his forehead seemed to suggest how he had lost his hair.

He indulged the habit disconcertingly as he sat facing The Tub. To Craig, it betrayed immoderate nervousness and determination.

"Now, Miss Walters," the psychiatrist proposed, "suppose you just relax and let me take over. We'll continue with erasure . . . Gentlemen?"

The girl's lips remained motionless. Craig made no effort to move them himself.

Dorfman shifted impatiently. "We'll take it along the chain of command. Paulson?"

The Tub's lips stretched taut. "Go to hell!"

Dorfman smiled. "That's more like it. But such vulgarity coming from such an attractive and otherwise well-mannered young lady! Gottweld?"

The nucleonist took over, seemingly grateful for the attention. The girl's form slumped languidly. Her eyes went indifferently out of focus and her mouth hung open awkwardly.

"Rub-a-dub-dub," she muttered in a thin, haltering voice.

"Excellent!" Dorfman exuberated. "I see we're not far from complete repression of the Gottweld impress. Now for the navigator."

Craig took over spitefully. "I'm with you, Doctor. Do your damnedest."

Dorfman rose and folded his arms pompously. "A bold challenge. But one which I promptly accept. It isn't often one man gets the chance to dissolve three personalities."

"Then climb aboard and have at it," Craig invited defiantly. "But let's call it what it is—legalized murder."

Abruptly he felt an inner burst of rage and recognized the particular brand of turbulence as Paulson's. But before the pilot could assume vocal control the girl took over.

"You don't have to be so brutal about it," she reprimanded the psychiatrist.

Dorfman's face twisted indecisively. "There are many things you don't understand, my dear. You'll have to trust me."

Then his eyes bored in severely. "You'll have to admit, Miss Walters, that we've almost completely removed the Gottweld impress. That's what you want, isn't it?"

She tried to turn her face. But Craig, interested, kept her eyes on the psychiatrist.

"All right, Paulson and Craig. You may withdraw." Dorfman slumped in the chair, crossed his legs and toyed with a pencil. "Gottweld?"

"Rub-a—"

"Stop that idiotic blithering and listen. What's your full name?"

The girl's lips quivered, then formed hesitatingly around "Gottweld."

"Is it John Harrison Gottweld?"

No answer.

"Remember anything about a ship? A tiny crew compartment—room for only one person—a small child?"

Still no answer.

The prodding questions made Craig restless and he wanted to seize control and storm out of the office.

The Paulson impress reached out to him: *Craig?*

Yes!

We've got to do something!

Like what?

"...one small child, Gottweld. A child whose brain was sufficiently undeveloped to house impresses of three personalities."

"Three men in a tub?" The girl's body stirred with eager interest.

Paulson: *We could try escaping.*

The Tub, Craig reminded dourly, *is stronger than the impresses.*

Not if we catch her off guard.

Dorfman straightened. "Three impresses on a child's mind. Three qualified, trained personalities. Three crewmen in one physical form to take the first starship to Centauri. It had to be that way. One hundred pounds of specialized crew in the form of a twelve-year-old girl would gain only an additional twenty pounds over eight years. A hundred and twenty pounds was all the ship could accommodate."

"Impresses? Centauri?" Gottweld murmured. "Who's Gottweld?"

See? Paulson offered desperately. *Gottweld's practically gone already. Only two men in a tub now. They won't stop until The Tub's empty!*

Where can we go? Craig asked hopelessly. *Where could we hide? Even if we can take over, she'll only foul up our control and eventually get back here. Anyway, we can't go on like this. It was all right for a specific purpose—as long as there was a job to do.*

You're not giving up?

Of course not. But the only way is to convince them we're real persons, that we can't be turned out like unneeded lights.

He could sense Paulson's contemptuous resentment, even before the pilot said: *That old integrated personality stuff again. All right. Go ahead. Try and convince Dorfman we can be welded into one. I've got other ideas!*

"You will forget, Gottweld," Dorfman was demanding. "You *want* to forget everything—who you are, where you've been, how you came about."

Craig was familiar with the theory: If you removed all memory, if you voided the psychic impression of every past experience, there couldn't be any surviving ego. It was simply a matter of discharging the molecular configuration of all the retentive cells.

"I *must* forget," the nucleonist agreed servilely in Vivien's slight voice.

Then Craig felt a jar of exploding violence as Paulson crashed through Gottweld's insecure control.

Vivien lunged from the chair and hurled herself on Dorfman, her thin fingers clamping vehemently around his neck.

But the attack died in the catalepsy of multiple purpose as the girl and Craig frantically tried to wrest dominance from the pilot.

Like a jammed machine, The Tub fell back into her chair and sat there trembling, arms hanging limp over the sides.

Dorfman raised exploring fingers to the scratches her nails had left on his neck. "That was Paulson, wasn't it?"

Regaining composure and straightening his tie, he promised vindictively, "We'll get around to you next."

≈≈

It turned out to be a long and arduous session and when it was over Paulson, who had taken the brunt of the psychiatrist's whip-lash onslaught, dropped exhausted to a non-communicative level of his conscious.

Craig, too, had doggedly fought the flashing lights and whirling discs and hypnotic monotone that scythed vital trunk lines of memory like stalks of wheat.

But he still lay awake, as did The Tub, when the nurse came around to turn out the light in their room.

Seconds passed before his eyes (*her* eyes, he amended enviously) became accustomed to the moonlight flooding into the room and bringing with it the redolence of the night jasmine blooming outside the window.

A dozen times since the session he had tried to contact Vivien, even calling out in her own voice. But there had been no answer because silence, he realized bitterly, was part of the "Treatment." Completely ignoring them, she had been told, would encourage voluntary detachment and hurry along the processes of total repression and erasure.

Finally he sensed the lethargy of sleep spreading evenly over her conscious. When her eyes closed he decided to leave them that way until she was deep in slumber. Then he could open them without disturbing her. After all, the sightless stare of a somnambulist was not incompatible with sleep.

He lay reflecting on his brief session with Dorfman and the hypnotherapeutical gadgets. And he felt certain that somewhere in that fateful office he had left behind a vital part of his psychic background and past experiences that would never again be available for recall.

Vivien's eyes opened and Craig tensed. But it wasn't the girl awakening. For he could still sense the indifferent calm of her slumber.

Craig. You with me? Paulson's searching thought was soft but sharp.

You mean about escaping?

What else? Another week or two and we won't even remember what the word means.

Somehow Craig could regard the hopeless future with an inordinate degree of objectivity, as though he weren't even concerned. After all, it would be the end of—nothing, a shadow of a personality, a collection of experiences, a group of concepts arranged into a pseudo being.

What will we do? he asked.

Lose ourselves in some isolated place—a cave, forest, swamp. Anywhere.

Then what?

We'll have to improvise as we go along. We might threaten to tighten up, stay there and starve if she doesn't see things our way.

But where will it all lead?

Good God, man! Your guess is as good as mine. Isn't it enough that every hour we stay away from here means an extra hour of existence?

Craig fought a paralyzing sense of futility. It was a numbing frustration that he should have foreseen eight years ago when he and Paulson and Gottweld had trained for the Centauri expedition.

But they had failed to consider the remote future. Instead, they had unsuspectingly submitted to impress treatment, allowing images of their personalities, experiences, knowledge and technical talents to be transferred to idle groups of memory cells and assigned unused synapses in The Tub's brain.

Only, no one had looked eight years into the future. No one had envisioned the time when the expedition would be over and The Tub, who would then be a mature woman, would have to be relieved of the impresses so she could take her place in society.

And no one, not even the three pseudo crew members, had even guessed that the impresses might learn to regard themselves subjectively as real beings.

Craig gave overt expression through the girl's lips to a sigh of resignation.

I'm with you, Paulson, he said. *Let's go.*

Imparting feather-smooth motion to the girl's body, Craig folded back the sheet and arose. It wasn't likely The Tub would awaken. She was used to somnambulistic motion while her faculties were controlled by other members of the quadrentity.

Unconsciously, he started for the locker where her clothes hung. But his motions slowed stickily, as though the very air were solidifying to offer resistance. Immediately, though, he recognized the partial immobility of conflicting purpose.

No time for dressing, Craig, Paulson cautioned. *We'll have to make the best of what we've got.*

Craig withdrew partially. *Very well. It's your show. I'll just tag along for the ride.*

Paulson slipped on a delicate, pink robe and stepped softly over to the window. There was a packing crate immediately outside and a smaller one next to it, simplifying their descent.

That's odd, Craig observed.

What? These boxes?

Not only the boxes. The yard lights are turned out too.

So what? So we're in luck.

They saw no one else in the grounds of the institution as they crossed the lawn and reached the main entrance.

Paulson, the gate's conveniently open. And nobody's in the guardhouse.

The Tub's body halted and stiffened—an overt expression of Paulson's sudden suspicion. *You suppose they're letting us escape?*

Damn if it doesn't look like it. But I can't imagine why.

Maybe we're just having an improbable run of luck. Let's hope so.

No time to stop and talk about it now.

They went swiftly through the gate and left the road, heading across rolling countryside towards the distant woods. More confident now, Paulson increased the sleeping girl's pace.

But as they passed under a tree, her foot rammed into an exposed oak root. The pilot swore and Craig reflexively executed the corrective balancing motions.

And still The Tub slept, even despite the sharp pain Craig could feel seeping through the thin curtain separating their egos.

If we can get to the woods, Paulson offered hopefully, *it won't matter if she does wake up.*

That's right. Without our consent, she couldn't return to the institution.

Or go anywhere else, for that matter.

She'd have to cooperate with us.

Or die in the woods.

In the distance a steady stream of cars hummed a monotonous drone along the highway, their headlights flaring suddenly and flashing into the girl's eyes as they swept around a curve.

At first Craig feared it would provide just the added distraction to awaken her. But he could still sense the vacuity of her sleepful state.

What's that? Paulson demanded abruptly.

Craig turned his full attention to the visual stimulus and saw what had attracted the other's interest—an anomalous Ferris wheel by the side of the highway.

It doesn't make sense, Craig said. *Out here in the middle of nowhere. Something's wrong—damn wrong!*

The buzzing of rubber on concrete was even more of a steady monotone than it had seemed before. It was oddly reminiscent of something, Craig thought.

And the lights of the cars, sweeping around the bend in the road, flashed with an irritating but almost enchanting regularity—with an almost hypnotic effect.

The shred of a scream came subvocally from some horrified depth of Paulson's conscious and Craig, staring through the same eyes, drew back in consternation.

There was only one occupant in each seat of the Ferris wheel. And they were all duplicates of Dorfman!

The psychiatrists leered down at them and each beckoned with a twisted finger.

And the wheel whirled and the traffic droned and the headlights flared and Craig felt himself being spun about in a nauseating vortex. And the Ferris wheel and cars and highway and countryside and Dorfmans chased one another into a monochromatic blur that left him almost senseless.

But suddenly all settled down and reshaped itself into one Dorfman bracketed by the flashing lights and whirling forms and other hypnotic instruments of his office. He touched a switch and the aggravating, high-pitched monotone that had been the hum of traffic slid down the sonic scale and faded out in a dull, bass groan.

"That'll be all for this session, gentlemen," the psychiatrist said. "See you again tomorrow?"

Craig was numb with despair as the purpose behind the hallucinatory sequence suggested itself with mock clarity. It had been a "show" put on principally to shock and demoralize Paulson. Craig had been implicated fully, though, because it was intended to contribute to his psychical disorientation as well.

Dorfman had painted a convincing illusion of escape and had snatched it savagely away from Paulson at the last moment. A sufficient number of such experiences would send any despondent person sulking into a schizoid shell.

Those tactics had worked so successfully on Gottweld that the nucleonist's impress was already almost totally erased.

They were succeeding eminently on Paulson, contributing to his gradual withdrawal from reality.

And, with slight variation to accommodate personality differences, that method would certainly achieve the desired results with Craig, too. It was just a matter of time.

It was difficult to believe The Tub had been a willing party to Dorfman's outrageous deceit. It was so unlike the child who had grown to maturity in the cold, grey womb of the Centauri ship and had achieved such an intense bond of pure understanding with the three men.

The memory of this relationship came back to Craig with poignant impact as Vivien walked aimlessly in the institution's garden the next morning.

The quadrentity, unique in the annals of psychology, had been a psychic union that had grown progressively more complete—until he had felt certain that full integration into a composite ego would be an acceptable alternative to erasure.

At one time he had almost convinced The Tub that such a consolidation would produce a pluralistic personality superior in capabilities, talents, knowledge and character to any being on Earth. And, since she was closer to him than the other two, she had listened.

But the endless voyage had ended and The Tub had begun examining herself in comparison with normal women. And she had begun responding to Dorfman's reassurances that the impresses weren't real persons at all.

Bruce, Vivien called softly.

Sulking, he ignored her summoning impulse. It was the fifth time she'd tried to reach him since breakfast. But the confusion and uncertainty surrounding the attempted contact left him without any hope that her attitude would be conciliatory.

A slight breeze wafted low-lying clouds overhead. With its promise of summer soon to come, warm sunlight spread a cast of gauzy softness over the garden.

Vivien paused in the shade of a tree and dropped to the lawn. She sat plucking pensively at tufts of grass.

Paulson? Craig tried.

No answer.

Paulson, you still with us?

Craig could detect not even a stirring from the pilot. The impact of Dorfman's hypnotic ruse must have been severe—as severe as some of the earlier disorientation tricks the psychiatrist had played on the nucleonist.

Craig reached out for the third man: *Gottweld?*

Bruce, I know you can hear me, Vivien pleaded. *Why don't you answer?*

Again he ignored the girl.

Gottweld? he repeated.

There was a brief murmur of despair.

Gottweld! Snap out of it!

Vivien: *I'm going to keep trying until you answer, Bruce.*

Gottweld: *Rub-a-dub-dub-dub-dub-dub...*

The nucleonist's irrational response elicited a disturbing picture in Craig's mind—a moist lower lip vibrating under the strumming motion of a thick, flexing finger.

You've got to fight back, Gottweld! he urged. *Don't let yourself go under!*

Under we go. The returning thought was thin, uncertain. *Three men in tow. There'll be hell to pay on skid row.*

Bruce! Vivien insisted. *I need your help!*

Craig resented the girl's petty, inconsiderate self-concern. It wasn't The Tub who needed help. It was Gottweld. And desperately. He needed someone to seize him by the shoulders and shake him back to sensibility, blister his face with jarring, back-handed slaps.

But the nucleonist had no shoulders, no face, of his own. There could be no such thing as physical interrelationship among the members of the quadrentity—only the tenuous, unsatisfying contact of words and concepts, vague attitudes and feelings.

Yet, Craig suspected, there must be some form of communication more complete than the mere transfer of ideas. In the material world you could stand ashore and shout directions to a drowning man. Or you could dive and bring him out.

Unhesitatingly, Craig plunged in. He struggled frantically through misty concepts of desperate purpose and uncertain dedication, floundering for lack of orientation. But if Gottweld existed, there must be some way of penetrating the monadic haze and finding him.

Gottweld! Where are you?

The desperate call drew another murmur of utter despondency, of abject submission.

Hold on! I'm trying to reach you!

Rub-rub-rub-rub-rub-rub...

There was a sense of direction now. The monosyllabic mumble beat out at Craig until the overwhelming volume of was like a thunderous peal—louder, *louder*, LOUDER.

Then abruptly his searching perspective probe crashed through a tenuous barrier and he was instantly caught up in exploding maelstrom of whirling, maddening concepts—impossible phantasmagoria of distorted mind-images and a terrifying cacophony of ideated sound.

In one corner of his field of psychic awareness was the warped perceptual vision that came to the Gottweld impress through The Tub's eyes.

But even as Craig looked, the horribly twisted vista of gnarled, motile trees and crazily tilted buildings and creeping, living hedges that harbored hideous and menacing things seemed to be drawing perceptibly away. The recession of all objects into the distance was like a slow-motion implosion, with all the material universe dwindling into a pinpoint of infinity.

He recognized a transcendent symbolism here—a rejection of reality, a drawing into itself of the Gottweld impress. It was as Dorfman had planned, as Vivien had sanctioned, as it must be if individuality was to be restored to The Tub's mind.

And all around the shrinking perception of reality, Gottweld's conscious was a festering place of terrified concepts and irrational fears, peopled by nightmarish things and unimaginable horrors.

All was tortuous disorder.

Gottweld was insane.

And his hope was in oblivion, in the promise that impress erasure would give him merciful release into the void of nonentity.

Bruce, Vivien importuned. *Please answer me!*

As though the girl's imploring thoughts were themselves a magnet, Craig was drawn up out of the whirlpool of Gottweld's depraved conscious. And, with a sudden scorn, he turned his attention towards Vivien.

Gottweld's insane. He's almost completely erased. What's left of him is something that wouldn't be at home even in hell.

Bruce, about Dorfman. That trick he pulled on you and Paulson—

Don't you understand? Gottweld's destroyed! Doesn't that interest you?

She was silent a long while. And in the hyperphysical stillness he was aware of strong emanations of uncertainty. Then there was a sudden unshakeable conviction.

Gottweld, she said firmly, irrefutably, *doesn't exist. There was a Gottweld—a real, physical nucleonist who went by that name. But he was killed in an accident—here on Earth—four years ago.*

Gottweld—the only one you and I know—is right here with us. And you're letting Dorfman and the institution murder him!

Don't say that—please. I've had a hard enough time convincing myself that's not true. But I'm certain about it now. And I don't want that belief to change. I wouldn't like to find out, instead, that I've got to be different from other people the rest of my life.

He detected only vague evidence of indecision—not even strong enough for him to play upon it in the hope of saving himself and the other two.

Do you actually believe I'm not real? he asked. *That I'm only a vague collection of impressions and attitudes?*

There was deep, distressful affirmation in her silence.

What do you want? he asked sharply. *Why do you call?*

You've got to believe I didn't approve of Dorfman's illusion of escape.

You were part of it weren't you? You went along with it.

I didn't know. I was under hypnotic compulsion, too. He told me what he was going to do, but that was after you and Paulson were under control. Then, before I could say I didn't like the idea, I was all wrapped up in the imaginary incident, too.

Craig swore vindictively. The minced phrases, coming anomalously from the girl's mouth, disrupted the stillness of the garden.

Dorfman's not really hateful, she said. *Just remember—there's a purpose behind everything he does.*

Of course there is. Sadistic torture.

No. You've got it wrong. He's told me things while the rest of you were subdued. Things I shouldn't repeat. If I could only be sure the others weren't listening—

Gottweld's totally repressed. Paulson's withdrawn, close to the brink of detachment. Even I can't reach him.

Again she paused irresolutely. And Craig waited.

Outside—to an even greater degree now he thought of "outside" as the vast arena of causality that excluded the intimate happenings within the quadripartite mind of The Tub—outside the sun drifted behind cumulus fleece and he felt a chill run through the girl's body.

Dorfman's being deliberately brutal with Paulson because that's the only way he can get the job done, Vivien explained. *Paulson's basic temperament calls for that kind of approach. With you it will be different.*

With me, he shot back, *it would probably be a horsewhip—if Dorfman could find a way to use it.*

The Tub rose and resumed her walk between the flower beds. But she maintained the thread of inner communication.

Bruce—am I doing wrong?

He produced the psychic reflection of a sour laugh. *You're asking me, who doesn't exist, to sit in judgment over whether you're wrong in helping to destroy three nonentities?*

She ignored his rhetorical question. *I want to be normal. But when I talk with you like this it's hard to believe you're just a complex of thought processes temporarily assigned to some of the idle cells in my brain.*

You didn't think that for eight years.

It was different then. There was nobody except the four of us—one quadrentity. The illusion came easily—when we were halfway to infinity.

But not now?

Yes—not now. They've proved what you really are.

Then why waste time talking with me—with nothing?

Her gaze swept the ground as she walked sullenly towards the fish pond.

Vivien, remember when we used to stand by the port and watch Sol grow against the background of stars and imagine we were two normal persons? You used to say—

She snapped: *I can't be held responsible for anything I might have said as a result of juvenile infatuation.*

But was it really juvenile infatuation? You were almost twenty.

He wasn't merely trying to play upon her sympathy. There actually had been a time when he was naive enough to believe things would work out somehow; that the end of the flight might, through some miracle, mean a new, normal relationship between him and The Tub.

She tensed angrily. *All right! I thought I loved you! Have it that way. But where could it lead from there?*

We could—

We could nothing! *There'd only be frustration. Where would there be any normalcy? It would only be an ugly and perverted form of narcissism.*

She drew to a halt before the fish pond and they stood staring unseeing into the deep, dark water, not even noticing the gardener who walked by and nodded a greeting.

To Craig, one thing was clear. She was right. Total erasure was the most merciful way out for all in the quadrentity.

Then he felt a spasm of erratic movement seize the girl's body and she hurled herself forward into the pond. Screaming, she sank below the surface.

Let's all be erased together! Paulson's mocking thought burst into the communal stream of conscious.

Desperately, Craig tried to swim back to the surface. But his attempted strokes only conflicted with the girl's frantic efforts to save herself. They sank to the bottom, arms and legs thrashing in futile, uncoordinated motion.

And from somewhere in the depths of the quadripartite mind came Paulson's sardonic laughter.

Water rushed into her lungs, burning, choking, suffocating. Then Craig felt the pressure of a firm hand gripping her arm and once more they were above the surface.

It was the gardener who had dived into the pond in time to rescue The Tub.

Dorfman dimmed the lights in his office and pulled a chair up in front of Vivien's. Her face seemed sallow and haggard as he reached towards the battery of switches on his desk. He changed his mind though, and folded his arms, staring intently into the girl's eyes.

"Paulson?" he called.

The Tub shifted uncomfortably. But her lips remained closed.

"Come on, Paulson. Quit sulking. I'm enough of a psychologist to know that you're watching with keen interest."

The girl's lips worked frenziedly, spitting out a barrage of coarse, whispered expletives.

"About yesterday's fish pond incident," Dorfman interrupted calmly. "Don't try anything like that again."

"Stop me!" Paulson challenged in The Tub's high-pitched voice.

"We intend to see—"

"That it doesn't happen again?" The words found a new level of sarcasm. "What are you going to do about it—*punish me?*"

Vivien's laugh was bitterly triumphant.

And Dorfman sank back into the chair, his face showing the disappointment of his first defeat since he had been assigned The Tub.

"You don't suppose I'm going to take erasure lying down?"

The pilot followed up his advantage. "If I have to die I'm going to see that everybody else goes with me, from The Tub on down!"

"There'll be guards standing by from now on," the other warned. "And I assure you that if you make trouble, the treatments from here on out can be much more severe than what has gone before."

Paulson buried himself in aloof silence.

The psychiatrist leaned forward, elbows on his knees and fists drawn up reflectively under his chin. "Well, fellows, I've arranged something of a surprise for today's session."

Craig could still feel the strong emanations of despair and fear and the deep desire for withdrawal that came from Paulson's conscious. But he nudged them aside and gingerly took control of The Tub's faculties.

"We could avoid all this," he suggested, trying unsuccessfully to impose a bass pitch on the girl's voice, "if you'd give us a few weeks to try integration."

The psychiatrist shook his head with adamantine smugness. "It wouldn't work."

"But it would! There's no impenetrable psychic shell surrounding our egos. Whatever it is that separates one from another can be pierced. I broke through it! I reached Gottweld's unconscious!"

Dorfman dismissed the proposition with a wave of his hand. "There isn't a professional roan in this institution or anywhere else who can conceive how that would work. Miss Walter's interest must be protected. Society owes her a debt. It can't consent to seeing her develop further as a psychological freak."

"But what about *us?*"

"Let me prime your memory—both yours and Mr. Paulson's. Some eight years ago three men agreed to the psychic impress process, as did the guardians of a twelve-year-old girl and the girl herself. The trio further agreed they would have no objections to any psychotherapeutic measures that might be required to correct results, traumatic or otherwise, that the subject might eventually suffer from the impress treatments."

"But you can't hold us to that! We thought she would simply receive a reflection of our knowledge and ability. We didn't know that a sense of awareness, our actual egos, would be duplicated, too!"

"Gentlemen," Dorfman said soberly, "the bare fact is that no duplicate ego was transferred—only the knowledge, only the talent, only the ability. The proposition that these collections of personality factors should consider themselves free entities is merely a case in faulty logic. Your awareness of being is simply an illusion. In short, you don't exist."

Paulson crashed through. "Damn you! Use any kind of logic you want. But you won't convince anyone but this girl!"

"Just the girl, Mr. Paulson?" The psychiatrist grinned self-indulgently. "Do you realize there are three real heroes of the Alpha Centauri expedition—Miss Walters and the *original* Craig and Paulson. Those two men, together with Gottweld who was subsequently killed in an accident, went through years of training in order to contribute the necessary abilities. Miss Walters is the one who made it possible for them to apply their talents aboard ship."

"But *we* made the trip! *We* took the risks!"

"Even now," Dorfman continued, unperturbed, "the whole system is waiting to honor Miss Walters and, to a lesser extent, Paulson and Craig. She has fired the imagination of all humanity. She has epitomized the spirit of valorous mankind on his greatest adventure. Do you want her to receive all that acclaim while her mind is cluttered with—with rebellious gimmicks?"

Craig could sense Paulson's utterly futile reaction, his dejected withdrawal into the shell of his unconscious. At the same time he was aware of his own desperate and hopeless response to the coldly logical argument Dorfman was advancing.

What he said might be true, Craig conceded resentfully. But the psychiatrist didn't have to say it. Humanely, he might have avoided the subject of their complete insignificance.

But that was just the point, he realized belatedly. Dorfman was pursuing a purpose with his eloquent, harshly impersonal words. He was merely wielding a psychological weapon intended to force the two remaining impresses further out of contact with reality.

"What about re-impressions?" Craig asked, seizing upon a remote possibility. "Can't you put us through the impress treatment again, in reverse—retransfer everything into the original Paulson and Craig?"

Dorfman tediously straightened the crease in his trousers. "We've explored that avenue. It's equally impossible. When the original impresses were effected in this girl's mind, they were only duplicates of a psychic totality that remained in the minds of the original men."

"If we were to re-impress on those original minds everything that was transferred in the first place, plus the experiences you've acquired over the past eight years, The Tub's mind would still be left with what's in there now. We would solve nothing. Only *reflections* of you would be passed back—just as only *reflections* of the original Craig were transferred to Miss Walters eight years ago. You, as you now exist, would retain your present status and would *still* have to be erased."

Dorfman rose abruptly. "Now for a surprise."

He crossed to the door and swung it open. A tall, angular man with crisp blond hair entered first. Apparently in his early thirties, he paused to stare inquisitively at The Tub.

Paulson was drawn curiously out of his shell. *What's all this abou— Good God, Craig! It's you!*

Vivien turned to watch another man enter. Slightly older than the first, he was accompanied by an attractive woman—his wife, evidently, and three children.

Paulson! Craig exclaimed. *The* real *Paulson!*

Dorfman settled back in his chair, not doing a very good job of choking back a laugh.

Paulson spoke softly to his wife and she took the children back into the corridor.

Craig, the Paulson impress cried out piteously, *I'm married to a woman I've never seen! And I've got* three children!

But Craig was too enveloped in his own emotions and in the tide of reaction that was welling in The Tub to notice the pilot's dismay.

"Bruce Craig!" Vivien exclaimed unbelievingly.

And he was even more deeply conscious of her emotional reaction as a flood of intense feeling broke through into the communal concept stream. It was a warm, poignant feeling—as though someone she had known only in a dream had become real after years of phantasmal existence.

He withdrew even more despondently, acutely aware of how impossible it would be to reach her after this.

Vivien, he called in quiet desperation.

Dorfman took the two men by the arm and brought them over to the girl.

"You three know each other," he reminded.

"Tub!" exclaimed the material Craig, with something more than casual interest. "It's been a long time. You put on a good show."

"Hi, kid," Paulson greeted, adding a suggestive whistle. "What eight years didn't do!"

Inside, the Craig impress sensed the swirl of Vivien's emotions as though they were his own. It couldn't properly be called a spontaneous affection, for there *had been* a fondness for a Bruce Craig that had developed over the years.

The psychiatrist tactfully retreated to an obscure corner of the room where he could silently witness the unfolding of the interlude he had arranged.

That damn, dirty, stinking Dorfman! Paulson swore.

I never figured he'd pull something like this, Craig said incredulously. *Hell—it's below the belt!*

It's a foul deal, all right. How can you go on believing in yourself after—this?

I'm sick. Dorfman's right. There isn't anything for us. Nothing. We can't ever get back.

Vivien! Craig pleaded.

Tub! God, Tub, answer us! Do something!

Hush! came an irritated aside from the girl.

But Craig pushed on. *Vivien, listen! Don't you see there can be two Bruces? Just because Dorfman produces a counterpart of flesh and blood, that shouldn't wipe me out as though I never existed, as far as you're concerned!*

Her reaction was a wordless, a most spiteful repudiation as she stared up into the physical Craig's face.

"What's this about you having trouble?" he asked.

"It's nothing."

"The impresses?"

She nodded, somewhat embarrassed.

"Dr. Dorfman said there were after effects," he prodded. "Can I do anything?"

She grasped his hand appreciatively. "You've done a good deal already."

Then she flushed with apology. "I'm sorry. You see, I feel as though I know you pretty well. After all, I've lived with part of your personality since I was a child."

The Paulson impress raved: *A wife and three kids! A wife and three kids! A wife and—*

It finally shattered the impress Craig's patience. *Oh, for God's sake! Shut up!*

Who is she? What's her name? Did I know her? Where—

Distraught. Craig started to cut him off. But he felt a sudden compassion for the pilot. Anyway, that was what Dorfman wanted—to have them shut each other out as a step towards rejecting the whole of objective reality.

Craig, can't you understand? A wife and three kids! A wife and three kids you've never seen! A—

The pilot was beginning to babble as Gottweld had. It was a disconcerting irritation and, reflexively, Craig blocked off the stream of conscious reaction.

"Since I know so little of you," the material Craig was saying to the girl, "maybe we can even the score."

They both laughed.

"Seriously, though," he went on, "would you mind if I came to visit you, Vivien?"

"You used to call me Tub during the impress sessions."

"All right—Tub. But you still haven't answered. I'd like to hear all about the expedition—how it went, whether my impress was on its best behavior."

Momentarily, a flood of rage choked Craig. He wanted to ball the girl's inadequate fists and lash out at the self-confident thing that called itself by his name.

But what was the use? What could he possibly gain, other than Vivien's scorn?

Thanks, Bruce. At least, the girl still recognized his existence. *I'm glad an impress can understand.*

There was a brief session before the flashing lights and whirling forms after the two men left. But, to Craig, it was as nothing compared with the traumatic effectiveness of the visit.

By contrast, he almost hadn't minded the recall erasure treatment. And, when it was over, it made no difference that he could remember nothing about his childhood, his schooling, his family.

Or, had he had any family? At least, he must have gone to school. Everybody went to school, it seemed. Or, did they? As a matter of fact, he wondered about "school"—some vague concept, no doubt, that wasn't even worth recalling.

Seeking company in his despondency, he penetrated the shrunken Gottweld impress's shell.

...a-dub-dub-dub. Tub. Rub. Hub. Free the three. Rub-a-tub-tub. Rub...

He snipped off the mournful rambling and reached out, instead, towards Paulson.

...kids and a wife. Who was she? And her husband—he seemed familiar too. Three kids and a wife. Three men in a Tub...

Craig shut him out completely.

In two more sessions of persistent ruthlessness, Paulson was beaten back into the desolate mist of schizoid existence. And Craig dismally realized the pilot would remain there, eating away at his own substance, until not a trace of that impress remained.

He also sensed that Dorfman had already decided upon the approach which would send him, too, shrinking back into his unconscious—like a cowering animal.

The psychiatrist, he suspected, would harp upon the threat that the Craig impress posed to the security and happiness of The Tub.

Such fears proved justified during the next session when Dorfman wheeled away the table with its battery of hypnotic gadgets and came back to perch on the edge of the desk in front of the girl.

It was then that Craig noticed the full-length mirror against the opposite wall, positioned so that he could see The Tub's reflection. He recognized it as a substitute device for the whirling forms and blinking lights.

For a long while he over-rode her control and forced her to stare at herself while he wistfully regarded the smooth flow of blonde hair that framed her pale face and billowed against slim but adequate shoulders. And he noticed for the first time how full and warmly curved were her lips and how smoothly chiseled was the small nose and proud chin.

"She is quite attractive, wouldn't you say?" Dorfman asked, studying the girl intently.

"There weren't any reflecting surfaces aboard ship," Craig said, nodding. "They planned it that way. It was easier without any mirrors around."

Dorfman laughed gently. "And now I'm using a mirror for the same reason they *didn't* allow one—to make it easier."

It was a gesture quite different from the derisive outbursts with which the psychiatrist had greeted Gottweld's and Paulson's desperation. It was obvious that Dorfman was pursuing a new tack.

He came over and clasped the girl's shoulders. Craig, aware of no reaction from The Tub, realized Dorfman must have dismissed her hypnotically before summoning him, to the surface.

"Craig, the time has come for a bit of frank confession. You probably think I'm a stinker of the first order for the way I disposed of Paulson and Gottweld."

Craig looked away contemptuously. "Bringing in the other gets us off to a nice homey start on the third erasure too."

"I suppose sadistic overtones *are* heavily suggested," Dorfman conceded.

Then he lit a cigarette. "You see, I have a tough job. It's been especially difficult in that I had to modify the means in order to arrive at the same end in each case.

"The end, of course, is erasure. Wait. Don't stop me, please. I think there's some intensely logical part of your mind telling you erasure is the only solution. But the requirements vary with different personalities. With Gottweld—and to a lesser degree with Paulson—I had to be contemptible, ruthless, unrelenting.

"You ever seen an animal trainer wield a whip to break a beast's spirit? Believe me, that was the only way erasure would work with the pilot and nucleonist."

Craig laughed spitefully. "But with me you're going to appeal to my better judgment."

"That's right. To an intensely logical part of your mind that has already admitted there's no other solution."

The navigator swore under the girl's breath. "And how can I square it with the *illogical* part of my mind?" he asked sarcastically.

"Look in the mirror, Craig. What do you see? A young woman. Fully mature. Beautiful. Yesterday she was a child—a child you knew more thoroughly than any man has ever known a child before. More thoroughly than you could have known even your own daughter."

"Daughter! I'm *only* thirty-two. She's twenty."

Dorfman leaned back, but continued staring severely at the girl. "I believe you are now bringing the issue round into its proper perspective. You imagine yourself in love with her, don't you?"

Craig said nothing.

"Then you do: Very well, let me supply a psychological interpretation of your motives—one you evidently can't figure out for yourself."

He rose and paced, stopped abruptly and said, "You only *think* you love her. Actually, it's nothing but sublimated self-pity. You feel sorry for yourself because you've got to be erased. So you arrange things mentally to make it appear that you've got a lot more to lose. With so much at stake—with a deep, abiding love also threatened—you'll fight all the harder."

It wasn't true, Craig told himself. He *knew* how he felt about Vivien. It was the way he had felt before the trip was over—before anyone realized the impresses would have to be dealt with.

"Because of a selfish, fallacious emotion," Dorfman went on more harshly, "you would deny this girl a normal life. Because you've forced yourself to believe something that isn't true, you're going to keep her in a mental condition that would, by all practical standards, justify her being placed in an institution. That, Craig, is irrational and unreasonable egocentricity."

"Go to hell."

"You're not going to reason this out with me?"

"Make me."

On his own, he would consider banishment into oblivion for The Tub's sake—maybe. But he'd be damned if he'd be driven into it.

"Very well, Craig. I'd hoped for your cooperation. Without it, the job will take longer. But it won't be any less effective."

Dorfman, projecting determination, trundled back the table with all its gleaming devices.

Craig trudged through timeless corridors of vague, distorted ideas and twisted concepts. He wallowed helplessly in a mire of fear and despondency and a myriad of emotions that tore at his conscious with shredding claws.

Lost, haggard, he pushed up one remote stream of thought and down another. In his frenzied wandering he tried to picture the physical equivalent of his psychic distress. It was as though he were a grimy, bearded and ragged recluse stumbling through a vast swamp with treacherous quicksand deposits into which he might plunge and never emerge.

And, always, it seemed to be only the hidden corridors of desperation that attracted his pointlessly ranging conscious.

But he could seldom be certain whether it was his own fear and depression or the dismal apprehension of one of the other walled-in members of the quadrentity.

Lost in the timelessness of thought duration, he plunged through a schizoid shield and blundered into a fringe concept of dire maniacal terror.

He was at the controls of the Centauri ship as it plunged past the innermost planet of the system and streaked bow-over-stern for the blazing sun. The bulkheads were melting. But the flowing metal metamorphosed into horrifying, threatening creatures that dripped beads of liquid fire as they advanced on the crew.

Paralyzed with a fear he recognized as belonging to the imprisoned Paulson impress, he bolted the phantasmal, self-torture chamber and banished himself to the infinite nothingness outside the isolated egos.

But, as though drawn by a magnet, he could sense the morbid attraction that was pulling him relentlessly into the Gottweld impress. His wandering subpercipient conscious pierced the tenuous curtain of no-concept, and was instantly enveloped in an even more maddening, more frenzied miasma of total disorientation.

The desperate Gottweld subconscious caught him up in an hypnotic grip and suddenly he *was* the nucleonist—Gottweld screaming as the ship's pile notched a step nearer run—away chain reaction; Gottweld as a meteor punctured the bulkhead of his compartment; as he went floundering out into the boundless vault of space; as a thousand life forms on an alien planet closed in, bringing their countless varieties of torturous death.

Craig may have spent a second as a captive of the nucleonist's impress. Or it may have been a year. There was no way of knowing. Nor was there any indication that the experience itself might not have been nurtured by Dorfman's commanding voice during one or a dozen psychotherapeutic sessions.

But finally he was free and wandering again. Now he was strolling up a corridor that led into a warm, breezy park where a score of children were happily at play. It was a nonsensical game in which the boys chased the girls until each had been captured. Only, he was one of the girls and the others called him Vivien as they urged him/her to run faster.

It was a poignantly nostalgic scene (as it came to him from the depths of the girl's unconscious) vividly etched in memory from some carefree era that predated her quadripartite life. And he lingered as long as he could—until the subtle compulsion seized him again and drew him back to his endless quest for direct sensual perception.

Always the objective was before him—some means of reestablishing contact with the outside world through The Tub's senses. But always there was the imposing bulk of Dorfman, blocking his paths, standing there adamantly and with a rigidly extended arm pointing the way back to schizoid imprisonment.

Sometimes, though, he succeeded. Sometimes he found a side corridor which the psychiatrist had overlooked. And during these rare instances he managed to reclaim his heritage of perceptual integrity.

And his reward was an occasional sensual impression—a faraway mumble of voices which he recognized as those of institution attendants, the occasional whiff of night air that came to him from the Tub's window, jasmine-scented and cool; and, more rarely, a glimpse of the walls of her room or of Dorfman's anxious face.

But there was another avenue to the world of objective reality—one that he stumbled upon quite accidently while exploring the pleasurable regions of The Tub's unconscious mind. It was only a secondhand means of perceptual contact with the outside world. But, in desperation, he accepted it eagerly.

It was the ever-running stream of impressions that cascaded from The Tub's senses into the vaults of conscious recall. Whenever the compulsion to withdraw into himself abated momentarily, he would seize upon the opportunity to invade the girl's mind and intercept this memory stream somewhere along its wending course.

It was a refreshing experience, with the sounds and tastes and smells and images fresher, more vivid, sharper as he neared the source of percipience. But always there was the distressing realization that the images were only delayed reflections of reality—that the farther he pushed up the bedstream of conscious time towards the sensual present, the more difficult it was to make additional headway.

Submerged thus in the memory stream on one occasion, he saw with The Tub's eyes and heard with her ears as the material Craig entered the solarium.

He tried to guess at the vintage of the memory, but abandoned the attempt as he felt himself being swept away before a dual reaction of self-compassion and interest in watching what would happen. (What *had* happened at some earlier time, he corrected himself, realizing he was dealing with a playback of the recall process and not contemporary events.)

The objective Craig crossed the room, held the girl loosely around the waist and planted a kiss on her forehead. And the casualness of the gesture convinced the impress that weeks must have passed since his last clearly remembered session with Dorfman.

The two sat by the open window and The Tub stared outside at the late afternoon scene with the lawn beginning to relinquish its verdure and an occasional browning leaf bowing to the onrush of autumn. And only then did the impress become acutely aware that *months* had passed since psychotherapy had begun on the girl!

The material Craig lit a cigarette. "By Christmas?"

"Dorfman hopes so," she returned dispiritedly.

"I thought he was sure."

"He was. But erasure isn't coming along as fast as he thought it would."

"Oh."

Forgetting that he was witnessing a transpired event, the impress Craig tried to seize control of Vivien's faculties just long enough to cry out, to let them know he was still there, to tell them how lonely he was. But there was no way now that he could control even her voice.

"Vivien, why the delay?" the smugly objective Craig wanted to know. "Has anything gone wrong?"

She shrugged her shoulders dejectedly. "No. But it's taking a lot longer than Dorfman expected. Bruce, do you suppose that means something? Can it be that the impresses actually did achieve entity?"

"Nonsense." He placed his arm reassuringly about her shoulder. "Like Dorfman explained, they were just rather complete bundles of knowledge and memory, ability and talent. It was your own synthetic influence that gave them the semblance of individuality. Dorfman isn't treating them, actually. He's treating *you*—trying to recondition the parts of your mind that were impressed with the past experiences of the three men."

She smiled appreciatively.

And the impress Craig could sense the gesture through the subtle undercurrent of well-being that suddenly dominated the memory stream at that point.

"You make it sound simple," she said.

"Then what seems to be the trouble?"

"Gottweld's taken care of. Dorfman says all the cells assigned to him have been cleared. And Paulson is completely inhibited. That erasure is over the hump. Even if it's left alone, it will fade out entirely on its own. But—"

Craig laughed. "Then it's *my* impress that's acting up. I might have guessed it. I've always been pretty bullheaded."

"Oh your impulse is shut out, all right. It's been over two months since Dorfman was able to make conscious contact. And even then the memory of that session was voided completely."

"Then what has you so concerned?"

"It—he, I mean it won't compact. It won't collapse in on itself. Dorfman calls it a 'Wandering persistence.'"

"You mean it can still contact you?"

"Of course not. It's shut off. But—"

"Could you contact it if you wanted to?"

"I don't know. I'm afraid to try. Dorfman tells me to leave it alone."

"Why are you so afraid, Vivien?"

"Maybe it's because I might break down in a sense of pity. Maybe I'm afraid I'll be convinced the impress does have distinct existence. That would ruin everything. How could the institution cure me if I'm working against it?"

She trembled and he put his arm about her. "Careful now. Remember, Dorfman said you had to guard against just this sort of guilt complex."

"I know, but—"

"But nothing," he said stubbornly, obviously bent upon changing the subject. "Tell me something—on Centauri II, was there a time when you were filling the water tanks and laughed at a leaf floating down the river with a sad-eyed little animal sunbathing on it?"

"Yes, there was! But how did you know? I didn't put *that* in the report."

"At one point, did Paulson have to fight his way on manual through a meteor swarm for over twenty hours because an auto-control circuit had shorted?"

"That's right!" She was surprised.

To the impress Craig the incident seemed, somehow, oddly familiar, as though he, himself, might have once participated in it long, long ago.

There was a sudden blinding flash of pure light that fiercely penetrated every area of Craig's conscious. And the subdued visual continuity of The Tub's memory stream seemed dim and inadequate by comparison. The inexplicable super illumination flared even more brilliantly, shaping itself into a startlingly beautiful impression of Vivien's face. It was like a transfigured intaglio, etched by lightning and drawn in sunken lines of frozen fire and deep, vivid patches of living shadow.

The splendid apparition that pervaded his entire being and occupied all of the vast stretches of the ethereal thought region was animate. And, although the eyes stared indifferently off into the distance, The Tub's lips seemed to be eternally poised on the brink of a tender word.

The image faded and, once again, Craig was left sullenly alone with the girl's memory stream, witnessing the incident which the physical Craig and Vivien had shared—how long ago?—in the solarium.

Slowly, the angular, intense face of the man drew closer and, at this point, the girl's stream of pluperfect conscious conveyed the subtle impression of capable arms closing around her waist and lips pressing hard against hers.

Despairing, the impress Craig drew away from the ironic interlude. Vivien was, had been his—Bruce Craig's. That much was implied, if not completely understood during the last year of the voyage.

111

And now she *was* Bruce Craig's. But it was a different Craig, while he, himself, had been banished to extinction.

He was torn inconsolably between alternate desires either to retreat, defeated, into the schizoid prison that was being prepared for him or to drift back down the stream of conscious and wistfully rewitness the humiliating incident.

But instead he plodded insensately upstream, bucking the orderly flow of stored incidents that comprised the girl's memory. Despondently, he stumbled awkwardly through the succession of days and nights, pressing ever forward in his quest for the present—for the direct sensual contact with the outside world that would come when he reached the fountainhead of the stream.

A sense of terrifying frenzy seized him abruptly and he charged more blindly now up through the sequence of The Tub's personal experiences.

The everyday occurrences of her pluperfect life, the indifferent comings and goings of the institution's attendants, the more than occasional visits by the objective Craig, the sessions with Dorfman, the afternoons in the solarium, the dark, sleepful, insensate nights—all blended into an inchoate phantasmagoria. Arid the endless successions of days, foreshortened by the impossible speed of his reckless dash through them, became but a flickering, grey blue as he swept on ahead.

God! How long had it been since a material Bruce Craig had taken Vivien in his arms on a serene October day in the solarium? There was only the vaguest of impulses to stop and examine a more recent stretch of the girl's conscious experiences and learn what he was afraid to know.

Bruce?

It was she! *The Tub* was calling *him!* After all these weeks—months? years?—of total rejection, of complete disregard of his existence, she was summoning.

Bruce.

Fiercely, he clung to the communicative thought impulse. It was a warm, solicitous voice come to dispel the loneliness of an abysmal, endless night.

Please, Bruce. I've got to know if you're still there.

He savored the poignant sensation of being wanted, of being recognized, afraid that should he answer he would satisfy the purpose of the voice and it would go away, never to seek him out again.

They say you're almost totally inhibited, Bruce. They say therapy is nearly over. But I've got to know if we're doing the right thing.

Therapy? He tried to imagine what kind of therapy she might mean. Then he puzzled over why she was calling him and, more pertinently, why he should be so exuberant merely to receive her thoughts.

Don't you see? I've got to know! If you're real—if you're actually something more than a bundle of personal experiences—I couldn't let them destroy you. That's why I'm trying to reach you before it's too late.

Now he remembered—the Centauri expedition, the institution, the impresses, The Tub, three men. It all returned gradually, indistinctly.

Bruce, don't let me do anything wrong. If you're still there, tell me. And I'll know that if they couldn't do away with you after all this time, they'll never be able to. I'll quit therapy. I'll help bring you back.

After all this time—he repeated the awesome phrase. But after *how* long? How much time had passed? And, if the real Craig had held her in his arms three weeks ago, two months ago, a year ago, what was the relationship between them now?

Was it that Vivien, in trying to contact him, was only seeking assurance that she was doing nothing wrong in submitting to the psychotherapy sessions? What if he answered her call? Would she then abandon the sessions? And would it mean the end of everything between her and the other Craig?

Bruce. Oh, Bruce! Can't you answer?

And, if he didn't respond, would she interpret that as signifying that nothing stood between her and his physical counterpart?

Bruce?

Furtively, he cowered behind the dismal, oppressive curtain of his own schizoid shell, eagerly seeking the resolution that would prevent him from ever straying out again.

Sometime later—an eternity later?—he started before a suddenly materialized scene that might have come to him directly from the objective world. It was as though he had again briefly been granted physical contact with reality through the girl's vision.

But somehow the perceptual scene that came to him didn't seem like something that would be witnessed in Vivien's realm of ordinary experience. Before him were arrayed the dull, grey bulkheads of an interplanetary passenger vessel's crew compartment, with its control instruments and screens and plotting boards.

The image enjoyed only ephemeral existence before it faded under a suffusion of nothingness. But so convincingly had it seemed a sensual impression that long dormant yearnings for physical existence weakened the schizoid wall and, more casually than otherwise, he struck out anew in search of objective perception.

Craig! BRUCE CRAIG!

It was a dull, booming omnipresence that penetrated every fiber of the ethereal thought region and suddenly stayed Craig in his quest.

Come out, Craig. I'm waiting.

All around, the black nothingness eddied in wild patterns of fear and defiance and spawned a myriad points of blinding, scintillating light. It was as though he were adrift in boundless space with an unrestricted vision that took in every coruscating star.

Craig!

The world thundered and the stars whirled in a macabre dance of tremulous terror, shifting, clustering into indeterminate blobs of light, dispersing, converging again.

Suddenly the radiant splashes were a thousand vaguely familiar faces—all demanding, all scowling, all identical.

I order you to the surface, Craig! All the lips moved in unison and legions of fingers, crooked and beckoning, materialized beside the faces.

Confounded, Craig fled desperately into the once familiar regions of The Tub's unconscious, seeking obscurity in the depths of a forgotten incident.

It was a warm, rainy day (in that stored recollection) and Vivien, scarcely five years old, was in the kitchen constructing islands of overturned bowls and pans on the sea that was the polished tile floor. The toaster was a ship and the girl's small hand was the zephyr that sent it sailing swiftly to its next port of call—the stained baking pan.

The cabinet was open, as it had been on his last exploratory visit to this memory excerpt. Only, now its once forbidding murkiness loomed as an inviting sanctuary.

But three of the leering faces were in there too!

Coordinately, they smiled in derision. *Don't be afraid, Craig. I won't hurt you. You must come out!*

Then he recognized the features. They were Dorfman's!

And, as he shrank fearfully, all the horrors of the institution and the sessions and the psychiatrist's relentless determination to destroy him were reborn with the force of an explosion in his memory.

He retreated frantically, the kitchen scene fading into nothingness as he plunged desperately down The Tub's fragmented juvenile recall stream towards the dead end of prenatal impressions.

Then he was lost in an incongruous region of repressed infant chimeras and fantasies, with nursery furniture that turned into friendly and threatening animals and adult voices that roared like ominous cavern winds and huge hands that caught and pressed like the relentless faces of a vice.

But he turned down the suddenly enticing corridor of a remembered nursery rhyme and hid among the soothing tones and rhythms of a maternal voice that fell upon him like a comforting spray of soft talcum powder and scented toilet water.

Surely Dorfman wouldn't find him here where Miss Muffet sat on her tuffet and all the King's horses and men took delight in trying to restore Humpty Dumpty's ovoid integrity. Surely the psychiatrist had never probed this deep into the obscure area of repressed urges and forgotten desires that was The Tub's psychic foundation.

But Dorfman *was* here!

Masterfully, vindictively, his great gnarled hands ripped through the thin veil of infantile serenity and stormed menacingly into the suppressed memory sequence.

Confounded, Craig plunged more frenziedly up the stream of childhood conscious, branching off into a dismal tunnel of long forgotten and primitive frustrations and fears.

Vivien was there—eight years old and in pigtails and with her eyes wide in terror, as she clung precariously to the ledge outside her window at the beginning of a traumatic experience.

Only, it was Craig who clung to the ledge in the child's pajamas and stared down in somnambulistic terror into the yard below where monstrous forms and amorphous, slimy things waited lustfully.

But abruptly each hideous creature was a replica of the psychiatrist. And all greedily extended their arms towards the child on the ledge.

In that moment of frozen terror, Craig heard the voices, sibilating harshly through the entire warp of intrapsychic space:

Mushily vibrant: *How much longer?*

Direct and massive: *Quiet! You'll ruin everything!*

Is she all right?

If you can't keep your mouth shut, then get out!

His/her fingers lost their final grip on the ledge and, suddenly incorporeal once more, Craig plunged towards the myriad waiting Dorfman's arms.

But the inertia of the psychical drop took him past the doctor and completely out of the suppressed incident and into the ebony infinity of the no-concept void.

But he couldn't stay there! There was no place to hide! And he mustn't return to The Tub's ego. For the psychiatrist had unrestricted access to every niche and facet of the girl's unconscious.

A giant, cold, steady hand emerged from the insuperable blackness, reaching out for him.

Come, Craig. Follow me to the surface—to reality.

But he lunged away, seeking out the subtle attraction of the Paulson impress's remnants so he would at least have a definite direction of flight.

Impetuously, he charged through the still coalescing shell of schizoid detachment. And the utter chaotic madness hit him like a blast furnace of air—stifling, damning, disorganizing even the tottering vestiges of his own rationality.

All was filth and horror and unimaginable gloom and despair. All was shrieking vituperation and agonized, mournful withdrawal. The recognizable characteristics of the pilot's personality were all gone. Left were only the basic libidinal drives—the destitute id—a cauldron of seething excitement and primitive feelings, of blind and raw impulses—a festering mire of hopelessness and ineffable despair.

And the bestial horrors and nauseous smells, the acrid tastes and torturous impressions of pain and thwarted desire were submerged under a basic, overriding concept of pitiable bewilderment over lost identity. Dismayed, Craig withdrew. And all the while he desperately resisted the hypnotic attraction as the shattered personality of the pilot seemed to reach out with clutching hands to sweep him up and make him an eternal part of the doomed Paulson malignancy.

Dazed from the impact of insane consternation, he broke feebly through the confining wall and drifted aimlessly, letting the psychic paralysis of the encounter play itself out.

Too late!

Before he realized what was happening, he sensed his involuntary passage through the now gossamer shell of the Gottweld impress.

Impulsively he tried to escape before he could be drawn inexorably into the expected maelstrom of violent lunacy.

But there was nothing here! Only the tenuous curtain and, within, the vague haze of a final, dwindling remnant of pure identity.

Like the echo of a lost soul, only the basic autoconcept resounded thinly within the Gottweld region:

I—I—I—I—I—I—I

And, even as he stood appalled at witnessing the ultimate destruction of a once complex ego, the last dying whisper faded out and the definitive curtain collapsed, like a veil of mist being wafted away on a suddenly stirring breeze.

Gottweld was no more.

Like lacy spray playing above the crest of a wind-driven wave, the mist eddied into nothing and in its place materialized the image of the psychiatrist.

Come, Craig. Let's quit playing cat and mouse. I'm taking you back to reality in order that I might take the final bit of reality out of you.

And abruptly there was a taste. The strong, biting acridity of tobacco on Craig's lips, the soothing swirl of warm, heavy, smoke in throat and lungs. Bodiless though he was, he reveled in the imagined, almost forgotten sensation of smoking.

Coming, Craig?

All psychic space gave mushrooming birth to a tremendous display of fierce luminosity that blotted out even the compelling image of the psychiatrist. The formless blaze of vacillated tremulously and reshaped itself into an objective scene.

Now he seemed to be inside Dorfman's office watching the psychiatrist who stood tensely before The Tub as she slumped in her chair. He was whispering urgent words and her eyelids flinched with each movement of his lips. But no sound came to Craig with the inexplicable vision from nowhere. For he certainly wasn't seeing through Vivien's eyes.

The scene faded and Dorfman's commanding figure loomed once more against a background of ebon velvet. *"Back, Craig. Back to objectivity."*

Then suddenly he realized he had not only sensed the words; he had also *heard* them! No vague thought impulses these. The sensation was also distinctly an auditory one.

"You may emerge," Dorfman coaxed magnanimously. *"The way is open,"* Again, both the thought and the sound.

There was another burst of light and abruptly Craig was fighting a dazzling luminescence that bathed every corner of conscious. The unbearable brilliance took solid form, shaping itself into the familiar features of the psychiatrist's office.

"That's better," said Dorfman, seated on the edge of his desk. "Glad to have you with us again."

Craig responded gradually to the kinesthesia of The Tub's body. And with the objective wholeness of physical awareness, with the sensations of heartbeat and pulse and breathing and warmth and skin pressures, came a more complete recollection of many of the things he had forgotten.

But remembering his identity as an impress and the persistent effort that had already gone into erasure was like reopening a severe, old wound. The warm blood of bitter, despairing memory flowed copiously.

"All right, Craig." Dorfman spread his hands tentatively. "We've had ourselves an amusing little game for several months. But it's going to stop now."

With the heavy curtains drawn open along the opposite wall, light flooded in through the window. Outside was the shimmering whiteness of a snow-covered countryside bathed in the thin rays of a winter's sun.

Once it had been spring and a young woman had been spirited out of a triumphant ship and brought to a sequestered institution, there to be "cured." But that had been an eternity ago. And now the crushing force of that eternity was like an unbearable weight that made Craig feel old and utterly helpless.

He shifted the girl's vision along the wall away from the window and discovered the material Craig indifferently smoking a cigarette, his foot propped upon a chair.

"I let it go this far," the psychiatrist offered disappointedly, "because I thought that in due course things would have worked out. But they haven't."

"I don't want to be erased," Craig said feebly, the words seeming even more ineffective and slavish in the girl's slight voice.

"You've no choice. You've been called back for a final session that will crush your bullheaded resistance—that will make you experience every form of imagined physical torture should you try to 'Wander' again."

"No!" Craig begged desperately. "No—please!"

Dorfman paced. "Evidently, despite our thoroughness, you've found some way of warding off schizoid compression. But we're going to correct that condition."

Hopeless, Craig tried to draw away, find temporary escape in the obscurity of his own psychic region. But Dorfman's magnetic stare held him helpless.

He wondered then how Vivien was reacting to his presence. But even with the most intense concentration he could make no contact with the girl. The psychiatrist had tactfully disposed of her conscious before beginning the session.

Dorfman approached and loomed over The Tub, fists pressed stiffly against his hips and legs spread superciliously.

"Over the past several months," he disclosed callously, "we've had a number of sessions that you know nothing about because we shunted out your conscious. We did that in order not to interfere with the withdrawal process."

He strode over to the closet and pulled open the door. "This one, though, you'll remember—for as long as you have memory, I assure you."

He trundled out the table and the suspended forms danced at the ends of their strings like the abstract elements of an intriguing mobile.

Impulsively, Craig lunged with all the strength of the girl's body. But there were straps holding her arms. Then his will to resist ebbed. He shrank futilely into the chair and a calming, almost pleasant lethargy stole over him.

For a moment he dwelt fondly on the radiantly luxurious feeling that was like a warm glow suffusing his being—the kinesthetic sensations of muscular movement, the reassuring rush of sensual impressions of sight and sound and smell, the magnificent realization that there were limbs which he could control with the mere volition of a casual thought.

But his euphoria fell away like a paltry veil, delivering him to an apathetic indifference. The design of fate, after all, stretched out before him now in incredible simplicity: Dorfman would put him through his paces of hypnoconditioning; he would return absolutely and completely into himself, like a snake swallowing its tail. And, in a short while, there would be...nothing.

The psychiatrist wheeled the table towards the center of the room and Craig started, suddenly attentive.

Why was he seeing *two* images of Dorfman—*two* images of the room, superimposed upon each other?

Fascinated, he watched the man and table progress across his field of vision in a direction normal to The Tub's perspective. But, as though in a double-exposure effect, a duplicate image of Dorfman confused the stronger visual impression by moving in the opposite direction. And each image had its individual background, one being the wall in front of The Tub and the other the wall behind her.

Then he sensed treachery and closed the girl's eyes against his tormentor's deceit. The psychiatrist had employed regression tricks before—illusions to strip away his defense and take him off guard so there would be less resistance to the hypnotic process.

Abruptly Dorfman's hand stung him across the girl's cheek. Her eyes blinked open instinctively and he was immediately captivated by the beguiling dancing forms and delightfully interesting light patterns.

Nothing.

Impenetrable blackness and vacuous silence—the impossible stillness and senselessness of profound psychic space.

Only the faint, false-real afterglow of past experiences. And even that mocking pseudo illumination was sustained only by a shred of faith, a failing belief that such abstract things as material objects and physical life and real light had once existed.

But he wouldn't go mad as Gottweld and Paulson had. Of that he felt an unbounded certainty.

Momentarily he considered trying to break out of his psychic prison. But even the suggestion brought hellishly real impressions of physical torture—slivers of burning bamboo under fingernails that didn't exist, bones breaking and muscles tearing on the rack, the lash of rawhide against an imaginary back, the agony of unreal skin being stripped away from nonexistent flesh with electrically charged forceps.

Forlornly, he dismissed the possibility of escape and, for the first time in eons, let all the tension flow out of him. It was like falling into a placid half-sleep after an eternity of trudging exhausted through a foul swamp.

He relaxed in the luxurious comfort of total apathy.

And suddenly there was sound—real, objective sound with the unmistakable fullness and consistency of outer-world origin.

It was the torrential swish of water spraying down in a thousand droplets and spattering against tile and flesh.

Craig drew back from the auditory impression, instinctively aloof, remembering the spurious effects that had come to him occasionally—the voices from nowhere, the images of faces, vague and distorted, the tastes and smells and sensations of touch, incongruous and inexplicable.

But they had meant nothing. They had probably been no more than merciless ruses intended to strip away elements of personality in the erasure process.

Curious, though, he relaxed again, wondering whether there might conceivably be some degree of valid significance to the manifestations. Would they have come more frequently except for the resistance of his constant tension over the past months?

And as though confirming his suspicion, there were other sensations—the pelting of tepid drops against naked flesh, the ticklish feel of rivulets coursing down cheeks and forming cataracts off tips of nose and chin.

The impression of warmth vanished and was replaced by an instant, wet frigidity that was like a thousand icy needles pricking his skin. It brought a breathless gasp from his throat.

And he retreated impulsively, like a furry animal darting back down its hole after being surprised by a child with a prodding stick.

But the sensations had been *that* real! He had almost felt the goose flesh and heard the reflexive sound as he imagined himself catching his breath!

In profound thought, he entertained a vast, unbelievable, dawning suggestion, too incredible to be true.

Yet...

He tried probing the schizoid shell.

Instantly the imagined tortures came.

He drew back, relaxed...and welcomed another sensual impression.

(There was a difference, evidently, between reaching out to intercept physical sensations, which brought immediate reprisal, and passively receiving those that came to him gratuitously.)

This time there was objective vision—the walls and effects of a bathroom, the blur of a cloth swishing about in his field of sight, the bulkiness of moist hands that drew up occasionally with a towel and brought darkness over the scene.

Then Craig tensed in disbelief. With the too-real vision came a mental reflection—an experience dredged from the past—*one of his own experiences!*

It was a recollection of the landing at Terraport following the Centauri trip—bands playing; dignitaries cheering; scientists and medical experts waiting to whisk The Tub away from the crowd.

The recollection had been complete and vivid. Only, *he* hadn't recalled it—not entirely on his own at least. There was a subtle but undeniable conviction that the thought had been somebody else's.

Yet there was no one else in the quadrentity who had that memory! Gottweld and Paulson had been withdrawn at the time of the incident, exhausted from the mental exertion of the approach and landing. And Vivien had been in a somnambulistic state, subdued by physical fatigue.

Only he, the impress Bruce Craig, the navigator of the expedition, had been conscious to direct the quadripartite Tub and experience the sequence.

And it was a memory that he recognized now, with its sudden return, as one of the first to be stripped away by Dorfman. But where had it been? And how had he recaptured it? Was the erasure process failing?

And the other memories that had been pirated away—he could sense the presence of them all now, lying in some convenient psychic vault and ready for instant recall.

The incoming physical sensations strengthened and expanded and now, beside the visual stimulus of the swishing towel and the auditory effect of water splashing in a face basin, he reacted to the impact of a burst of kinesthetic awareness on his conscious. And he could feel the strong, capable body of which he seemed to be newly possessed.

A mirror loomed suddenly in his line of sight and he stared incredulously at the features of the material Bruce Craig.

Confounded, the impress drew back into itself, secure in the knowledge that it could recapture the physical sensations at will.

Some of it was beginning to appear rational now. Hadn't he once heard Craig tell Vivien that he was somehow receiving memory impressions of the flight?

Wasn't it possible that *all* of the recollections which he, as an impress, had lost had been transferred through some emphatic means to retentive cells in the other Craig's mind?

And, with such a transference, wouldn't it be logical to assume that the complete experiences of the Craig impress, the sum total of the ego as modified over the past eight years, was subtly being reincorporated into the personality of the physical Craig? Was disintegration in the impress synonymous with reintegration in the original?

Such a transfusion, he conceded, would seem plausible on the basis of the overwhelming psychic affinity and the occasional physical proximity of the impress and its material counterpart over the past months.

The concept was vast and incredible. Yet, nothing else could explain all the anomalous sensations he had experienced in his inhibited state but had been too dazed to question:

The physical sounds of detached conversations that had pervaded the isolated thought region from time to time.

The occasional valid sensations of feel and smell.

The authentic visual impressions—the flashes of faces, the double-negative effect of watching from two different perspectives as Dorfman trundled the table into his office.

The material Craig had been in the office then; had witnessed the same scene. And, in emphatic counter-relationship, his perception had been transferred to the impress's conscious.

But the other hadn't been aware of the emphatic effect because there had thus far been only a transfusion of recollections while the displaced conscious of the impress had remained separate.

Now; however—now that the impress had ascertained what was happening—there could be a total reunion of the split Craig personality.

The two parts—the original, with its individual experiences of the past eight years, and the impress, with its separate and distinct memory during the same period—could blend once more into the reconstructed whole.

Experimentally, he tested the hypothesis by summoning a recent recollection from the distinctive objective-Craig segment of the dual personality.

And he thought of the previous evening—a drive through the moon-bathed country—Vivien close beside him as the wind swept her hair back, her face uptilted to drink in the freshness of the night.

It was a wonderfully gratifying recollection and it was his as much as it was the material Craig's.

They/he stood before the mirror and adjusted the knot on his/their tie.

The experience was real. The sensations of manual direction, of participation in the action were strong.

And, as yet, he (the other Craig) hadn't begun to suspect the process of reintegration. Perhaps he never would. Perhaps it would come off so smoothly that there would be only a subconscious awareness of temporary duality until unification was complete.

He tried to withdraw. But he achieved only an approximate degree of detachment, of walled-in isolation. Sensing a growing resistance to such unnatural dissociation, he felt himself being forced back involuntarily to objective status as part of the duo-personality.

They/he finished dressing and went down to the reception room of the institution's guest building.

Vivien was there. She smiled at him/them and came over.

"Hi, Tub," he said. "It's been a long time."

She lifted an eyebrow dubiously. "Yes," she said facetiously, "—all of twelve hours."

He took her arm. "Now why do you suppose I said something like that?"

REIGN OF THE TELEPUPPETS

"The way this thing shapes up," Director Gabe Randall of the Bureau of Interstellar Exploration was saying in his usual manner of understatement, "it will be our most important trouble-shooting mission to date."

He stood cranelike, one leg hooked over a corner of the desk, as he whacked his thigh with an illuminated indicator rod. With purposeful eyes, he sized up the other three men in the briefing room. Lean and alert, he held himself straight against the encroachment of age that was evident in a fully white shock of hair and a brow furrowed with decades of executive responsibility.

"I suppose," he digressed, smiling, "that we'll have to get along without our Maid of the Megacycles."

Dave Stewart, Randall's assistant, glanced at the empty chair. "Carol said she'd be along shortly." Actually, she hadn't. But, if the situation were reversed, she'd cover for him.

"Woman's prerogative," the director observed, shrugging phlegmatically. "Gentlemen, I submit that the greatest deterrent to progress in BIE is the fact that direct radio empathy can be developed only in women—and young ones at that."

But Stewart recognized the imperceptible jocularity in the other's stare. It contrasted the sobriety with which he had said only a moment earlier that the nature of the mission required top personnel.

At half the director's age, Stewart had earned his recognition as logical successor to the seat of executive authority. And, in Carol Cummings, Randall had selected the most capable radio empathy specialist BIE had produced in years. The prettiest, too, he added as an afterthought.

But there you could draw the line. Below was the *Photon II*'s crew. At forty-four, Nat McAllister, pilot, was well past the age when he might look forward to a supervisory position, thanks to a rash of bad-judgment accidents and a general absence of ambition. And Ship Systems Officer Mortimer, ten years younger, seemed anchored to his niche by an equal measure of minimum ability—if not by the sheer weight of his two hundred and fifty pounds.

"Top" personnel for a "priority" job? Stewart shook his head dubiously.

Randall rapped the desk and the sharp sound snapped McAllister's chin from his chest, where it had gradually descended.

"Since it appears we'll continue to be disfavored by Miss Cummings' absence," the director resumed, "we'll proceed."

He touched a button and darkness filled the room. Another stud hurled into existence a ten-foot sphere of galactic luminosity, ablaze with motes of scattered brilliance.

Stewart located the coordinate axes and traced them to Sol. Nearby was Centauri, ringed with a halo to signify location of Headquarters, Bureau of Interstellar Exploration. Mortimer's corpulent face took on a Buddha-like appearance in the illumination from Alpha Hydrae, hovering near his left cheek.

"All right, Stewart," Randall gestured with his rod. "Suppose you identify that star immediately behind your shoulder for McAllister and Mortimer's benefit."

"Alpha Tauri."

"Right. Aldebaran—where you made a telepuppet drop on Four-B two years ago."

"Just before Harlston and I pushed on out to explore beyond Aldebaran."

Randall directed his next words at the pilot and ship systems officer. "What Stewart did not know as he ranged outwards was that the Aldebaran telepuppet team, for some reason, stopped transmitting—less than a year after the drop."

Stewart finger-combed a spray of blond hair off his forehead. In the pseudo galactic illumination his face, tanned from exposure to a score of suns radiating heavily in the ultraviolet range, appeared cinnamon in hue.

Randall glanced back at him. "Tell them what we're going to do on this mission."

"Unknot the puppet strings," he said laconically, becoming impatient with his dutiful recitation to enlighten the other two.

The director glanced off to his right, eyebrow raised to compound the eternal ridges of his forehead. "I see we've got our Maid of the Megacycles with us at last. Couldn't you tear yourself away from a Terracast, Miss Cummings? Or did you bring it along?"

Carol advanced through a patch of projected galactic nebulosity. Ebon hair sheening with the reflected glow, she smiled saucily and tapped her temple. "It so happens I *am* peeking in on a videocast," she bantered. "And I'm learning more about what's behind this briefing than if I'd been here all along."

Groping for her chair, she weaved between the steady, cold points of suspended light that represented Epsilon Scorpii and Eta Orphiuchi. "Don't look now, Chief," she added, winking, "but I'm afraid this newscast shows you've got a leak in your bureau."

Stewart caught her arm and guided her towards the chair. His hand held the coarse texture of fatigue coveralls that did little to obscure the shapeliness of her lithe, five-foot-four form. She returned his greeting with a spirited, "Hi, glad to have you aboard. Not planning to lead us off on a two-year jaunt?"

Randall tapped the desk with his rod. "If Miss Cummings is willing to forego informalities, we can get along with our briefing."

McAllister tossed his head erect, but started nodding again almost immediately. Mortimer looked up tolerantly from contemplation on the orbiting of one of his stout thumbs around the other.

The director touched another button and the celestial sphere expanded to twice its diameter, encompassing another seventy light-years in all directions. "Again, directly behind you, Stewart, is—what?"

Enthusiastically, he sat erect. "The Hyades Cluster."

Randall laid down his rod. "Stewart, as you are aware, completed his expedition two weeks ago—in a ship stripped down for maximum range. Now he's going to tell us something about his experiences."

Mortimer, finally interested, glanced over at McAllister. The pilot, however, was dozing.

Stewart stared at the cluster of four stars huddled together in the still air of the briefing room. "We found the Hyades rich in Earth-type worlds. Seven—" He paused. Was it seven, or eight? "Eight of them are more like Terra than Terra itself. Four others are more suitable than anything we've run across in a century and a half of galactic exploration."

His eyes clung to the brilliant specks, set like jewels against a velvet background. They *were* jewels—cold and glittering and beckoning. And he could almost feel their attraction—like a magnet tugging on filings of hope and ambition. Yet, somehow he felt dejected, as though he were reluctant to reach out for them.

"You did *all that* in two years' time?" McAllister asked.

"Why yes, of course. I—" He could understand the other's skepticism, however. He *had* covered a lot of interstellar space.

"You know what this development means," Randall said.

"That our expansion will be concentrated in a new direction!" Carol volunteered hopefully.

The chair creaked its complaint as Mortimer shifted his weight. "And the Aldebaran telepuppets?"

Randall gestured for emphasis. "That robot team is now of first-rate importance. We'll need a full analysis of Four-B in the shortest time possible. The Hyades are a hundred and fifty light-years away—too far for direct development. But a halfway base in the Aldebaran system will open them up to us immediately."

Carol found Stewart's arm. "This one is really worthwhile. Think you can get your puppets back on their strings?"

"I suppose so. There can't be too much wrong with them." But still his thoughts were on the Hyades. Somehow they left him with an emptiness, a bittersweet taste. Whereas he knew he should feel only enchantment and the satisfaction of accomplishment in his discovery.

"That all there is to this mission?" McAllister, fully awake now, asked disappointedly.

"I thought it was going to be a challenge," Mortimer complained.

Randall played the buttons on his desk as though they were a console keyboard. The celestial sphere deflated, then collapsed. Room lights blazed, harsh and intense. "Everything clear?" he asked.

Then he added, "We'll assemble at oh-eight-hundred Octoday at the *Photon II* dock. My gear is already packed."

Carol's eyes widened. "You're going, too?"

"Yes, finally. About time I got out in the field and see how our new generation of—ah, specialists handles things."

Stewart only stared at the director. On the latter's desk were mountainous stacks of back work. Yet he was finding time to get away.

Rationalization circuits working sluggishly as he surveyed his realm, Bigboss dredged from the fragmented impressions on his memory drums his most fascinating, most disturbing subject for speculation:

In all Creation, there was nothing superior to Him. This material world that stretched out around Him, everything in the celestial reaches as far as infinity itself—all *His*! He had brought it into existence, although (confound those faulty drums!) He might not be able to recall the specific acts of Creation.

Yet He sensed, with the nagging certainty of conviction, that somewhere in His Universe, there was an insolent creature or creatures who would dare challenge His infinite supremacy.

Well (He generated power so fiercely that he had to shunt the excess to ground), let them! He could desire nothing more. And His only hope was that they would confront Him personally to express their insolence. *Then* there would be opportunity for an accounting!

Remembering his blaster, he swung around, aimed it at a boulder and, vengefully, fed it an enormous surge of power. Angry liquid light streaked out from the intensifier and crashed against the rock. The concussion sent him skittering back several meters.

Bigboss was by far the most magnificent member of the clan if indeed, he should condescend to regard himself as belonging to the set at all. Fully twice the size of any of the others, he reared pompously erect on four stout appendages. Through its ports, his central section offered glowing evidence of the nuclear processes within. Majestic in stance, he swung a pair of formidable members—the auxiliary blaster and a massive, extensible vice.

Assuring himself that the insolent creatures were *not* spurious impressions on his drums, he blasted another boulder. *That* for the pretenders, should they ever decide to contest His Reign!

Bigboss reacted abruptly to the realization that Minnie was watching him. No longer was his digital subsystem receiving her stream of telemetric signals. Relays clicked within his control section and video gain brought intensified visual awareness in all four quadrants. Immediately he spotted Minnie, immobile and ungainly as gyros balanced her elongated metal form on six jointed legs.

Her drill head, held high above the outcropping on which she had been working, glinted in the light of a shimmering, golden sun. Her single, wide-angle lens, set like a Cyclopean eye in its chrome-plated forehead, was focused intently on him.

Interrupting his subliminal correlation of data from the other workers, he sent Minnie an indignant "back-to-work" impulse. Reluctantly, she sank her bit into the rock.

But she had ingested only a slotful of fragments when the ground bulged beside her. Displaced soil slid away and Screw Worm erupted, carrying in his thread pouches mineral specimens for her analyzers.

Bigboss generated more easily as he watched Worm at work. Not that the menial helper, who occupied the lowest rung on the ladder, was worthy of speculative attention. But a laboring borer meant Minnie was preoccupied with her limited supervisory function and couldn't be plotting to supplant him.

Working near Minnie, Seismo squatted at his sedentary task. Sensor rod sunk to bedrock, he was proudly purring an encoded disclosure of distant rumblings beneath the surface. Less than a hectometer away, Sky Watcher's tripodal locomotive system was bringing him carefully up a rise. Arriving, he assumed the location Sun Watcher had only recently abandoned. He adjusted himself on dead level, then thrust out a number of lensed tubes that locked on a referent star, three distant planets and a smaller satellite.

At that moment came an excited eureka impulse from Breather, posted outside a cave and briskly inflating and deflating the external pouches that bracketed his long, cylindrical form. The impulse proudly told of his detection of oxygen traces.

Nearby, Scraper diligently shoveled soil into his scoop in an endless search for microorganisms and DNA molecules. Grazer munched on a growth already identified as lichen. Peter the Meter sat on a knoll scanning the sky with his battery of inferometers, radiometers and bolometers.

Of the distant workers, Bigboss was most sensitively aware of the volant signals from Maggie. Kilometers away, she was covering the ground in great, leaping strides of abandon as she sought out and traced down each fascinating iso-magnetic line of variation.

Work, work, work. Get the job done. Shake a leg. Shoulder (whatever that was) to the wheel. Dig in and pitch. But—for *what*?

What was responsible for the irresistible compulsion? Was it *his own* idea? But of course, it must be. For, how could there be any power capable of directing Him? Unless, perhaps, it might conceivably be the insolent creatures who lurked like vague shadows on the fringe of his almost obliterated memory. But, no!

He, Himself, was the Supreme Being of All Creation!

His master timer peaked in its four-hundred-cycle sine wave, reminding him of the chore at hand. The sun had set and the huge, pink planet had already laid claim to the night sky. Just below it was the special grouping of stars that matched, point for point, the referent pattern on his orientation drum.

Programmed functions took over. Sensors hunted out the bright central star and aimed his parabolic antenna at the designated spot seven degrees south-eastwards. Then he loosed his transmission into subspace. Data stored over long hours of tedious sequencing surged from the tape, bringing a euphoria of relief.

Eventually telemetric transmission ended and Bigboss, as had become his custom, automatically turned his thoughts to the Totem.

All metal it was—sleek and sheening and shaped like a truncated cone as it lay powerless on the plain beyond the hill. How akin it was to him and the clan! Why, it even seemed he could almost *remember* having once been a part of the huge, polished thing. Perhaps it was the very vessel He had used on His Celestial Tour of Creation.

Yes, it was time for Pilgrimage to Totem. And a fitting reward it would be, as always, for successful transmission.

He mustered the volition required to break functional compulsion. Then he sent the "fall-in" impulse to his subjects. Eventually the line of march took shape, with Bigboss leading his analyzers up the first hill and calling for the proper reverential attitude.

Behind him lumbered Minnie, her thick neck weighted by the bulky drill and swinging awkwardly with the sway of her six-legged stride. Seismo, encumbered with a faulty, dragging sensor rod, was having some difficulty maintaining a straight course.

Sky Watcher came along in lunging motions, a natural consequence of his tripodal system. Immediately to his rear, Sun Watcher, who held the fifth rung on the ladder, moved smoothly ahead with all his instruments retracted except the solar plasma detector.

Then there was a break in the line for Maggie, who could now be seen galloping along on an interceptive course. Peter the Meter, lurching from the imbalance of an extended boom-and-ball sensor, appeared somewhat like a many-spiked sphere on spindly legs.

Farther down the file, no deference was extended in the form of gaps for those missing workers who had yet to join the march.

Bringing up the rear were the diminutive Scraper and Grazer, resembling a pair of scurrying crabs, and Screw Worm, using his blade-like jets to propel himself in a rolling, transverse motion.

Aware of commotion behind him, Bigboss continued unconcernedly up the rise. Sky Watcher, interpreting Seismo's faulty motions as an opportunity for his own forced ascendancy, had drawn back a photo-multiplier tube and sent it crashing into the other's rear plate.

The attack, though, was only self-thwarting, since it jarred a servo unit into retracting Seismo's dangling sensor rod. His locomotive integrity restored, he kicked out with a pedal pad and sent Sky Watcher flailing back into Sun Watcher. The latter rammed forward with his plasma detector's boom-and-ball shield, managing to knock Sky Watcher back into his proper position.

Finally fearful of damage to instruments, Bigboss gruffly radioed "cut-the-comedy" impulses, then trained his rearward lens on Minnie. She had inched furtively forward and was now menacing his upper section with her drill head.

He considered wielding his blaster but rejected that expedient as an excessive and unnecessary ostentation. Instead he countered by raising his extensible vice. The lesser show of strength sufficed to discourage Minnie's ambition, for the moment at least.

How foolish she was to imagine she could supplant Him as the Supreme Being!

Let her try.

Even if she succeeded, he would merely deny her a place at the trough next feeding period.

Then where would she get the vital charge for her batteries?

II

The *Photon II* groaned, heaved and popped out of subspace for a fix before striking out on the last short leg of its journey. As Stewart had feared, they were five light-years off course.

Ship Systems Officer Mortimer's thickly-fleshed face struggled with an embarrassed smile. "Well, you can't hit 'em on the nose *every* time out," he rationalized, waddling back to the charts.

Stewart reflected that rare indeed were the occasions on which Mortimer came anywhere near the nasal target. Conceding the loss of nearly an entire day, he waited for Director Randall's permissive nod, then joined Mortimer in cutting the new navigation tapes.

It took two hours to process all data and feed them into the SCC-772. When the computer burped out the new heading, Stewart threaded the tape into the control programmer and decided to spend the uneventful period of subspace travel in his bunk.

Sleep came swiftly, but it was shallow and restless. More than once over the next several hours, as he plummeted down a chasm of nightmares, he regretted having left the control compartment.

First his dreams brought him back to the Hyadean Cluster, as they had on so many occasions during recent weeks. And, for a while, he drank in the blue-green beauty of the seven—or, was it eight?—worlds that seemed to beckon with all their irresistible allure.

They were incredibly splendorous, these planets that would soon embrace man and feed and clothe and shelter him. But, as he admired them in his dream, a sort of astronomical surrealism bunched them together—all in orbit around a central, massive sun—until it seemed they were occupying so compact an area that they must surely crumble under the weight of their mutual attraction.

And, as though upon his suggestion, crumble they did. Only, it was no pulverizing force that scattered them into fragmented rings, such as those around Sol's Saturn. Instead, each planet cracked like a hatching egg, its crust stripping away and exposing beneath a gruesome Harpy that was all razor-sharp talons and vicious beak and slime-filled, ruffled feathers.

Stewart tried to scream himself awake but couldn't. He only flailed helplessly in the void while monstrous wings thrashed space into a frenzy, producing great currents that set the stars themselves to eddying and swirling.

They dived at him, but before their talons could sink into his flesh he awoke trembling and cold in his twisted, moist clothes.

For a long while he merely lay there trying to wash his mind of his horror. But the steady whine of the subspace drive reminded him that the *Photon* was streaking in the direction of the Hyades. That it would end its headlong plunge in the Aldebaran system, only half-way there, brought no relief from his baseless, unreasonable fear.

When he returned to the control compartment, the ship was back in normal space and within Aldebaran Four-B's gravitational field.

He joined Carol Cummings in the forward section, hooking his arm through a view-port strap and mooring himself against null gravity.

"You suppose we're home free?" she asked uncertainly.

Her normally effusive smile, he noticed, had moderated considerably. "If McAllister doesn't louse up his landing."

"I take it he's not very efficient."

"Pure and simple understatement. Last time out he missed an entire continent. It was a case for Search and Rescue."

Carol pressed forward and soft light from Aldebaran Four, off the port bow, warmed her sculpturesque features with primrose highlights. "I should imagine he would have been cashiered."

"But he wasn't. Instead he turns up on this crucial mission."

He busied himself with frequency adjustment on his portable transmitter. With it he would be able to tell, soon after landing, whether the Operations Coordinator could still be reached orally through its command discriminator circuit.

He flicked on the power switch, positioned the microphone comfortably against his larynx and sharply intoned a series of numerals. An oscilloscope faithfully traced the amplitude pattern verifying effective transmission.

Down the companionway in the pilot's compartment, he could see McAllister anchored in his acceleration couch. He was drifting back and forth between padding and slack restraining straps, vicariously lost in the blood-and-guts action of a dramatape feeding into the view slot of his helmet.

Stewart read the label on the empty container—"The Kowalski Bros. in the Korean War."

"Always has his head buried in one of those escapist tapes, hasn't he?" Carol observed, still staring out of the port.

"I don't think he ever grew up," Stewart agreed. But, again, even the Bureau seemed to contain its share of coasters who had never quite reached maturity, he remembered.

"Even in the Bureau," Carol observed thoughtfully, "you'll find coasters who've never reached maturity."

Intuitively, he tensed. Was it just coincidence that she had repeated, almost word for word, his own thoughts?

"I've never looked at any of those warfare tapes myself," she said. "But I've heard about them. Do you suppose armed conflict was really that horrible?"

"Pretty rough, according to the historians. It's not the sort of thing I'd like to be mixed up in."

"And McAllister?"

"Him? He's just building up a reservoir of false courage through his viewer." Yet, in fairness to the pilot, Stewart had to admit that he, himself, felt a deep and reasonable gratitude that wars were a thing of the historic past.

Carol sighed and glanced at him. "I'm certainly glad," she said, straight-faced, "that wars are a thing of the historic past."

He seized her arm. "Carol! Do you realize you're repeating *everything I'm thinking*? You've gone a step beyond radio empathy! You can pull in *thought* waves too!"

"No-o-o, you're joking!"

"No. Honest, I—" But his words were lost in her welling laughter.

He followed her amused stare to his portable voice transmitter and the mike that still clung to his throat. And instantly he realized that his subvocalizations, being picked up and broadcast, were to her like a window opening on his thought processes.

"Why, you—" Feigning indignation, he caught her around the waist and pulled her towards him. Weightless, she drifted forward and spread out conveniently across his knees.

But before he could bring a hand down resoundingly on the curvature of taut coveralls, Randall drifted in on the scene.

Still laughing, Carol straightened and announced, "Saved—by the great, white-haired protector."

Randall grinned benignly, lit his pipe and stared out of the port. "Couldn't help hearing your conversation about the horror of warfare. I've seen all the documentary tapes. It *was* rough."

"Thank God it's a closed book," Carol said seriously.

"But *is* it? There's still a large and articulate school that regards armed conflict as an instinctive human mechanism."

"We've had no war in two hundred years," Stewart said.

"Only because political subdivisions haven't had time for one. The instinct is blurred as a result of our expanding into a vacuum."

"I see." Carol's eyes strained with disillusionment. "And the question is—what happens when we run out of galaxy?"

"Fat chance." Stewart laughed. "We've got a few billion years to go before we find ourselves short on worlds."

Having apparently lost interest in the conversation, Randall was staring ahead at the onrushing satellite.

"That's one way of looking at it," Carol said pensively. "But there's also another possibility—resistance to the expansion."

"You kidding? In two centuries we haven't run into a single life form that's the intellectual equivalent of a Terran fiddler crab. What do you think, Chief?"

The director blew a stream of smoke at the swiftly expanding disc of Four-B. "I think our Maid of the Mega-cycles ought to start sniffing for that telepuppet team. I wouldn't want to rely on Mortimer's locating them with directional gear."

Carol faced the view port with her eyes closed for perhaps three minutes. Then she grinned. "I think I've got it! Not just a single, strong signal. Bundles of weak ones."

"It figures," Stewart verified. "The OC wouldn't be transmitting now. But the lesser puppets would be funneling the stuff into the CXB-1624. Can you identify any frequencies?"

She hesitated. "I'd say they're spaced out between fifteen hundred and two thousand kilocycles."

"You're a bit off. Should be sixteen to twenty-four hundred."

She opened her eyes, studied the rugged face of the satellite, then pointed. "Three—near the end of that mountain range."

He handed her a mike and earphone set. "I'll tell McAllister you're ready to guide him in."

As Stewart had feared, McAllister's landing turned out to be a real corker. It even started with a three-gainer flip, rather than a simple end-about maneuver, when he first applied braking thrust.

Bigboss responded automatically to the abruptly peaking sine wave that reminded him it was time for feeding. Summoning the clan with a brisk flow of "come-and-get-it" signals on all command wavelengths, he strutted to the center of the clearing and prepared the trough. Squatting, he switched on all outlet circuits and directed bristling current into each jack.

The workers came from the cave, over the hills, out of the shadowy depths of fissures, from behind grotesque outcroppings. Illuminations piercing the twilight gloom, they extended retractable electrodes and converged on Bigboss.

One by one, plugs slipped into jacks and steadily increasing drain gave assurance of an orderly distribution of current.

Minnie was late arriving. She came along clumsily, massive drill head bobbing with her awkward stride. Had Bigboss's memory pack been serving him more efficiently at the time, he might have realized her gyros couldn't be overcorrecting that radically without triggering a "fix-me-I'm-broke" impulse.

But, as it was, she completed her apparently innocuous approach with impunity. Taking a last, measured step, she toppled over backwards on her posterior analyzing chamber. An ostensibly helpless victim of imbalance, her neck teetered skywards and her drill head hovered over Bigboss's upper section.

Then it crashed down, the drill bit shattering his port video pick-up lens. Instantly he lost visual contact with one quadrant of his surroundings. He reacted at once, though, swiveling his upper section around ninety degrees and bringing Minnie back in sight through another lens. Guarding against repetition of the accident, he reached out and gripped her neck in his vice. He guided her plug into the proper jack, maintaining his purchase just to be sure.

Accident? he asked himself.

It was an unfamiliar concept, at best. Then he recalled that "mishap" was a notion not applicable to members of the clan. Perhaps other beings in other universes were given to blunder. In His World, though, He had arranged it that His intellects would be without error. Here the concept "intent" had no polar opposite.

Which meant that Minnie, not having reported malfunctioning gyros, had *planned* the destruction of one of his video sensors.

Vindictively, he started to turn upon her. But he realized he would be circumventing the primary compulsion—work, work, work. She was, after all, diligently discharging a worthwhile function in unraveling the secrets He had so cunningly hidden in His Creation.

Feeding finally over, he signaled a general "back-to-work" order on all wavelengths and watched his subjects return to their chores, motions brisk with restored energy.

For many sine wave peaks thereafter, Bigboss fretted over the ramifications of having lost visual contact with a ninety-degree wedge of his environs. Had Minnie intended that effect? Did her rationalization pack have the capacity to reason out such a complex cause-and-effect relationship? Had she anticipated his resulting vulnerability?

Oh, he was compensating readily enough through self-reprogramming: stability for five sine wave saliences; activate upper section's horizontal servomechanism; circumrotate ninety degrees; stabilize; count five more waveform saliences; reverse procedure. That way three video sensors did the job of four.

It gave him adequate coverage. But there were those times when the demands of function modification required the full output of his PM & R pack and his defensive scanning had to be sacrificed.

Such as now—when he was receiving Screw Worm's clear and frantic "save-me" signals.

Activating his directional gear, he lumbered over to the precise spot—a gentle rise of topsoil not far from where Minnie herself was chipping away at a boulder. Engaging his ventral illuminator-sensor, he located Worm's most recent drill hole. The borer's distress impulses were issuing with great amplitude from the opening. Bigboss unfolded his scoop and went to work.

It wasn't long before he had uncovered the borer's rearward axial protuberance. Extending his ventral vice, he gripped Worm securely, heaved to free him from the rock formation in which he had become wedged, and brought him back to the surface.

Released, the lesser worker scurried off to rejoin Minnie.

Bigboss realized only then that, during the entire rescue operation, he had neglected his defensive scanning procedure.

Restoring his upper section's quarterly rotational motion, he regarded Minnie warily. Was there any significance to the fact that she was facing him from the other side of the boulder, such that each time she elevated her head her field of vision swept over him?

Experimentally, he moved twenty meters to his right. Compensating, she skewed left, maintaining her visual advantage.

A calculated maneuver? Of course, it *had* to be. Perhaps her insolence should be dealt with summarily. But how could that be done without reducing the clan's over-all efficiency as a team dedicated to the compulsion of work, work, work?

At that moment Peter the Meter, busy scanning the sky with his battery of instruments, loosed a shrill eureka signal.

Bigboss thought for a moment that one of the latter's gamma ray spectrometers had been swamped. But, on monitoring Peter's telemetered stream, he discerned that the impulse was from an infra-red photometer. A check of coordinates showed the source of disturbance to be skyward, with a dead zenith orientation.

He commandeered one of Sky Watcher's planetary telesensors and redirected it at the source of new emanation. Now there were additional data to throw light on the manifestation.

The disturbance was in the visual range; classification—material. A rapidly shifting parallax suggested either constant location and swift expansion, or steady size and brisk approach.

Sky Watcher, on his own adaptive initiative, settled that uncertainty. His radar gear calculated a variable approach momentum averaging twelve-hundred kilometers an hour and decreasing.

Peter also improvised on his function, bringing into play a photometer that instantly gauged the emissive intensity of the disturbance: comparable to the parameter for solar brilliance.

The object had shifted from zenith and was drifting over into the quadrant wherein the clan's Totem was located. Bigboss responded with some degree of concern to this development. Did it represent a threat to their revered symbol of metallic kinship?

Then he had the object in his own visual field. It was a great, blazing ball of brilliance that extended a flickering tongue downward. Atop the sphere of fiery energy sat a shining silver needle that resembled nothing as much as it did *the clan's own Totem!*

Evaluation circuits frozen in a confusion of indecision, he stood there fully unaware that he had discontinued his protective scanning and had not brought Minnie into one of his lines of sight for a number of sine wave epipeaks.

He was shocked back into action, however, when an equilibrium circuit tripped the alarm that his attitude was unstable and beyond compensation within the limits of gyroscopic control.

He pivoted sharply and planted two pedal discs down in the direction of fall. As he did so, his upper command section swung around, bringing a video lens to bear on Minnie. Refocusing, he saw she had crept up from his blind quadrant and had begun drilling into his powerplant section.

Fool. In her thirst for supremacy, didn't she realize she could touch off an explosion that would hurl them both halfway to the pink planet?

He pulled away from the grinding bite of her drill and brought his vice swinging forcibly upwards. It slammed into her forward

141

analyzing compartment and sent her reeling backwards. Her equilibrium system overextended, she toppled sideways and lay there
kicking ineffectually.

By then, the great blazing light had disappeared beyond the hills
at almost the exact site where the Totem was located.

He left Minnie to her struggles and went eagerly forward. Eventually, she would evaluate her position and hit upon the proper combination of responses to right herself.

Meanwhile the now Surface-borne needle was a new environmental item that cried for analysis, with eureka signals already coming in from several workers. Maggie, for instance, was covering the
ground in lurching strides, honing in on one of the new lines of force
the object had established.

Seismo had recorded and sent along exciting data on tremors that
could be interpreted in terms of a number of closely-spaced, localized
impacts. Even Minnie—despite her predicament and in response to
the basic compulsion of her function—was using her high neutron
tool. Evaluation circuits humming, she was sending a stream of signals that fairly screamed, "Pure metal!"

And Grazer, abandoning a patch of lichen, was scrambling up a
hillside in the direction of the recently arrived object. His eureka was
the most frenzied of all. Which was understandable, since he was
sensing DNA molecules for the first time in his memory!

The best Bigboss could surmise, from a precursory correlation of
data, was that Grazer had detected the molecules in a substance that
wound helically around the great needle-like form.

Then his rationalization circuits labored under peak voltage as an
obscure memory fragment thrust itself up from one of his drums.

Again, it was a vague bit concerning his suspicions on the existence of insolent creatures who might imagine themselves superior
to Him—might even be presumptuous enough to give orders to the
Supreme Being!

If such creatures were more than spurious impressions, he reasoned, then wasn't it likely that they, too, could move about in celestial
vessels? Hadn't He all along feared that if they came to contest His
Reign they would come from the sky?

142

Voltage regulators clicked frantically as he shunted aside raging current and averted damage to his rationalization pack. But he could hardly consider the beings without over-generating. They were *that* infuriating.

Had the contemptuous creatures come at last, as he had always supposed they would? Was his period of agonizing vigilance at an end? Could this be the final accounting he had anticipated so anxiously?

Enraged, he lumbered forward, his blaster extended rigidly before him, as though it were a lance.

III

Stewart dug out from under the miscellany of dislodged gear that had buried him in his acceleration couch.

"Good landing," he grumbled at McAllister, whose hands were still trembling at the controls, "—all six of them."

White-faced, Carol recovered her composure by releasing her hair from its free-fall net. "I wasn't sure," she whispered, "whether he was going to land or just play bounce."

Randall tested his legs. "Well, at least we *are* here."

He crossed over to the external view console and threw a switch. One of the screens flickered, then steadied with a wide-angle image of the sky, framed in the sweeping curvature of the horizon. Aldebaran, setting, was bisected by a serrate mountain range, while its fourth planet was rising in all its brilliant immensity.

More interested in their surface surroundings, however, Stewart brought another screen into play and aimed it at the ground. The lens swept across, then came back to focus on a silvery form that reared skywards beyond a nearby hill.

"At least McAllister put us down in the right place," he conceded. "There's the telepuppet barge—right where I left it."

He swung the lens on around and picked up movement on the ground almost in the shadow of the *Photon*.

"And there are our puppets!" Carol announced.

The Operations Coordinator, its laser intensifier evidently locked in the ready position, was leading a march towards the ship. Some of the team were not in evidence, as was to be expected after a year of managing on their own. But there was the Seismometer, the Astronomical Data Collector and the Solar Plasma Detector.

Trailing behind were the Atmosphere Analyzer and the Radiometer Complex. Stewart could make out even the lesser forms of the Microorganism Collector and Analyzer, the Flora C & A and the Subordinate Mineral Specimen Collector. In the distance, the Roving Magnetometer was homing in on the rest of the team.

He opened the locker and selected a hostile-atmosphere sheath. "This shouldn't take long. Just a matter of replacing the OC's malfunctioning unit. It's either a thermal increment problem or a component that's been ionized by particle radiation."

Reluctantly, Randall turned from the zenith screen. "How are you going to go about it?"

"Try a few oral commands on the OC." He slipped into the rubberized suit. "Trouble's probably in its CXB-1624 digital system."

"You picked up anything, Carol?" Randall asked.

She tilted her head alertly. "Just the subordinate stuff. I can't tell if the CXB's functioning 'til big boy starts transmitting to the relay station. However—"

She paused to stare curiously at Randall, who was still scrutinizing the sky. Stewart wondered momentarily whether the director might not be wrestling with a morbid fear of the astronomical distance separating him from home. It was possible, with Sol and Centauri far less prominent than Aldebaran's minor companions in the field of brilliant stars.

"However," Carol resumed, "I'll put on a sheath and go with you. Out there I might tap the predigital spill-off and find out whether it's correlating and sequencing properly."

"You'd better stay aboard for a while," Randall advised. "Those puppets haven't responded to human direction for over a year."

"You mean there might be danger?"

"Let's just say their behavior may not be entirely predictable." He gestured towards the screen. "Like now."

The vanguard of robot explorers, led by the towering Operations Coordinator, had reached the ship. The Magnetometer began darting around one of the hydraulic fins, charting lines of isomagnetic intensity. The Mineral Analyzer had already sunk its drill into the broad, flat surface of the stabilizer. And the Flora Collector and Analyzer was being boosted by the OC to the lowest spiral of the ship's subspace drive intensifier. Deposited upon the ceramics-insulated coil, the crablike puppet was doing its best to flake off some of the outer surface for testing.

McAllister laughed. "Look at those mixed-up machines! They're trying to *analyze* the ship!"

"That's what I mean," Randall pointed out soberly. "One of their inhibitions is to ignore refined metal. That's how we keep their barges from being pecked to pieces."

"You don't think we can run into trouble out there, do you?" Mortimer asked, concerned.

Randall hesitated. "No, but we won't take any chances, although it's doubtful that loss of contact has obscured their *basic* inhibitions."

"Of course it hasn't. Nothing like that's ever happened."

"In that case, you won't mind accompanying us outside."

Mortimer stabbed his chest with a pudgy thumb. "Me?"

"Right."

McAllister, Stewart noticed, was frowning in front of the screen as he watched the Flora C & A munching away at the subspace drive coil. "That thing can't do any damage, can it?"

"Not as long as the current's off," Stewart assured.

Mortimer paled as he lunged for the subspace drive switch.

But just then there was a thunderous concussion and the *Photon II* lurched and swayed on its hydraulic fins.

Randall shrugged. "Well, there goes our subspace drive."

"And our long-range transmitter too," Stewart added. "They both work off the same generator."

Outside, the puppets were withdrawing.

Mortimer, pulling up short of the switch, spread his arms apologetically. "I forgot to turn the circuit off."

Stewart grimaced. "Well, one thing's for sure: We're not going to finish up in a couple of hours and head for home."

Aiming the pickup lens more directly at the damaged area, Randall filled the screen with an image of shredded cable and shattered ceramics. "It'll take a week to repair that."

McAllister's face had whitened, caused the veins in his forehead to stand out under taut skin. "You mean we're stuck here?"

"As far as subspace is concerned. And I can't think of any lively spot we might want to visit in the Aldebaran system."

Keeping a ridge of hills between themselves and the robots, Stewart trailed the telepuppet team towards their working area.

Randall stumbled and fell against him. Glancing back, he saw that the director had lost his footing because he was still staring at the sky. Within the helmet, his face appeared harsh and grim in the profuse coral planetlight.

Stewart shrugged, deciding to let the other wrestle in silence with his phobias, whatever they might be. As for himself, he had his own brand of jitters to worry about. And what made things worse was that he had no idea what was behind them.

Not that he hadn't been afraid before. One could hardly put in twelve years with the Bureau of Interstellar Exploration without getting his courage sullied somewhere along the way by a cliff-hanger or two. But, in each of those cases, the menacing factor had been vivid, easily recognizable, something he could put his finger on.

The apprehension that lurked in the back of his mind now, however, was something he had never encountered before. Vague to the point of being mysterious, it seemed to be hardly more concrete than a fear of itself. But he felt that at any particular moment, if he found the right curtain to draw aside, he would expose a darkened recess filled with horror.

Was this dread something that was reaching up from the depths of his phantasmagoric nightmares? Was his subconscious, for some reason, handing up reservations on the acquisition of the Hyades as pearls on the string of galactic expansion? Intuition? Hunch?

Whatever it was, he didn't like it. And he cared for it even less now—as he trod the surface of this remote satellite and stared hypnotically ahead at the brilliant stars of the Hyades, well above the horizon. For how could he be certain *this* wasn't a nightmare and that in the next instant the stella ova wouldn't hatch and hurl their fierce Harpies at him?

"Why don't you try the big boy with a few commands?" Mortimer's voice rasped in his earphones. The ship systems officer, pulling up the rear, resembled an overinflated balloon as he gestured at the line of telepuppets through a breach in the ridge.

Satisfied with the concealment their present position offered, Stewart flipped on the command transmitter and intoned, "Supervisor to OC. Stabilize and remain where you are."

The master robot didn't even break stride.

He tried the order again, then repeated it several times as he tuned slightly up and down the band.

"It's no use," he said finally. "Either the thing's slipped frequency, or it's not receiving at all."

"Carol will spot any new wave length," Randall assured.

"What we ought to do," Mortimer proposed impatiently, "is show that thing who's boss."

Then Stewart caught the motion in the corner of his eye as the ship systems officer struck out for the marching file of puppets.

He intercepted the line near the tail end and tried to force his way in between the Solar Plasma Detector and the Magnetometer so he could close in on the OC. But the SPD kicked out with a stiff pedal pad and sent him sprawling in the path of the Magnetometer, which simply strode over him.

The Atmosphere Analyzer nudged him aside with an inflated air pouch and, in its turn, the Radiometer Complex compounded the indignity by planting a motor appendage in his abdomen. Mortimer rose screaming, circled wide around the Microorganism C & A and the Subordinate Mineral Specimen Collector and raced for the ship.

"This," said Stewart, "may not be as simple as we thought. Evidently some basic inhibitions have faded."

"We can't risk getting in range of one of those large puppets, especially the OC," Randall agreed.

Abruptly the master robot stabilized, swung sharply to face the horizon and adjusted its parabolic antenna.

"Look!" Stewart pointed. "The thing's transmitting! But it's not properly oriented! *It's beaming in the wrong direction!*"

"Where's it transmitting to?" Randall asked anxiously.

"Can't tell without point-to-point astrographs. Anyway, what difference does it make? It's only a random misorientation."

On the way back to the *Photon II*, Stewart lost himself in confusion. Random misorientation? Of course. What else? But why should he even consider the alternate possibility—that the misorientation was *not* random, as suggested by the director's question?

Bigboss completed transmission and burst into an instant fury of thwarted purpose. He leveled his blaster and annihilated the ridge behind which the defiant mobiles had recently hidden.

He swiveled his central section, redirecting the blaster at a boulder that lay between him and the needle and destroying it in a fiery eruption of light and heat and pulverizing forces.

Fuming, he paced forward, stopped and paced back again. He had *seen* the audacious creatures who were bold enough to invade His Realm! But He had been able to do nothing about them. For at that moment the irresistible compulsion of function had taken over and He could only orient and transmit all the data from his master tape.

Surlily, he bled off excessive current in his reaction circuits and watched his workers going dutifully about their business. Inactivity was frustrating, of course, but it was not entirely unwelcome. For there was much now that demanded evaluation, even though his urge to pursue the contemptuous mobiles and blast them from their needle was almost overpowering.

For one thing, there was the needle itself. Had He made it? (Oh, why couldn't he remember these things?) Of course, He must have, although He couldn't recall the specific act of Creation. And He must have produced the arrogant mobiles too, even though they would probably claim *they* had created *Him*.

But the needle itself was *metal!* Even a precursory analysis with Minnie's high neutron flux tools had established this. It was so much like the clan's Totem it must be Totemic.

The evidence was undeniable. Every member of the clan was metal. The clan's Totem was metal. Therefore the new thing from the sky was to be revered as the traditional Totem was.

Hence he had been justified, he assured himself, in issuing the "cease-and-desist" order that had brought an end to destructive analysis of the needle.

But, still, it was providing sanctuary for the detestable little mobiles. Which comprised a frustration that was almost unbearable. A venerable Totem offering protection to the arrogant non-Totemic creatures that had to be destroyed so His Universe would be cleansed of their blasphemous impudence!

The demands of logical deduction fully served, he published on each wavelength an order that amounted to: "Vigilance is to be maintained against the non-Totemic mobiles. Report instantly on their reappearance."

That taken care of, he reduced current in his rationalization pack. But the pleasant calm of abstraction did not last long. Peter the Meter began flooding his allocated frequency with eureka signals from an infrared photometer. And once again the source of disturbance was at a remote distance in the sky.

Oh Bigboss, he invoked himself. Not *another* Totemic-non-Totemic complication!

As before, Sky Watcher accepted the reported coordinates and trained a visual telesensor on the indicated position. But nothing was there. His Doppler radar gear, however, did manage to pick up a blip at many hundred kilometers distance just as it vanished.

Only a meteor, Bigboss decided, relieved. He let the evaluation stick, even though Peter the Meter had detected no ionized trail that would have verified that type of disturbance.

And Bigboss generated a good deal more easily, satisfied that the new manifestation had not, after all, been *another* needle.

His peace of rationalization pack was fleeting indeed, however. For in the next moment it required the full versatility of all his servomechanisms to maintain balance against a sudden upheaval of the ground beneath one of his appendages.

Tottering precariously, he engaged his underslung illuminator and video sensor. Screw Worm, having evidently bored a great distance, was emerging at the spot where his foot pad had been planted.

Fifty meters off, Minnie was expectantly rigid, her lens aimed in his direction. She was poised for a running start towards him should the opportunity present itself.

Screw Worm finally surfaced. Angrily, Bigboss kicked him back towards Minnie, who returned—disappointed, it seemed—to her work.

The huge Tzarean ship, bristling with the most formidable weapons its makers had devised in millennia, recovered from subspace emergency, adjusted its concealment shield and slipped into orbit.

Assemblyman Mittich, second in command, used a stout tail to brace himself against shifting inertia and watched Vrausot, Chancellor of the Tzarean Shoal, hiss his nagging instructions.

"The data, Kavula!" he demanded. "Punch out the data!"

Cowering before the impatience of the Tzarean World's highest authority, the pilot beat upon the control computer with a taloned fist. "It will be feeding out soon—I hope."

Mittich pressed forward into the anxiety that filled the compartment with hydrostaticlike intensity. It was well past time for his isotonic saline soaking and already the coarse drying process was chafing his chitinous skin. He was even sensitively aware of each scale as it grated against the one beneath it.

But he couldn't withdraw. Not when they were so close to determining whether an eons-old culture was doomed to extermination.

The computer clacked its readiness and belched out the new data. Vrausot snatched up the perforated strip and his massive head swung up and down in satisfaction.

"The orbit's absolutely synchronous," he disclosed, "We can keep the alien landing site under constant observation. And our position is additionally camouflaged by those peaks."

He used the scales of an abbreviated forearm to scratch his lower jaw. With all the authority vested within him as Chancellor of the Shoal, Adviser to the Curule Assembly and leader of the current expeditionary force, he directed the pilot to order gunnery practice.

Assemblyman Mittich swallowed incredulously. "But the aliens! Aren't we going to observe them? That's what we came for!"

"Not now." Vrausot waved him off. "Preparations first. Anyway, we *know* they're aggressive."

"We don't. That's what we have to establish."

The Chancellor shifted his tail from left to right. "We've observed their machines. They fight among themselves, don't they? And isn't it a fundamental fact of design that automatons are fashioned mainly after their creators, even in matters of temperament?"

"Yes," Mittich admitted. "But we *interfered* with those machines. We interrupted basic behavioral patterns. Our automatons, too, would show primitive social tendencies if the same thing happened to them."

Vrausot exposed a jagged array of teeth that conveyed his displeasure. "I'm in no mood for interference, although I might have expected only forensic exercise from the Leader of the Opposition."

"In that capacity, I'm here to offer suggestions." But it was more than that, Mittich reflected. The Assembly had been quite leery of the compromise plan. The Chancellor had wanted an awesome display of force; the Opposition, a try at peaceful contact.

They finally concurred in: observation, evaluation and application of force *only* if required. And it was hoped that, on the expedition, the Chancellor and Assemblyman would restrain each other.

But how could *anyone* restrain Vrausot?

"Prepare for gunnery practice," the Chancellor directed.

"But," Kavula protested, "that will produce observable missions beyond the concealment of our shield."

Disappointed, Vrausot leaned back upon his tail. "Very well, then—we'll go through the motions. Order a wet run."

Kavula relayed the order and scores of hatches swung open, baring to space the glistening intensifiers of high-powered weapons. The ship reverberated with the hiss-click articulation of military command and response.

Pivoting on his massive tail, Mittich went over to the teleview screen. "I have your permission, of course, to take a look at the alien vessel?"

"Suit yourself," the Chancellor grumbled.

The screen hunted out and steadied upon the alien ship.

"It's clean!" Mittich exclaimed. "They're *not* armed!"

151

"Nonsense," Vrausot said, coming over to see. "They've got to be. Why else would they come here?"

"The hull is sleek." The Assemblyman pointed with his long shout. "I see no gun-hatch outlines."

The Chancellor produced the Tzarean equivalent of a humorless laugh. "They're aliens, Mittich—with an alien technology. "Perhaps we wouldn't even recognize their weapons if we saw them."

"But, if they were hostile and furtive, would they have exposed themselves helplessly on that plain—like sitting *uraphi?*"

Vrausot's eyes intensified with resolution. "We're going to strike them—*now!* We're not going to wait and take the chance of having them slip from our grasp."

Appalled, the Assemblyman drew back. "But that's just what we're *not* supposed to do! We might touch off a war that will annihilate either or both of two cultures!"

"If we don't strike now it'll be our culture that will be annihilated. I wouldn't want that, Mittich. Just think of the glory and honor and tradition of conquest that would be lost forever. What we do here is being watched, indeed, by our ancestors who gave their lives in the final battle for total consolidation of the Tzarean Shoal!"

"But—"

"Our opportunity now is to live up to the finest military examples set by all Tzarean heroes who ever aimed an intensifier out of love for homeworld. Mittich—*This is a time for empire!*"

It was no use, the Assemblyman saw. Vrausot would have his way. He would wear his shining, imaginary medals and order his attack and bring doom to—oh, how many worlds? And the Curule Assembly could only give his leadership the support it would need after he presented them with the *fait accompli* of this treacherous deed.

"Kavula!" the Chancellor hissed. "Order the gunners—"

But Mittich nudged him in the back. "It could be a seine."

"I—what?"

"We may be swimming into a seine. Perhaps they're just toying with us—waiting to see if we are foolhardy enough to attack."

The scales above the Chancellor's eyes stood on edge as he pondered the ramifications of the other's suggestion. Finally, "We'll hold off for a while, perhaps."

Mittich had put him off for a moment. But no gain against Vrau-sot, political or otherwise, was ever more than temporary.

The Assemblyman was jarred from speculation as one of his major scales split with aridity. He hurried off to his isotonic saline tank.

Rested, although no nearer a definite plan for re-subjugation of the telepuppet team, Stewart cautiously watched the robots from behind an outcropping. To this concealed vantage point he had led Carol, Director Randall, and McAllister while the automatons had been occupied with recharging.

"You're going to try some more voice commands on the OC?" Carol's voice came softly through the earphones as she squirmed to find more comfort within the folds of her over-sized sheath.

"We're not doing *anything*, Stewart said firmly, "until that thing is well occupied with transmission."

McAllister's boot came in contact with something hard and he bent down to inspect it. "Say, what's this?"

Randall went over to see. "A burnt-out telepuppet, obviously."

Steward had a look too. "It's an Algae Detector. But, since there's no water around here, it hasn't had a chance to exercise its function. Electronic atrophy must have set in."

"It's riddled with drill holes," McAllister noted. "Looks like one of those other puppets worked it over."

Stewart examined the thing. The pilot was right.

"At least *one* of our robots seems to have overcome its inhibition against analyzing pure metal," Randall observed, prodding it.

"Or maybe something else has been around here," McAllister said.

The director looked up sharply.

"Something else? Like what?" Carol laughed at the pilot's unreasonable concern.

McAllister only hunched his bony shoulders.

It was not difficult for Stewart to see that McAllister was afraid. Neither the pilot nor Mortimer was generally known in the Bureau for his courage. That their apprehension had grown to visible proportions out there on this Godforsaken edge of infinity was merely an expected extension of their characters.

Rather, it was Randall's fear—Randall's and his own—that concerned Stewart. Both seemed incommunicable. Stewart's reticence was involuntary, stemming as it did from his inability to find words for his incomprehensible dread. And he wondered whether the director's fear, too, was that inexpressible.

He picked up a clod of soil and crumbled it in his gloved hand, as though symbolizing his anxious desire to come to grips with whatever it was that bid behind a veil in his mind.

Randall lowered himself on his haunches. "Don't we have any *emergency* means of bringing that machine under control?"

"Oh, there are a couple of tricks. Manhandling it is one."

Carol hugged her knees and laughed skeptically. "*That* thing?"

"There's a recessed deactivation switch in its lower section. All I have to do is get my hand on it."

"And all *it* has to do," she retorted dubiously, "is to get one of its fifty-pound vices on *you*."

She seized his hand and, through two layers of rubberized material, he sensed the unsteadiness of her grip. "Do be careful, Dave."

He was impressed. It wasn't often she allowed her more serious nature to show through candidly.

She rose suddenly and turned to face a distant mountain range.

Randall tensed. "Yes, Carol—what is it?"

Profuse light from the primary etched lines of concern on her brow. "I'm sensing electronic spill-off from somewhere up in those peaks—perhaps beyond."

Randall's breath rasped in the earphones. But he only said, "Spurious stuff. Reflections caused by a dense magnetic field can throw you off like that, you know."

She nodded—not enthusiastically, however.

Stewart glanced at the director, who looked swiftly away. But their eyes had met for an instant and, in Randall's, Stewart wondered whether he hadn't detected something cunning, elusive. Or was it just the same nameless fear that he, himself felt?

"There it goes!" McAllister exclaimed. "The OC's getting ready to transmit!"

Elbows splayed along the ridge, Carol watched the huge machine steadying its parabolic discs on a spot close to the horizon.

"See if you can pick up some of the spill-off," Stewart urged.

She waved for silence. "I'm beginning to get it "Now."

"Can you pinpoint the frequency?"

"Just a notch above one thirty-six point two MCs."

"On the nose, isn't it?" Randall asked.

"Close enough. How *are* the signals, Carol?"

"They seem shipshape, well modulated, crammed with data. I can even read some bits having to do with oxygen—plenty of it—in that cave over there, I believe." She pointed then glanced at Stewart. "There's no malfunctioning at all!" He retrieved his transmitter and switched from MCW to CW. "That simplifies our task. When we re-establish control, all we'll have to do is reorient the OC."

Randall walked several feet away, kicked a stone, glanced up at the sky and returned. "What now?"

Stewart retuned his transmitter; "Penultimate emergency procedure. I'm going to come down with both heels on the frequency at which it received code signals from the relay base."

"But can you give it *coded* commands?"

"I'm just going to lock the sending key on a steady impulse. It's a 'stop-everything' order." He hit the lever.

Carol winced. "Ouch. I wasn't ready for that."

"What's it doing now?" he demanded.

"Still transmitting. No interruption."

He released the key. "Well that exhausts our bag of tricks. We'll have to do it by hand."

Just then Carol's amused laughter tinkled in the earphones. "Why, that harebrain machine thinks it's God!"

Randall started. "What?"

"I'm having a peek at its PM & R pack spill-off. It's lord and master of the universe! There's only one thing worthy of touching its pedal pad—the puppet barge. That's because the barge, being metal too, is a *totem*!"

The director shook his head and mumbled, "Most unusual." Then, "Carol! Can you see anything at all significant in its memory pack? Any evidence of—"

But in the next instant she screamed and lunged back away from a foot-long metallic crab that had drawn up before her.

"The Flora C & A!" Stewart made a grab for the thing, but it skirted his gloved hand and started forward again.

McAllister backed away until he came up against the out-cropping beside the girl. Squirming qualmishly, he kicked out and caught the crab broadside, sending it skittering back.

Then he shouted in pain and gripped his instep with both hands. "My foot! It's broken!"

But a moment later, Stewart was certain the injury was negligible, judging from the adequate support the foot provided in McAllister's spring for the Photon.

Bigboss completed his transmission and turned full attention on the eureka signals coming frantically from Grazer.

Interested, he inspected the sequenced data and took note of the modulation peaks that exactly duplicated the C_5H_8 parameter.

Grazer had sensed *hydrocarbon*! More important, one of his spectrometric biodetectors was getting a whiff of DNA molecules!

Even those significant findings, however, accounted for but part of the frenzy with which Grazer was transmitting his impulses. There was much more behind the eurekas than that. But all the lesser worker could convey telemetrically was his general excitement, for these were no parameters dealing with the third element of his discovery.

Perplexed, Bigboss pondered this inadequacy of communication between him and his servitor—until a rationalization circuit came up with the recommendation: tap in on Grazer's direct video system.

He did.

And Bigboss went momentarily irrational as motor circuits fought one another to express the exultation flooding from his evaluation pack. He leaped three meters high. His upper command section turned up a hundred revolutions per minute in triumphant delirium. He extended and retracted his vices, leveled his blaster and spat out a lance of vicious destruction that slashed a concentric trench in the ground about him.

Then he damped all activity and steadied himself with a sober appreciation of the telemetric signals Grazer had contributed. The servitor was confronting three hated non-Totemic mobiles!

They had emerged from their needle! They had come finally to hurl direct challenge at the Supreme Being!

Circuit currents surging once more towards irrational levels, Bigboss calmed himself with dedication to the vengeful destruction of those insolent creatures.

He transmitted a "stop-what-you're-doing-and-follow-me" order and headed into Grazer's telemetric signals. Every twenty meters or so, a discrimination circuit peaked in its erratic pattern and he hurled out a bolt of raw energy, annihilating a boulder here, leveling a rise there, pulverizing an occasional crag.

In his excitement, however, he had neglected the environscanning procedure he had devised to compensate for his damaged video sensor. And he didn't realize that, while he had been stabilized for transmission, Minnie had almost reached him in a stealthy advance. But now he was pulling steadily away from her.

Ignoring their order of social priority, the workers converged on the nearby outcropping. Some bore to the right around the rock formation, while others joined Bigboss in a flanking maneuver to the left. The long-legged Maggie and Peter the Meter evaluated the slanted stone as comprising no barrier and proceeded directly over it.

When he finally swung around and brought the contemptuous mobiles under direct visual observation, Bigboss paused to evaluate the situation. It required no small amount of self-control to restrain his motor circuits. But he *had* to. For he was determined the arrogant mobiles would not again reach the sanctuary of their Totem.

Grazer stood before the three creatures, his servo units idling as his transmitter continued to send frantic eurekas. And now his excited impulses were joined by those of other servitors who had formed a half circle around the out-cropping—Peter the Meter, boasting of excitation of an infra-red radiometer; Breather, reporting traces of both oxygen and carbon dioxide in the immediate atmosphere; Minnie, whose high neutron flux instruments were beginning to identify concentrations of calcium, potassium, carbon.

Sequencing and storing the data, Bigboss sent out a curt directive that amounted to: Do not analyze! Just stay out of the way!

The ring of clansmen remained poised. Several times one of the nonmetallic captives attempted to force its way through the workers, but was pulled back by another mobile.

Bigboss brought up his blaster and loosed a vicious, blinding charge that swamped half a dozen unretracted photometers and pulverized the top of the outcropping. He adjusted his aim, compensating for the crouching, huddled position the interlopers had assumed, and fed renewed energy to the blaster's condenser.

By the next sine wave peak, however, he regretted his preoccupation with the mobiles. For, at that moment, Minnie's drill head, sweeping through one of his fields of vision before he could discharge the blaster, crashed into video pickup lens Three.

He sprang back, rationalization packs coming frantically to grips with this further loss of visual integrity. Through luck rather than intent, he brought one of his still-functioning lenses to bear on the advancing Minnie.

She let her entire drill head fly in a bludgeoning blow, but he parried it with his vice while he reasoned out the modified swivel motion now required to provide adequate coverage with only two lenses.

But the attack had touched off a number of other clashes among socially ambitious workers. Seismo turned on Minnie's exposed flank and sent a pedal disc crashing through her after analyzing chamber. Sludge spilled out upon the ground.

Peter the Meter swung his boom-and-ball gamma ray detector against Breather's air pouches while Maggie straddled Sun Watcher and proceeded to stomp on one of his telescopic instruments.

In the midst of all this confusion, Bigboss was only vaguely aware that the three impudent mobiles had slipped out of the ring of servitors and were returning swiftly to their Totem.

Infuriated over the imminent loss of prey, he swiveled around in their direction. Again, however, he neglected his defense.

And before he could trigger a charge at the fleeing things, Minnie's drill head whipped around in a level arc that snapped his blaster off at its socket and sent it hurtling across the plain.

As she drew back for another blow, he lunged over and managed to grip her bit in his vice. With a violent twist, he broke it off at the chuck.

Subdued finally, she withdrew.

"You saw it, didn't you?" Mittich demanded.

Vrausot scratched his jaw with a rigid talon. "Interesting—that trouble between the aliens and their automatons. What interpretation do you put on it?"

Pivoting on his tail, the other spun around from the screen to face the Chancellor. "That they don't even carry side arms. They had no defense whatsoever against their machines. If they were here looking for a fight, wouldn't they be armed at all times?"

Vrausot expressed ridicule by tracing a circle with the tip of his tapering snout. "Mittich, you amuse me. Only one sunset ago you were bending my tail to make me believe they may be cunning; that they might have strung out a seine for us."

"Yes?" the Assemblyman prompted, expecting more.

"Now I simply extend your own logic back to you. They prepared that drama down there for our benefit—just in case we were watching. They *want* us to believe they are stupid and helpless."

Assemblyman Mittich faced the other with a calculating stare. He was aware of the heavy irony in Vrausot's hisses and clicks and he knew the Chancellor was only deriding him.

"If I had to arrive at an alternate assessment, Assemblyman—" Vrausot paused and Mittich braced himself for more scorn. "It would be that the aliens are stupid, inept, blundering, defenseless. Actually, it would seem that they must have gained interstellar status only through accident."

"Oh, no. We know *that* isn't true."

Ignoring the interruption, the Chancellor continued. "And they *were* foolish enough to come here unarmed, apparently."

But Mittich broke in again. "If I had attracted more votes in the Curule Assembly, we would have come unarmed too."

"Ah! But we didn't. And do you know why? Because the Assembly really believes as I do, even though they might not have the courage, to vote their convictions. That's why I'm going to exercise my own judgment—because I *know* their subliminal disposition in this matter."

Mittich unhinged his jaw, conveying dismay. There was no doubt now what the Chancellor's intentions were. Oh, he would probably swim around cautiously for a while. But his final determination was already cloaked with inevitability.

Eventually—how soon?—he would lash out at the aliens with all the ship's invincible firepower. And nothing else could be done to delay that treachery. For Mittich couldn't conceive of another last-*purai* diversion, such as the suggestion that the aliens may have strung out a seine, to forestall the tragedy Vrausot was determined to perpetrate.

Lumbering over to the ship's control panel, the Chancellor directed his pilot: "Advance five degrees westward along our orbital path then restabilize."

Kavula's hands darted here and there and the vessel resounded with the *thuds* of great tails thumping down on the deck to maintain equilibrium as new velocity came in surges.

"This will put us below the aliens' horizon," Kavula noted.

"Of course it will," the Chancellor hissed back at the other's impertinence. "And we'll be in such a position that they won't be able to observe our artillery emissions."

He turned to the intercom. "Gun Crew One, prepare for firing."

"Action?" Mittich asked, fearing the worst.

"Of a sort—preparatory." The Chancellor studied the teleview screen and once more directed the gunners:

"I'm designating a target circle on one of those peaks down there. You may fire at will."

He touched a button and a green halo flared on the screen. He adjusted it to encompass the surface prominence he had in mind. The ship shuddered as the gunner punched his firing stud.

Mittich watched the surface erupt in a brilliant display of angry energy—a thousand kilometers off target.

The Chancellor received the fire control officer's apology, together with a request for permission to try again. The latter he denied.

"They evidently need the practice," Kavula advised.

The Chancellor fumed at his pilot's insolence. "They'll do better at close range," he promised. "Meanwhile, I want this ship stripped for action. I've reached my decision. One close pass is all it should take. We strike after sunup."

Desperately, Mittich hurried over and swung his small arms imploringly. "You can't do this thing!"

"Oh, quit being such a floundering minnow! Nothing's going to happen. They're quite defenseless, I'm convinced."

"If that's the case, then you are under injunction of the Curule Assembly to make peaceful contact!"

"Drown peaceful contact!" the Chancellor swore. "I'm supposed to exercise my judgment out here!"

"But—"

"Flotsam! There will be no peace. If that's what the aliens wanted, they wouldn't have come out here in the first place. We are going to blast them. And from here we'll go on!"

"Go on?" Mittich repeated cautiously. "Where?"

Vrausot's eyes glazed over and his disarray of teeth were exposed to the gums as he paced the deck and beat his arms against his side in a fit of frantic expectation.

"We know where their relay base is," he explained, "We'll strike that next! Then, capitalizing on the element of surprise, we'll continue to their World Of Origin and destroy it outright. On the way back we'll probably knock out one or two other planets."

He turned on a dumbfounded Mittich. "The war—if there is to be one—will be short. We'll have only to return to the Tzarean Shoal and muster a fleet before we wipe out the rest of their civilization. And once again ours will be the glory of conquest—such as we have not experienced in, oh, how many millennia?"

Stewart woke up shouting the next morning.

Perhaps the nightmare had been brought on by his previous day's experience with the telepuppets. For, in his dream, there had been the OC, again spitting out deadly fire that missed the targets only by inches before gouging great craters in the plain beyond.

Suddenly the master robot vanished, taking all the lesser automatons with it. In the suspenseful stillness that followed, Stewart could only stare in bewilderment at Carol and Randall. Then it came—the blazing, naked light, together with the stentorian roaring that filled the sky and shook every rock.

Terrified, he huddled with the other two, his eyes searching desperately for some place to hide. But as he spotted each gaping fissure, each yawning cave entrance that might offer concealment, it too vanished. Until they were left with only a smooth, featureless plain extending to infinity in all directions.

Eventually the mighty ships—hundred of them, it seemed—landed. And down debarkation ramps poured thousands of hideous Harpy-like forms, their gigantic claws magnified in his fancy until they were even larger than the bodies they supported and, by their sheer weight, made flight impossible.

This vast army assembled before its ships in the center of the plain and started forward.

But there was a blur of motion on the right and left extremities of Stewart's field of vision and he watched great, gauzy curtains draw together from opposite horizons, meeting directly in front of him. Like dazzling auroral streamers, they hung from a rod located so high in the stratosphere that it was lost in the blackness of space. Diaphanous though the drapes were, they appeared to be adequate, as if through some magical power, to hold back the horde of vicious Harpies on the other side.

But even as Stewart shuddered with the thought of what would befall Randall, Carol and himself should the almost intangible barrier fail, the director charged forward and drew the curtains aside.

Instantly, the monstrous creatures poured through.

But in the next moment Randall was beside his bunk, shaking him awake and regarding him quizzically.

Dismayed over the continued evidence of a lurking inexplicable fear, Stewart ate breakfast mostly in silence while he cast about for a reasonable interpretation of the nightmare.

It was almost as though the auroral curtain represented the mental vein that hid a horror-filled recess of his mind. The content of that fissure—was it something he didn't want to face? Something he had *intentionally* hidden? Was it actually that Randall could, if he desired, draw back the curtain? Why Randall?

He brought his cup to his lips and almost gagged on an icy bitterness. Carol chided him for his abstraction, dumped the coffee into a disposal slot and gave him a refill.

Randall slapped his thigh. "Well, we still have a telepuppet problem on our hands."

Mortimer sat up sharply. "You're not going to fool around with those damned things any more, are you?"

"Don't see how we can avoid it. We've got several days' repair work on that subspace drive coil—*outside* the ship. That's the only way we can either get out of here or recover use of our long-range transmitter. But I wouldn't want to turn my back on those puppets while they're out of control."

"You won't catch *me* out there again," McAllister vowed.

Randall went over to the external view screen and spent several minutes scanning the sky, bright now with the dawning light of Aldebaran.

"You won't find the puppets up there," Stewart said, finally intolerant of whatever phobia Randall might be pampering.

The director turned guiltily away from the screen. "Anybody have any ideas on what we can do about those robots?" Stewart went over to a second screen. "After having slept on the problem, I think I might be able to contribute something."

He focused on the telepuppets, attending to their various exploratory chores out on the plain. "Carol gave me an idea with something she said yesterday. We may be able to solve our telepuppet worries within five minutes' time."

"Bring the OC back under control?" The director arched his thick brows. "How?"

"We might succeed in immobilizing it. That'll deprive the other puppets of their source of power. Within a few hours their batteries will drain and we'll be able to go work on the OC without any possible interference.

He indicated his hostile-atmosphere sheath slumped in a corner of the compartment. "Won't need that. But I will have to have a deep-space suit—heavily shielded against solar storm exposure. You have one aboard, McAllister?"

The pilot nodded. "Standard equipment. But you'll think it weighs a ton. It's designed for null-G use."

Carol's puzzlement drained away. "The suit's *metal!* Which means, as far as the puppets are concerned, that it's *totemic!*"

"That's what I figured," Stewart said. "Wearing it may give me status as one of the boys."

⇌

McAllister had been right. Against the relentless tug of gravity, the armored suit felt as though it weighed not much less than a ton. Laboriously, Stewart planted one thick-soled boot ahead of the other and moved at a snail's pace across the difficult terrain.

Through a separation between two boulders he could see the telepuppet team. The machines were hard at work, with the Operations Coordinator majestically surveying its charges.

Stewart's legs strained under the great weight as he struggled over a rise and stepped out upon the plain.

Pausing, he stared at the mike recessed in the inner curvature of his helmet. It was dead and his resulting loss of voice contact made him feel lonely and inadequate. But the suit was not equipped with radio, since its wearer would normally be plugged into the ship's intercom system through an anchor line.

Inching across the plain, he closed in on the puppet team. Thus far he had not been noticed.

Cautiously, he skirted the knoll on which sat the Solar Plasma Detector. Even now its boom-and-ball sensor was swinging around to point towards a rising Aldebaran. He was certain he had passed in the SPD's direct line of local sight. But it only ignored him.

Twenty paces farther he gave a wide berth to the Atmosphere Analyzer. Here, too, he had to go directly in front of the thing's video sensor. But the AA obliged by making no move towards him.

So far, so good. But he had approached only those robots which would ordinarily show no interest in him, since he was neither celestial nor gaseous. A minute later, however, when he was cleared through without incident by an indifferent Mineral Analyzer, he was certain his totemic qualifications would bring him to his objective without picking up a challenge along the way.

He crested a rise, trudged between the Astronomical Data Collector and the Seismometer and, more certain of his immunity, stepped over the crablike Microorganism Collector and Analyzer.

Then he stood hesitating before the master robot.

Ports ablaze with luminous evidence of faultless power generation, the huge automaton ignored him. Shorn of its laser intensifier, it appeared somewhat pathetic. But Stewart was inclined to waste no sympathy. It stood swinging its upper command section, first right, then left, to compensate for loss of two video sensors. But he was more interested in the under-slung, recessed compartment whose outline he could now see. He had only to flip open the lid and throw the switch in order to deactivate the OC.

Suddenly the thing reacted to his presence. One of its lenses swept over him, stopped, swung back, overcorrected, then steadied. And he couldn't guess what analytical criteria were being applied in the general assessment.

The robot raised its vice-equipped appendage. A hostile gesture? Defensive move? Or merely one of the symbols of communication it had devised during its independent reign?

There was swift movement in the periphery of Stewart's vision and, instinctively, he dropped to the ground as a great clanking form swept past him.

Rolling over, he saw it was the Mineral Analyzer, boring in for another attack. The six-legged automaton drew up in front of the OC and swung its stout drill head in a sweeping arc.

He ducked under the gleaming neck and watched it crash into the bigger machine's lower section, sending it bouncing rearwards on stumpy legs. The master robot lashed back, slashing a gaping slit in the MA's neck.

Into this fury of swinging appendages Stewart decided he would have to hurl himself if he expected to immobilize the telepuppet team. As unpredictable as the robots were, he might never get this close to the master automaton again.

The flow of battle, however, made his decision unnecessary. For the grappling machines were now sweeping over the spot where he lay and a huge pedal pad barely missed him as it thudded down.

For a fleeting instant the recessed compartment was immediately above his head. Overcoming the ponderous weight of his mailed arm, he reached up and flicked open the lid. At the same time he managed to get a finger on and throw the switch.

One final kick by the OC hurled him from beneath the tons of metal. Meanwhile, the thing's thrashing vice caught the MA broadside and sent it flailing backwards. Then the master puppet toppled over like a towering tree being felled by an ancient woodsman's chain saw. The ground trembled violently with the impact.

Stewart rose and wiped dust from his helmet's view plate.

The monstrous robot lay motionless, darkened ports evidencing its lifelessness. Close by, the Mineral Analyzer stumbled around in looping circles, one of its gyros atilt. The other puppets continued their work, unaware that when all stored energy was depleted there would be no opportunity to recharge their batteries.

Exhausted, his face filmed with perspiration and his hip aching beneath the dent the big machine had kicked in his armor, Stewart headed back for the ship. But his release from urgency lightened his steps somewhat. Now there would be little to do but wait until the lesser puppets ran out of power.

An automatic erector leveled Minnie's tilted gyro. Another emergency maintenance circuit cut in and compensated for precession. Finally her sense of balance was restored.

Rationalization circuits reasoned out the precise maneuver necessary to bring her upright and she rose upon her motor appendages, expecting at any moment to be bludgeoned again by Bigboss's vice.

Slowly she turned and sent her restricted field of vision sweeping across the ground. And her video lens carne to focus on—

Bigboss!

In a most unusual position! And—*motionless!*

He was stretched out on the ground, extensible vice limp as it lay half covered by the soil into which it had dug. One of his antennae was crumpled beneath him while the other was bent and twisted. Hardly able to accept as valid the visual data she was receiving, she transmitted an unwarranted "please-verify-that-instruction" impulse at low volume.

Her evaluation circuit was thrown almost into a frenzy when there was no response. At maximum gain, she repeated the signal.

Still no response!

Cautiously, she went forward and stood over the Supreme Being. She lowered her hitless drill head and nudged one of his motor appendages. Drawing away, she watched it swing back and forth in smaller and smaller arcs until it finally came to rest.

166

Then she went into a limited ecstasy of reaction. She whirled around in circles until she became afraid she would tilt another gyro. She reared up on her two posterior appendages and thumped back upon the ground. She swung her drill head up and down, back and forth, around. Through her rear slot, she exhausted all the sludge from her analyzing chambers.

She had won! She had supplanted Bigboss!

She had climbed to the top rung of the ladder!

And now She was Supreme Being!

That she had been able to succeed, despite Bigboss's overwhelming superiority, was a datum so questionable that she almost decided to reject it before storing it away.

Minnie went into another triumphant dance, but suddenly came to a rigid halt. Her head held high and Her lens aimed in the direction of the non-Totemic mobile that was withdrawing towards its needle.

There was something *wrong* in Her Universe! It was not at all as it had been before She had conquered the Supreme Being!

Tensely, She recalled for review impressions only recently implanted on Her drums. And she recognized immediately what was missing.

The telemetric chatter of all the workers was gone! Nor could she detect the constant exchange of directive and acknowledgement that had always flowed ceaselessly between Bigboss and each of the workers. Yet, all the analyzers were there, continuing their chores as though nothing had happened.

Apprehensive now, she assigned her meager rationalization capacity to the task of deducing the reasons behind the startling change. And many sine wave peaks passed the judgment was handed back up to her main circuits for storage on a memory drum.

Bigboss had *justifiably* been the Supreme Being! For He had, indeed, been Supreme. The workers had voices, of course. But they were isolated voices that could be heard by other members of the clan only because they were passed along by Bigboss.

Minnie's drill head sagged until it rested on the ground. She was Supreme Being now. But it was only a hollow distinction. For she had fallen heir to none of Bigboss's authority. That authority had been lost forever in the neutralization of charges which had rendered the former Omnipotent One impotent.

What *had* she done? How could she have been so irrational? Why hadn't she more thoroughly evaluated the consequences of bet forced ascendancy?

More for consolation than for any other reason, she transmitted a desperate "where-are-you" impulse to Screw Worm.

The directional signals that returned brought with them a great sense of balance to the circuits in her PM & R pack. She was not, after all, alone! She still held the supplemental function of supervision over her sole helper!

She watched Worm approach, kicking up clouds of dust with the jets that propelled him across the ground on his rolling treads. When he arrived, she sent him a "hold-everything" signal. As he remained motionless before her, she lowered her drill head until she could sense the slight change in capacitance values that indicated physical contact with him.

No, even though she had destroyed the Supreme Being and, by that action, had forever shut herself off from the other members of the clan, she was not alone. She still had her Worm!

But within the limits of those circumstances, she resolved suddenly, she would try to *act* like a Supreme Being!

She drew herself upright and remained rigid while she drove her rationalization circuits at a furious pace.

How *did* an Omnipotent One act?

Judging from Bigboss's behavior, a Lord or Mistress of All Creation should go about destroying non-Totemic pretenders.

Was that what *She* should do?

Realizing the decision would require much more concentration, she retired from the site of operations to consider all the factors.

Halfway back to the *Photon*, Stewart paused and leaned against a boulder, exhausted. The muscles of his legs were flaccid from lifting the great weight of hermetically sealed plating with each step. Now he fully understood that the suit was *not* made for walking.

Ahead, the ship was a beckoning silvery pencil that glittered in the harsh, golden light of Aldebaran and cast its blocks-long shadow on strange, bare soil and rocks.

Then he saw it—the elongated, symmetrical shape that seemed to spring up from beyond the horizon and expand explosively as he watched in dismay.

It was a *ship*—the likes of which he had never seen before! Or, then again—

Bewildered, afraid, he could only stand there trying desperately to pierce the veil in his mind, to equate this incredible thing that was happening now to the inexpressible fear he had felt for weeks.

Meanwhile, the strange ship, gliding smoothly in its horizontal attitude that gave evidence of some highly developed type of anti-gravity drive, surged forward. Its smooth, dark undersurface, he could see, was broken by twin rows of open ports that extended from bow to stern on either side. And deep within those circular recesses bristled scores of elongater metal structures that could only be—*linear intensifiers for laser weapons!*

Then Stewart realized this could only be another nightmare and he sickened at the horrible prospect of being drawn further into the dream. The ship would land, of course, and out of its hatches would pour streams of vengeful, grotesque Harpies.

But, instead, the sky was lashed by scores of fierce, dazzling beams that streaked from the vessel as it passed overhead.

And he sensed that this was no nightmare, no mere symbolic expression of the vague dread that had harassed his thoughts all along. This was real! This was actually happening!

Bolt after bolt rammed down from the open ports, scorching the ground, blasting great holes in solid rock formations, leveling hills, raking huge furrows where before there had been only level soil.

One of the laser beams—perhaps the fiftieth or sixtieth—took the nose section off the *Photon*, leaving only jagged metal as an undignified crown marring its architectural integrity. Another found its mark too, annihilating one of the helpless ship's hydraulic fins and tearing a gaping hole in its engine section. The *Photon* tilted precariously, but somehow managed to remain upright.

Then the assaulting vessel was gone, swallowed from the sky by the ridge of hills over which it had passed in completing its low-altitude sweep.

Minute followed minute in the breathless silence that punctuated the impossible attack. Stewart knew he should be pushing on to the *Photon* to see if Carol and the others had happened to be in the demolished nose section.

But he only stood there, paralyzed. For, as he looked back on the unbelievable action, he realized that the vicious attack had, after all, *come as no surprise to him!*

He had expected it all along!

That must have been the nameless fear lurking behind a curtain in his mind. And abruptly he knew with a certainty that expectation of this assault had been the basis of his indescribable apprehension.

He had *known* that a ship—*an alien vessel*—would be here waiting for them!

And the *Photon's* crew would be taken all the more off guard because it was incredible, in the first place, that the galaxy might have spawned two intelligent, star-seeking races within the same sector.

But, if he had had that knowledge, how could he have *forgotten* anything so crucially important?

IV

Stabilizing itself once more in synchronous orbit, the immense Tzarean ship generated internal gravity and meted out isotonic saline solution to a number of tanks in crew's quarters.

In the central compartment it was a triumphant, impassioned Chancellor Vrausot who turned his massive bulk on Mittich and hissed-clicked, "There! I told you they had come unarmed! There was absolutely no response to the attack!"

Grim-faced, the Assemblyman only stared at him.

Vrausot paced, thumping his stout tail against the deck with each stride. It was a gesture that expressed anxiety.

"Don't you see what that means, Mittich? They *knew* we would be out here. They had independently corroborating evidence to that effect. Yet they came unarmed. They are a peaceful, naive, unsuspecting race of sitting *uraphi!*"

170

Very weakly, the Assemblyman reminded, "Our purpose, then, is to make amiable contact and determine—"

It was no use, though. The Chancellor wasn't listening. He had absolutely no sense of humor or ethical appreciation. But, Mittich reflected, that should have come as no surprise. It was to have been extrapolated from the Chancellor's political history. And now the distressing fact had to be faced. Vrausot was a megalomaniac.

The Chancellor drew proudly erect and his tail stiffened. "But *we're* not weak! Kavula—see that all gun crews stand by. We're going to finish them off now that we've established their inability to inflict damage on us."

Mittich drew back, appalled at the fierce determination behind the Chancellor's driving ambition for conquest, disgusted with his own inability to turn Vrausot's purpose aside. How to stop him?

It was Mittich who paced this time, helplessly wrestling the impossible problem of preventing the Chancellor compounding Tzarean dishonor.

Frustrated, he pivoted on his tail and returned to the telescreen. Focusing on the landing site below, he zoomed in for an extreme close up. The aliens were still scurrying around outside their crippled ship, glancing occasionally into the sky as though terrified over the possibility of another assault.

Mittich adjusted the instrument to its operational limits, as he had wanted to do on so many occasions since they had brought the aliens under observation.

Two of the creatures were facing the mountain range behind which hid the Tzarean ship. Anxiously, the Assembly man moved in and studied their heads, clearly visible through transparent helmets.

He drew a startled breath. He must be mistaken. Of course he was. He could see that now.

Yet, there *was* something fascinating as he compared one of the heads with the other. What impressed him most was the contrast. There was an indisputable difference—many differences. Then he tensed with sudden realization. Perhaps he *could* forestall their fate.

171

"Chancellor," he called out softly. "Don't you think it might be a good idea to take prisoners?"

"Drown the prisoners!" Vrausot swore. "We don't need them."

"Yes, I realize that. But—well, look at the screen."

The other studied the picture. The scales of his forehead strained erect as he pondered the contrast Mittich had already noticed.

"Observe the one on the left," the Assemblyman suggested.

Interested, Vrausot bent forward. "You don't suppose—?"

"Yes, I do. This is our chance to study *both* sexes."

"I—" The other hesitated.

"There could be significant psychological differences, you realize." Mittich pushed ahead while he had the other's attention. "Why, we can't even be sure which is dominant!"

The two alien creatures had gone out of the picture, leaving only the empty image of soil and rocks.

"It would be nice to display a *pair* of them at the Curule Assembly, wouldn't it?" the Chancellor said thoughtfully.

"That's what I had in mind. A positive demonstration of our superiority. So much more convincing than empty hisses and clicks."

Vrausot drew himself to his full height. "It will be done. Kavula, assign twenty men to a landing party to accompany myself and Mittich out on the surface. A stun gun for each man."

The pilot turned from his controls. "You'll need something heavier than that if you're going among those machines," he said officiously.

Vrausot displayed his teeth in an expression of uncertainty.

"But the robots won't be a factor for very long," Mittich pointed out. "The principal one has been deactivated. The others depend upon it for their power. Soon they'll be immobile too."

"How soon?"

"By next sunup, I'm sure."

"Very well. We'll go asurface then." Vrausot withdrew for his isotonic soaking.

Mittich turned back to the view screen and worked with its controls. Finally he located the aliens—five of them—trudging across the ground. They were headed for a nearby cliff in whose face yawned the mouth of a cave. It was the same cave one of the automatons had reported filled with oxygen. And he further recalled that oxygen was the basic requirement of the aliens, just as it was the Tzarean's fundamental necessity too.

Evidently they feared another assault on their ship. For they were carrying a number of supplies.

"You don't much approve of what the Chancellor is doing?" Kavula asked, drawing Mittich from his troubled thoughts.

"*You* do?"

The pilot flicked his tail rashly—a gesture usually associated with independent thought. "If he pushes on into the alien sector, it will be genocide. Those creatures are helpless. It isn't the sort of operation I'd care to be in on. *Anyway*, there's no reason why Tzareans and the aliens can't live side by side, even in one small pocket of the galaxy. We have different requirements. I don't think they would even be interested in the type of world we need."

Mittich eyed the pilot gravely. "We *could* assume command from the Chancellor."

"You do that. I'll watch. There are just enough glory hunters in the Assembly to have my head if I tried and failed."

And Mittich was intensely dissatisfied with himself over the fact that he, too, valued his head dearly.

Aldebaran Four, rising in all its primrose splendor, cast eerie splotches of light among the tumbled rock formations outside and thrust a brilliant planetbeam boldly into the small cave.

McAllister and Mortimer were huddled against the wall, still assuring each other it must have been some mistake, that there just *couldn't* be an alien race anywhere around.

Randall sat glumly on the emergency transceiver set, salvaged from the *Photon* in order that they might contact a rescue ship—should they be able to hold out long enough for one to be sent.

Still in his suit of armor but minus the helmet, Stewart sat trancelike near the cave entrance. He hadn't said a word in hours. Nor had he uttered half a dozen words since the attack.

Beside him, Carol murmured, "It's going to be all right, Dave. Everything's going to be all right."

She placed a hand on his forehead, then looked worriedly at the director. Stewart, however, wasn't even interested in the fact that she had misinterpreted his numb silence.

For the thousandth time he searched his mind for all its hidden knowledge of the alien space ship, of how he had gained that information, how he could have forgotten it.

Carol tried to console him again, as though he were a child. "We'll get home all right. Then we'll get out of the Bureau. We'll go to Terra—you and I—and you'll see how happy we'll be."

On any other occasion, those words would have sent him into handsprings. But now they just bounced off his traumatic shield.

Then, suddenly, he had it. He *knew* what had happened. He rose, fully in command of himself finally, and struggled out of the heavily-shielded space suit. Then he faced the others.

"I've known all along," he said, "that we might be attacked out here by an alien ship."

Carol gasped. McAllister lunged erect. Mortimer, puzzled, started forward. But Randall stopped him.

"Wait," the director urged. "We may want to hear this."

"I said," Stewart continued, "that I knew it all along. But I didn't *know* I knew it."

He looked away from their bewildered expressions. "Harlston and I made an advance exploration trip to the Hyades, all right. But we *didn't* find seven—or was it eight?—Earth-type worlds. We didn't even drop back into the continuum. Because we found evidence of bustling subspace travel and communications that indicated a vigorous culture of star-traveling Hyadeans!"

McAllister swore. Mortimer came forward, perplexed. "But—"

Randall motioned for silence. "Let him finish."

"We got the hell out of there," Stewart said, "Without even having seen a Hyadean. We figured that if there was another intelligent race in this part of the galaxy, it might be a hostile one. And our worlds had to know about it. We couldn't chance being captured.

"So we started making subspace leaps back home. One of those jumps ended here—where we had dropped off the telepuppet barge on our way out. At long range, we had a look at that team. And there was an alien ship down there—maybe the same one that attacked us

174

this morning. It could only mean that the Hyadeans were expanding into our sector of the galaxy."

Stewart paused and stared at the cave floor, still confused over what had made him forget all that. Then he went on, but only surmising the rest:

"Don't you see? That ship must have captured us—removed from our minds the fact that we had discovered their nest in the Hyades. That way, we would never suspect we were about to run into opposition in our expansion. We'd be caught off guard, while the Hyadeans would have time for arming!"

Again, he paused uncertainly. "They must have also planted the false impression that there were many Earth-type worlds in the Hyades—so they could pick us off, ship by ship, as—"

But Randall was shaking his head miserably.

"No, Dave," the director said finally. "The Hyadeans did not brainwash you. *I* did. I also planted the false impression—to justify this mission. It was necessary that only *I* know the true situation."

Stewart staggered back.

"Yes," the other went on, "after you and Harlston told me there was another culture out there of undetermined size and intentions, I almost hit the panic stud. Two cultures expanding towards each other, previously unaware of each other's existence. The wrong move could be the shot heard around the galaxy.

"What to do? Report it to higher authorities? No. For I saw immediately what would happen: 'menace from space;' Terra and Centauri Three, our other worlds—'helpless before an unknown terror;' all that sort of stuff. Anybody could appreciate what the consequences would be.

"Send out a single ship to try for peaceful contact? But who would buy a scheme like that? Instead it would have been: Send out a thousand ships armed with laser intensifiers of every caliber, all manned by green, trigger-happy kids who had never fired a shot in battle back to the eighth generation before them."

Stewart realized there was no reason not to believe him.

For, all along, Randall had acted as though he *expected* to run into something like an alien ship.

The director lowered himself wearily on to the transceiver and folded his hands. "Anyway, from what you reported, I had hopes that there *could* perhaps be peaceful contact—between two single, unarmed ships. The evidence seemed to point in that direction.

"There were our telepuppets, for instance. The OC had quit transmitting—a year ago. Later you tell me you sighted an alien ship on Aldebaran Four-B. If you put two and two together, you come out with something that looks like a logical four."

He fished for his pipe, stuck it between his teeth, but forgot to light it. "If we have hostile aliens working in our direction and planning on surprising us, would they interfere with our robots? Of course not. For then we would send a trouble-shooting gang out here to put the puppets back on their strings. And we might discover them and mess up their strategy.

"So, since the Hyadeans weren't aware you had discovered them in their own cluster, the malfunctioning telepuppets could mean only one thing: They had stumbled upon our robots, reconciled themselves to the existence of another intelligent culture, and *purposely* interfered with the operation of our team."

"But why would they do that?" Carol asked, perplexed.

"As I figured it, that action practically amounted to an engraved calling card—requesting our appearance in the interest of amiable relations."

His final words rasped in his throat and he added remorsefully, "But I was wrong—oh, so wrong! It was only a trap. They just wanted to get us here so they could fire their opening shots!"

McAllister cut loose with a string of expletives. Mortimer only shook his head despondently.

Carol spread her hands. "But why didn't you tell the rest of us what we were getting into?"

Randall laughed in self-disparagement. "Oh, it was part of my grand strategy. I didn't want anybody along who knew what the real setup was. If this was going to be a try for peaceful contact, there'd be no room for possible hostile predispositions built up during nervewracking weeks of suspense while traveling to Four-B.

"You see, I even allowed for the possibility that the aliens might be telepathic, or at least have long-range instruments which could dig into our minds. If so, I was determined they would find nothing there to touch off an incident. I went out of my way to pick McAllister and Mortimer, who wouldn't *fight* their way out of a torn paper bag. I didn't want any triggerhappy, eager Bureau boys who might start fissioning at half critical mass."

The pilot and ship systems officer grumbled, but sat still.

"I wanted you along, Dave," Randall went on, "because you are dependable and reasonably pacifistic. And since you already knew, subconsciously, what the setup was, you'd be useful. Because if trouble developed it would break your conditioning."

"And Carol." He smiled at the girl. "I brought her because I was aware of the tender sentiments between you two—perhaps even more aware than you yourselves were. If those Hyadeans *could* see inside us, they'd know something of our gentler sentiments."

Randall snorted. "But I guessed wrong. My entire strategy wasn't worth the brain it was dreamed up in. I led us into a trap. It was the Hyadeans who turned up in a ship bristling with laser weapons. They had not, after all, sent us an engraved come-and-get-acquainted card. Instead, it was come-into-my-parlor."

Stewart was still having difficulty getting it straight in his mind. Somehow, it seemed there were still unanswered questions. But he felt too numb even to wonder about his dissatisfaction.

"The upshot of everything," he said, "seems to be that we've had it. Even if that Hyadean ship doesn't finish us off, there's no way we can get a warning back home."

The director smiled finally. "Give me credit for at least one redeeming bit of foresight. I *did* conceive of the possibility that something like this might happen. So when I conditioned you and Harlston, I arranged it that the conditioning would break down in another three weeks. Harlston will then report everything. And the Bureau will guess why they haven't heard from us."

To Minnie's utter confusion, the great pink sphere had risen yet there had been no subsequent Pilgrimage to Totem. She spent an eternity, it seemed, pondering that enigma but getting nowhere.

Eventually Screw Worm erupted from the ground—oh, so slowly, so sluggishly—and rolled towards her with his load of mineral specimens. When he tried to force the substance into her intake slot, however, she only turned away dispiritedly, still mourning the loss of communication with all the others.

Screw dropped his specimens and squirmed around, tilting feebly into the attitude for boring down again.

His jets came on weakly, managing to rotate him only three or four times before giving out completely. Then he fell into a strange motionlessness.

Minnie prodded him with her chuck. He toppled over, but did not stir. Disturbed, she sent a "report-your-location" command.

But there was no response.

Like Bigboss, he was totally inoperative. Like Peter the Meter and Maggie and Grazer and Breather and all the others, he, too, was now a victim of the stubborn stillness.

Confused, Minnie stumbled forward, realizing that her motor circuits were not responding as lively as they always had. Too, she was having some difficulty evaluating and rationalizing.

Then an odd thought occurred to her: She had devoted most of her time since becoming Supreme Being to considering how she should act. Her motor activity had been at a minimum. The other members of the clan, on the other hand, had continued their physical tasks. And now they were all motionless. Only she had any power left. Could the formula be: Motion minus the presence of Bigboss equals eventual immobility?

If that were the case, then how hollow, indeed, was the distinction of being the successor to the Omnipotent One!

If she was going to act like a Supreme Being, she decided suddenly, she would have to do so in a hurry. But do—*what*? Then she finally hit upon the answer: She must be about Bigboss's work of destroying non-Totemic pretenders.

And she knew just where to find *five* of the despicable things!

V

Exhaustion blunting the bite of sharp rocks into his back, sleep finally overtook Stewart. Despite his plight, he had not resisted. Four weeks had passed since his slumber had not ended in terror brought on by some form of the horrible nightmare.

But it would be different now. The Hyadean ship had torn aside the curtain behind which the suppressed knowledge had lurked. And his subconscious was rid of its awful burden.

He had been wrong, however. He knew that much when the army of hideous monsters sprang up from subliminal depth to fill the cave with their vile, menacing forms.

Only, it wasn't a cave in which he found himself now. It was a huge chamber whose vaulted ceiling was supported by ornate columns. In the center of the room was an immense table, surrounded by thousands of—chairs? Standing on stout legs evidently intended to bear ponderous hulks, the artifacts consisted of paired buttock rests merging into a large, tapering chute that curved down to the floor.

It was as though the chairs had suggested a shape for the monsters in his nightmare. For abruptly the chamber was filled with scaly creatures only remotely resembling the Harpies of his former fantasies. The head was a grotesque pair of jaws, lined with jagged teeth and resembling that of a massive crocodile. Resting in each chute was an immense tail that seemed as large as the body itself.

Then he was caught up in a vortex of blazing light and incredible sounds. He spun from fear to terror, from incomprehensible concepts to semantic confusion. The air about him was a sonic battleground of *hisses* and *clicks*. But, occasionally, one of the noises seemed to convey meaning of a sort.

The cave floor jolted beneath him and Stewart instantly sprang up, welcoming the abrupt awakening no matter what new complication had caused the tremorlike shock.

Then Carol screamed and lurched back against the far wall. There was a blur at the mouth of the cave and the Mineral Analyzer's huge drill rammed in—until its forward test chamber was blocked by the narrowness of the entrance.

Backing off, the robot charged again; withdrew and came forward once more. Then, apparently satisfied it couldn't get through, the thing directed its drill head in a series of determined, chopping blows that sent fragments of rock hurtling in all directions.

McAllister sidled along the wall. "That thing's got the same compulsion the OC had! It's trying to reach us!"

179

Randall stood in front of the transceiver to protect it from flying chips. "But I don't think it'll get through," he said uncertainly. "How does it look to you, Dave?"

"All depends on the amount of power it has left." Stewart drew Carol farther from the entrance.

Between blows, he glanced outside. Dawn was beginning to tinge the sky. "But it's been almost a whole day since it's had a recharge from the OC," he added hopefully.

The MA's drill head slammed down again and knocked loose a section of rock the size of Mortimer's head.

Carol dropped to the floor and sat with her arms wrapped around her knees.

Stewart leaned against the wall above her. "You said something about leaving the Bureau—maybe going to Terra—you and I—"

Her face was rigid, though no less attractive than he had remembered it when good-natured jest was her principal mannerism. "Talking about that is only an exercise in futility now," she said.

"I won't argue that point. But I want you to know the words weren't wasted." He took her hand. "It was something I had in mind a long time."

Abruptly he realized the MA was no longer chipping away at the cave entrance. When he looked up, the robot was withdrawing towards a mound of tumbled boulders perhaps a hundred yards off.

He slumped down beside Carol, his sense of relief dulled by renewed concern over the nightmares. Had *everything* in his subconscious come to the surface? Could there be more?

Carol gripped his arm and he looked off in the direction of her extended finger. Seeping in through the entrance, the gathering light of day was dimmed by a dark form descending silently to the surface.

He lunged up. "The Tzarean ship!"

But it wasn't until several seconds later that he realized he had used two *clicks* of his teeth and a *hiss* to pronounce the strange word between "the" and "ship."

Chancellor Vrausot was even more imposing in his home-environment suit. The helmet made his head seem twice as large and the clear-plastic snout cup enormously magnified his craggy teeth.

Just inside the main hatch, Assemblyman Mittich regarded the other and swallowed a strong taste of neglected opportunity. He had soaked awake all night, trying desperately to muster the will to accuse Vrausot of malfeasance and assume command.

But he had to face the bitter fact that he lacked sufficient courage. And, even more distressing, his cowardice was something he would have to live with for the rest of his life—as he watched the destruction of many worlds and billions of their inhabitants.

Odd, he thought, how so much could hinge on a single twist of circumstance. Vrausot would return to the Shoal and become a symbol around which Tzarean determination would rally.

On the other hand, if he, Mittich, were leader of this expedition, he too would receive a hero's welcome. Only, his praises would be hissed in the same breath with glorious tribute to the concepts of peaceful contact.

Vrausot turned to check the readiness of his landing party.

"All stun weapons loaded and set?" he asked, his voice sounding coarse both in Mittich's earphones and through a bulkhead speaker.

He received twenty affirmative tail flicks.

Of the pilot, standing by the hatch control switch, he demanded: "Status of the aliens' robots?"

"They are *all* impotent," Kavula reported back into the bulkhead speaker. "The last one used up its remaining power as we descended."

Vrausot stepped towards the hatch, but hesitated again.

"Kavula, you will double check the detention compartment and see that the proper protein nutrient is being synthesized."

The pilot acknowledged with a thump of his tail and opened the hatch.

A short while later the landing party was making its way across the plain towards the area strewn densely with boulders and the cave in the cliff beyond. Formality was strictly observed. Vrausot went first. Twenty paces behind him came Mittich; then, at intervals of ten paces, the remainder of the detail.

For Minnie, impotence was a strange and bewildering sensation as she stood paralyzed out among the boulders.

Equilibrium gyros spinning too slowly to accomplish their function, she had tilted over against a rock. In a final and desperate spasm, her drill head had swung upwards, toppled over, fallen a few centimeters and come to rest precariously against a ridge.

Frantically, she fought relentless inertia. She opened special circuits that would ordinarily have flooded her balancing system with emergency current. But servomechanisms failed to respond and her chrome-plated neck remained thrust towards a sun now well up in the sky.

Gears whirred faintly and her head turned ever so slowly on its axis, bringing its video sensor to bear on the cave entrance.

It had been her determined efforts to reach the non-Totemic mobiles, she reasoned, that had drained off all her energy. She had been aware of the imminent power failure even during her last, frantic blows at the rocks. Then, retreating, she had struggled desperately against terrifying paralysis.

And now she stood almost powerless, whereas before her forced ascendancy she had imagined she would be *All* Powerful. It was an ironic turn of fate indeed. Oh, how she longed now for the telemetric voices of the clan, the crisp orders from Bigboss, the obedient, sometimes plaintive responses of Screw Worm to her own directions.

Incapable of movement, she sensed finally and with much distress that her rationalization processes themselves—were becoming—sluggish, weak. She could hardly—think coherently—or with rapidity—any longer.

Slowly her head responded to the pull of gravity and turned once more on its axis, the weighty chuck arcing down like a pendulum. It reached the nadir of its swing and momentum carried it up in the other direction. In a desperate effort, she locked the servo unit.

In that position, her video lens took in the huge, new symmetrical form that had come to rest out in the plain.

It was—another Totem! And approaching—in her direction now were—many other non-Totemic creatures—somewhat different in form—perhaps, from—the ones Bigboss had—pursued. But—still insolent, despicable—things, nevertheless.

Was it—possible that she—could still—discharge her—function as—Supreme Being? If they—passed—close enough, it—would require—only one—final—desperate—impulse—to—"

With the others, Stewart crowded into the cave entrance, careful not to let Carol press too far outside where she would no longer be in the stream of oxygen flowing from the bowels of the satellite.

"They're coming!" McAllister exclaimed, withdrawing. Mortimer retreated with him, striking out for a small passageway that fed from one of the side walls.

Stewart strained forward, shading his eyes against the glare of Aldebaran. The landing party's advance was half concealed by the mass of rocks and outcroppings that hid most of their ship. Only occasionally could he see part of a space-suited Hyadean form as its clumsy, swaying stride brought it more completely into his line of sight.

And vision was further complicated by the glint of sunlight off the Mineral Analyzer's upthrust drill head, which had finally come to rest against the rock.

Carol tilted her head attentively and frowned. "I'm picking up the *oddest* radio stuff. The modulation breaks down into nothing more than clicking and hissing sounds. I can't seem to get any meaning. It's too—alien!"

Randall reached back into the cave for his hostile-atmosphere sheath. "I'm going out there and see what happens. After all, I'm responsible for our predicament."

But just then the first alien figure pulled into view, coming around the boulder and pausing. Apparently sighting Randall's movement in the cave entrance, the Hyadean raised a stubby arm that held a gleaming instrument.

Randall pulled Carol back into the subterranean chamber. But Stewart only stood there frozen in bewilderment.

Then the Mineral Analyzer's ponderous drill head slipped from its perch and came plunging down. It shattered the Hyadean's helmet and almost tore his grotesque head off, sending his weapon flying out across the plain.

The creature lay there writhing for a moment, then was still, its hideous crocodile head turned lifelessly towards Aldebaran.

Stewart, his eyes locked hypnotically on the prostrate form, could only watch with shocked fascination as the other members of the landing party appeared from behind the rocks. They stood silently around the body, then turned back towards their ship.

"Tzareans"—"Tzarean Shoal"—"Curule Assembly"—"Vrausot"—"Mittich"—*"uraphi"*—

Strange words and phrases whirled about in Stewart's thrashing thoughts as a great flood of deeply buried experiences rushed with cyclonic fury into the conscious levels of his mind. And he realized that, just as the sight of the Hyadean ship had swept aside the conditioning Randall had imposed upon him, so was the sight of Hyadeans—Tzareans—hurling aside another, denser curtain of conditioning.

He staggered back into the cave and fell sitting against the wall as all the suppressed knowledge and memories engulfed him.

Stewart and Harlston were seated beside the table in the Great Hall of the Curule Assembly. They were having some difficulty making themselves comfortable in chairs designed to accommodate Tzarean buttocks and tail, rather than support the human form. They were manacled, but only symbolically—with flimsy crepe paperlike handcuffs.

"Our problem," Mittich, the Hisser of the Assembly was saying, "has been clearly defined. We have captured the expeditionary ship of an alien culture that appears to be expanding in the direction of the Tzarean Shoal. We have taken pains to teach its two crew members the rudiments of our language. And we have found that the official alien response to this situation may or may not be hostile."

"Kill them! Kill them!" one of the Assemblymen clicked out as he sprang up on his tail.

The Great Hall resounded with click-hisses of approval and disapproval—an equal measure of each, it seemed to Stewart.

He watched Mittich smile—at least, it passed for a smile in the Tzarean Shoal—tolerantly at the excited Assemblyman.

"Killing our prisoners," he chided, "will not alter the fact that alien expansion is under way in the direction of our Shoal."

Chancellor Vrausot lumbered down the central aisle, defying the independence of the legislature as he had during all sessions which Stewart and Harlston had attended as Exhibits A and B of the "Alien threat" issue.

Whacking his tail against the floor for attention, he stood before the table and hissed vehemently, "We must arm to the limit of our potential. We must dispose of these prisoners. We must attack their centers of civilization before they attack ours!"

Another Assemblyman rose imploringly. "But how can we do that? We haven't fought a war in countless millennia! Once we were many and mighty, as they are now. But while they have grown, we have shrunk. Why, our entire Shoal consists of only two civilized worlds. All the others have long been in decay."

"Oh, we could take them by surprise and inflict much damage on their worlds," Hisser of the Assembly Mittich agreed with Chancellor Vrausot. "But they would recover. And we would be annihilated."

"Then what," the Chancellor asked scornfully, "would you propose that we do?"

"Our choices are innumerable:

"One—we kill these captives and prepared a surprise attack. Two—we condition our captives to return to the center of their civilization and report that they found no worlds worth possessing in this sector."

Vrausot reared erect in protest. "But eventually the conditioning will break! They will remember! And their race will then fashion an attack!"

"If we are to assume that they would attack in the first place," Mittich pointed out. "Our prisoners themselves aren't certain whether their race would or would not."

"Three—we could try instilling fear in them. Condition our captives to go back home and report a powerful, vast Tzarean Shoal culture. But that, I suspect, would only drive the aliens into a frantic arming effort. And, once a formidable strike potential is accumulated, use will be found for it—believe me.

"Fourth—we could let them return and tell the truth—that the Tzareans are a declining culture on its last tail, so to speak."

Again Chancellor Vrausot erupted in a series of violent hisses and clicks. "But that might only encourage them to attack!"

"Precisely. So the only course left is Number Five. That is to condition our prisoners to report indications of an interstellar culture in the Tzarean

Shoal—nothing precise, nothing definite. Our prisoners will say they made no visual observations. We thus present the aliens with neither the temptation of our actual weakness, nor the fear of our pretended strength.

"At the same time we interrupt communications between them and the robots they have stationed in the system halfway between their center of civilization and ours. We shall hope they interpret that action as signifying we have discovered their automatons and desire to meet them in peace on that satellite.

"We shall go there prepared for friendly contact. If they come unarmed we shall know there will be no fighting; that perhaps they will even provide the stimulus and inspiration for regeneration of the Tzarean culture. After all, it's a pretty big galaxy and there's plenty of room for two interstellar races."

"But," Vrausot hissed grimly, "what if they come armed?"

"Then we shall know what fate holds in store for us. We will prepare to the limit of our resources and acquit ourselves honorably."

Stewart watched Vrausot thump his tail on the floor in an expression of displeasure.

"The administration," click-hissed the Chancellor, "will agree to that plan with two modifications: one—that the Tzarean ship we send to contact the aliens will itself be armed so that the lives of our brave men will not be jeopardized; two—that the highest administrative authority be appointed to lead the expedition."

"Dave! Oh, Dave! What's wrong?"

He opened his eyes and stared up into Carol's solicitous face. "I'm all right," he said numbly.

Randall was tinkering with the transceiver, while Mortimer and McAllister were moving about excitedly in the cave entrance.

"Come and see what those Hyadeans are doing!" the latter exclaimed.

Stewart went over. In front of the cave, obscuring the formation of outcroppings and boulders beyond, was a pile of shining, metal instruments that looked like—

"The linear intensifiers off their laser guns!" Mortimer revealed. "They've been stripping them off the ship for the past half hour. And look!"

He pointed off to the side, indicating another mound of weapons that were quite obviously of the class the landing party had worn as side arms. In between the two piles and lying directly in front of the cave's mouth was the body of the Tzarean who had been slain by the fall of the Mineral Analyzer's drill head.

Even as Stewart watched, other Tzareans brought more weapons to add to the two stacks.

"Dave!" Randall's voice sounded excitedly back in the cave. "Come and listen to this. I've tuned in on their frequency!"

Stewart accepted the earphones and listened to the clicks and hisses that translated readily into:

"How many gun batteries left?"

"Two more and they will have all been dismantled."

"And the stun weapons?"

"There isn't a single one left on the ship."

Stewart tensed. The questioning voice—it couldn't be—

Anxiously, he picked up the microphone and ignored the bewilderment on Randall's face as he hissed, "Mittich! Is that you?"

And the Tzarean who had practically been his companion during the Curule Assembly hearing phase of his captivity answered with a series of startled clicks:

"Friend Stewart? It's not *really* Stewart, is it?"

⌦ PROJECT BARRIER ⌫

"**C**ulture," said Chimur pompously, "is built on technical knowledge and social virtue. Never on technology alone. Otherwise there would be stagnation."

Self-satisfied with his dissertation, the Chief Ursa relaxed in his chair and complacently folded his great stubby arms.

Savorn shifted uneasily. "But that's exactly my point. Our world is some one thousand miles across and—"

"And is sorely beset," Chimur broke in bluntly, "with internal disruption. In that five-hundred-mile radius there are four hostile nations."

"You don't follow me, sir. Celestial measurements show the Shimmering Cliff encloses but a small portion of the surface of a great sphere. What's on the other side of the Cliff? What's—"

Chief Ursa Chimur brought his paw down resoundingly on the desk. "And you, sir, don't follow me. With war staring us in the face, there is little time to think of such academic issues as what's beyond the Cliff!"

Savorn glanced away impatiently. He could almost see back through the curtains of time to some dim prehistoric era. There must have been many like Chimur—great shaggy beasts, sharp-taloned, long-snouted, bigoted, squatting smugly around their primitive fires, blindly proclaiming their implements couldn't be improved upon.

"But don't you see?" he pleaded. "If we could negotiate the Cliff we'd be invulnerable! If any nation attacked, we could strike back directly at its capital—from *beyond* the barrier!"

For a moment the Chief Ursa sat back and pensively ran his closely cropped claws against his jowl. Then he snorted.

"Nonsense! I know what this is leading up to. You want more funds for your pointless research. But this time I won't go along. Not when we have to budget so much for weapons."

The Chief Ursa was quite indignant. Savorn's sensitive nostrils quivered as he detected the subtle odor of the other's anger.

"I'm on a new project, Chimur," he confided anxiously.

"So I understand. Something about breaking water down into its elements." The other disinterestedly straightened his collar.

"It's an extension of the electrolytic process. I'm refining hydrogen and oxygen."

Chimur flicked his paw disparagingly. "And of what practical use is refining these elements?"

"Hydrogen is lighter than air."

"So?"

"If we gather enough of it in a light container, it might be made to lift an observer."

"And what," the Chief Ursa growled, "will the observer observe?"

Savorn leaned forward tensely. "The thing might rise *over* the Shimmering Cliff!"

Chimur sprang up, baring his vestigial fangs. "You meddling young cub! No matter where you start, you always get back to that damned barrier!"

Savorn backed off as the other shook a trembling paw in his face.

"I'm serving warning," the Chief Ursa rasped, "that I'll fight any request for more appropriations for your bumbling research bureau!"

Outside, Savorn disgustedly thrust his paws in his pockets and signaled for a cab. He was tall and supple, having not yet acquired the excessive proportions of ursine maturity. Cinnamon was the color of his down, vestige of a once-lush coat of ancestral hair. It made a striking contrast with the rich tan of his nose.

"Barrier Park," he directed sullenly, getting into the cab.

The vehicle backfired and stumbled off over a cobblestone street that had only in the past decade watched the ox-drawn cart bow out in the march of progress.

The cab turned on to a broad boulevard and headed towards the Shimmering Cliff, scarcely three miles away.

Impressive was the barrier—all coruscating and pulsating, like a splendid cataract that sent its silvery water cascading down from a mile-high altitude. Breathtakingly beautiful and challenging. Derisively challenging to Savorn. He had spent half his life, it seemed, standing at the foot of the barrier, awed at its magnificence, trying again and again to push into the delightfully tingling matter-that-wasn't matter. Always, however, it repulsed—gently but relentlessly.

Thiebok and Cella, the latter in a light print dress, were waiting at the park entrance. They cuffed one another friendlily, then withdrew to a terrace flanked by rows of tall cedars.

"Well?" Savorn prodded.

"You first," Thiebok smiled. He was not quite as tall as Savorn, but the principal difference between the two was one of coloration. Thiebok's down, which he flaunted with pretended ostentation, had a bluish cast.

Savorn glanced disconsolately at Cella. "No luck. Chimur's going to fight any more appropriations."

"Oh!" exclaimed Cella sympathetically. "Does that mean the end of your work?"

He shook his head uncertainly. "The bureau hasn't been disbanded—yet."

He turned anxiously towards Thiebok. "What did you find out about Councilor Murdas?"

"Nothing. If Murdas is a subversive agent, he hasn't done anything to arouse the suspicion of the ministry of security. Cella and I haven't come across anything in our files."

"But he is from a border area. And he has been influencing the Chief Ursa to oppose more research on the Cliff."

"Quite true."

"And every time the council cancels one of the bureau's projects, we find the Southern Nation has started identical experiments."

Thiebok spread his paws. "But that still doesn't prove subversion. His conviction might be sincere. There are plenty of diehards on the council."

Savorn's shoulders slumped.

Thiebok cuffed him encouragingly. "Got to get back to the ministry before they find out I'm conspiring against a councilor. Watch it with Murdas. Don't forget, if you make any rash charges he's entitled to physical challenge. He's the *last* one I'd want to see you tie up with."

"But you'll have the ministry on your side," Cella offered hopefully, "if you can convince them he ought to be investigated."

"That's right, Savorn." Thiebok backed towards the park entrance. "But they won't accept intuition as evidence."

Savorn watched him leave then turned to gaze at the Shimmering Cliff. Viewed so close, it appeared to tower menacingly overhead. The vertiginous effect was almost overpowering. It seemed as though its majestic bulk was toppling over and would crush all civilization.

A lance of yellow light broke loose from the top of the glittering cataract and streaked upwards until it disappeared in the azure depths of the sky. And from the unknown reaches beyond the barrier came the faint muffled roar of thunder. The streaking lights and rumbling sounds were not uncommon. And it must be, Savorn reflected, that they only *seemed* to surge up out of the very top of the Cliff. It must be that the barrier hid the lower part of their trajectories.

He made a mental note: Put the rumbling lights down as Barrier Research Project 1-B.

Cella cuffed him gently. "It's not all that serious, is it?" she asked facetiously.

She was tall but elegantly proportioned. There was a harmony of rhythm in her movements and, altogether conforming with the tenor of her other features, her coloration was a warm yellowish white.

He seized her paws. "I want to get on the other side of the Cliff, Cella—more than *anything* else."

Her eyes laughed. "More than anything else?" she nuzzled his ear coquettishly and nipped him lightly on the jowl.

Then she backed off, ready to turn and sprint gleefully should he show signs of giving chase. But the set lines in his face rejected the invitation. So she reluctantly altered mood and stood by his side. He took her arm and they walked across the terrace.

But she drew up suddenly, pointing ahead. "What's that?"

He glanced down at the reddish-brown animal that sat on its haunches and surveyed them inquisitively. "A prairie dog. There's a colony of them in the park."

The creature ambled off in a three-legged gait and Savorn saw the reason for its limp. It was dragging a long hooked twig with its right forepaw.

Drawing up before a bed of sunflowers, it used the crude implement to pull one of the seed-heads down within reach.

"Oh, it's darling!" Cella exclaimed.

"Witness the forgotten prairie dog," Savorn offered philosophically. "It's got a long standing section option to fill the niche occupied by bearkind."

She crinkled her snout questioningly.

"Unfortunately," he expanded, "only one species can hold the scepter of civilization at one time. If it weren't for that fact, we might discover that 'darling little creature' building cities alongside ours."

Savorn threw the switch and listened to the whine of steam-driven generators. He made several notations on a pad, then paused to survey the laboratory scene. Satisfied that everything was functioning properly, he returned to his office.

An assistant came in and laid a square of dark cloth on his desk. "Here's the sample."

Taking the material between his paws, Savorn stretched it forcibly. "We've made all tests?"

The assistant nodded. "It's the same stuff the army uses as tent material."

"Hermetic?"

"Completely. It's rubberized. Stands up under seventy-five pounds of pressure. It'll do for your hydrogen bag, all right."

"Order a hundred bolts. And have Axeru send in those samples of wire for the reinforcement net."

Savorn dismissed him and tried to get the North-eastern Production Unit on the voice-receiver. But the diaphragm only made a squawking noise and he regretted having let them replace his sending key.

He was still shouting impatient "hellos" into the mouthpiece when his secretary announced Councilor Murdas.

Like Chief Ursa Chimur, the huge Murdas only seemed clumsily stout. Actually, untested power lurked behind his deceptive appearance of ursine plumpness. Also like Chimur, his vestigial down was dark brown.

"I've come to find out something about this electrolysis thing," Murdas disclosed perfunctorily.

"I didn't think you were interested," Savorn said guardedly, appreciating the advantage the councilor's position of authority would afford him if he were a foreign agent.

"I'm concerned with all ways in which treasury funds are spent."

Savorn led him to the main laboratory. "The work we're doing here is similar to what's being done at five other regional facilities."

He made the tour short—brief almost to the point of rudeness—and they ended up at the main cell.

"Here, an electric current runs through the solution. You can see the hydrogen collecting on those cathodes. From there it's funneled off to a chamber and pumped into portable steel capsules."

The councilor grunted his disapproval. "And this is the stuff that's going to make a bird out of a bear?"

Savorn regarded him appraisingly. Why, he wondered, was Murdas *opposed* to research? If he were siphoning off the results of the bureau's experiments and relaying them to the enemy, shouldn't he want to see the bureau continue?

The councilor started back for the office. "Have you ever got the impression, Savorn, that what you call progress is carrying us, like an overwhelming tide, towards oblivion?"

Savorn started to answer, but tensed instead. Suddenly it occurred to him that Murdas would want to halt the bureau's research *if he knew war was imminent*! For then his line of communication would be broken and data gained future experiments would remain the exclusive property of the Northern Nation.

"Do you realize," the councilor continued, "that two hundred years ago the bow and arrow was seldom fatal? But now, with the blessings of knowledge and progress, we can kill thousands in no time at all?"

"The bureau's function," Savorn protested, "isn't to make war more horrible."

"But your Cliff research is intended to do just that. You're seeking a way to attack beyond the barrier so we can inflict greater casualties."

"But I'm just using that as an argument to get more funds!"

Murdas laughed throatily. "Just like the bureau supervisor before you wanted metal-plated cars to try to push through the Cliff. We got the armored cars, all right. But they couldn't penetrate the barrier. And now what do we have? Gun-mounted armored vehicles! It's going to be hell when they tie up with the cars of the Southern Nation."

Savorn stiffened. How did *Murdas* know the Southern Nation had armored cars? Intelligence had established that fact only hours earlier. And it had come as a surprise. Thiebok had confided at lunch.

Savorn parked the car on the edge of the theater district and escorted Calla down the crowded sidewalk, ignoring the tug of abandon and excitement that seemed to be part of the gay night throng. He was impressed, though, at the predominance of uniforms, realizing only now that the war emergency must be serious indeed.

Cella nodded ahead. "There's your culturally precocious creature."

A cinnamon-hued music-box grinder was the center of attraction among a nightclub and theater crowd that had collected at the next corner. He churned the handle of the hurdy-gurdy, strapped to his shoulders, and a lilting tune accompanied the gyrations of a prairie dog on a leash.

The animal, dressed in a mock military uniform, pranced on its hind legs and extended a tiny cup towards the delighted onlookers.

Savorn and Cella skirted the assembly and entered one of the less pretentious nightclubs. They ordered honey-fizzes and he sat back reticent, staring unseeingly through the congression of individual dancers who lurched and whirled and surged in time with the blaring orchestra.

Cella leaned across the table and gripped his paw. "You're not keeping your promise," she chided.

He started, then smiled. "But I don't have my mind on the bureau."

"Then what do you have it on?"

Her stare was severe, yet tender, both accusing and solicitous. Dim, revolving reflections threw sparkling highlights against the soft, yellow hair that fell down on her shoulders.

"You," he said, laying a paw on her arm. But then he slumped. "No, that's a lie. It's on Murdas."

"But don't you see there's still nothing you can do about him?" she asked earnestly.

"I could report he knew about the Southern Nation having armored cars."

"Not without betraying the fact that Thiebok passed confidential information to you. That would cost him his job—maybe even a prison sentence."

Savorn sipped his drink. "I suppose you're right," he admitted grudgingly. "If I could only find Murdas's equipment!"

She frowned. "What equipment?"

"I don't know, Cella. But he must have some way of getting information to the Southern Nation. It can't be through agents. Too risky that way. And I know he doesn't have a private telegraph line running under five hundred miles of landscape."

"But what other way is there?"

"Wireless transmission."

She drew back skeptically. "I've never heard of that."

"No doubt you haven't. It was killed in the experimental stage almost four years ago. It's a theoretical way of transposing voice impulses into electromagnetic vibrations that can be sent through the air."

She hid her confusion behind a tactful burst of laughter. "I haven't any idea what you're talking about, darling."

He leaned back and laughed too—at himself for having thrust fleeting concepts of abstract science on her. Yet, he reflected soberly, that was the trouble with the world—too many were willing to accept the comforts afforded by research while they reacted indifferently to further progress.

But science—even what Murdas has called an overwhelming tide of it—was good. It had accepted the candle in trade for the incandescent bulb; the courier for the transmission cable; the oxen for the motor car.

Cella was serious again as she reached across the table and took both his paws. "I wonder, darling, if you aren't just fashioning a paper dragon. Doesn't a councilor doubling as a subversive agent seem a bit melodramatic?"

He laced her with a protesting stare.

"Why don't you go out and dance?" she suggested. "Have fun. Don't even think about going before the council tomorrow."

"I'm thinking about something more important than that," he said obscurely.

"What?"

"Whether or not the council approves more funds, at least one hydrogen bag will be built. And I'm going to ride it over the Shimmering Cliff."

The meeting was uncomfortably formal as Savorn shifted restively before the challenging stares of Chimur and Murdas.

"...And even the Chief Ursa," he concluded, "has conceded that culture is built on both technology and social virtue. So there must be more funds for new undertakings by the bureau of scientific research."

"True, I admitted that much," Chimur said. "But things are different now. We must show we are willing to practice pacifism by not pursuing more horrible means of waging war."

Several of the councilors nodded in studied agreement.

Murdas clasped his paws together soberly. "Just what are these new undertakings you're considering?"

"For one thing, we'd like to push further into the hydrogen bag experiments. Even if the device fails to rise above the Cliff, it might still be used as a means of rapid, direct transportation. Engines could be attached in some way to drive fan blades and give the thing a forward impetus."

Murdas lurched up. "Another form of intimidating the other nations! Troop vehicles that could rise *above* their lines of defense! Why must you insist on such provocations?"

Chief Ursa Chimur rapped the table. "It seems to me that if the research bureau operated under a tight control authority which would determine the course of its work, then there would be less objection to its existence."

Murdas shook his head. "That's not enough. We've got to prove our peaceful intentions. I move that we disband the bureau and put research back on the plane of private endeavor where it belongs."

"What individual," Savorn asked bitterly, "could undertake anything the size of the hydrogen bag project?"

"That," said Murdas, smiling, "is exactly the point."

The motion was carried unanimously.

The forest was dense and shadowy and, being only a few miles from the capital, was ideally located for Savorn's purpose. It stretched like a great, green finger along the inner curve of the Cliff, ending at a point due north of the city. And the deserted shack which it concealed couldn't have been more suited to his needs had he supervised its construction himself.

Walking along the row of benches in the shanty, he watched the workers cutting and sewing, patching and pasting. When he reached the end table, he waited until Cella finished tracing the pattern for one of the lower panels of the bag.

Then he took the pencil away from her. "You're far enough ahead of the others now."

She smiled wearily and followed him outside.

Above the trees, the Shimmering Cliff soared up like a huge, quivering blanket of luminous fibers, outshining even the lunar disc.

"It's wonderful, Savorn," she said.

"The barrier," he agreed, "is the most wonderful and challenging thing in our world."

"I wasn't talking about that. I meant the loyalty of all these people from your bureau." She motioned towards the workers in the clearing who were stacking tall cylinders of compressed hydrogen.

He nodded. "They all wanted to help. I had to turn down half of them. But they understood when they realized somebody had to go through the motions of disbanding the research centers."

The deadened roar of distant thunder erupted again and again. Savorn looked up to see a whole string of brilliant lances shoot up from beyond the barrier and finally snuff themselves out in the far reaches of the darkened sky.

"That's your whole life, isn't it?" Cella asked remotely. "The Cliff and the soaring lights."

He stared into the distance. "When I was a cub, my grand-sire used to say, 'Savorn, those shooting lights are the Gods beyond the barrier going off to their altar homes among the stars.'"

He glanced eagerly at her. "Now I want to go beyond the Cliff and see if that's true."

She grasped his arm. "But, Savorn. Even if you can get over the top, how will you ever return, with the wind blowing northward at this time of the year?"

"Do you want me to come back?"

In answer, she nuzzled his ear affectionately.

"Then I'll be back. You believe that, don't you?"

"Of course I do. Like all these workers, I have faith in you, too. Would I be practically deserting my job with the ministry to come out here and help if I didn't?"

In the distance, a motor-bike *putt-putted* along the road paralleling the forest. The sound grew louder and Savorn stiffened. But he relaxed when he realized the driver was heading too unerringly for the clearing to be anyone but a member of the secret project.

The cyclist finally broke into the glade and cut off the engine. It was Thiebok.

"Sorry I couldn't get away sooner," he explained as Savorn and Cella came over, "but intelligence is going full blast. How's the barrier effort coming along?"

"We'll be ready to go in a few days."

"Will you have enough hydrogen?"

"Yes, with the cylinders we were able to pull in from the regional centers."

Thiebok drew back and stared up at the Shimmering Cliff. Its gentle coruscations, like blobs of greenish white fire chasing one another up and down the luminous surface, gave an eerie cast to the blue down of his face and bare arms.

He glanced towards the center of the clearing, with its winches and ropes for holding the bag down until it could be filled. And his snout wrinkled meditatively.

"Won't the hydrogen keep lifting the bag? How will you get back to the surface, provided there is a surface on the other side?"

"There'll be a valve in the top to release a little of the gas at a time. The bag should float down gently."

The other nodded thoughtfully.

"Are we still safe out here?" Savorn asked.

"I don't think they suspect anything. At least, security hasn't got any orders to investigate 'curious activity' at a shack in the forest."

Reassured, Savorn fixed the barrier with a mocking stare.

Thiebok dropped a paw across his shoulder. "I sometimes wonder whether you aren't attaching too much significance to the Cliff. There are other barriers, you know—just as provocative."

Savorn squinted at him.

"There's the barrier of the past that hides the origin of the ursine race. The barrier of the future, concealing the destination of bearkind. And all the barriers of social and political differences that divide us into antagonistic nations."

"What are you trying to say?"

"That the council might be right. Maybe we should leave the Shimmering Cliff alone until we've overcome the barricades that exist *within* our world."

Thiebok mounted his motor-bike and drove off. After the silence of the night had folded over the staccato of his departure, Savorn took Cella's arm and they strolled through the forest to the base of the Shimmering Cliff.

A meteorlike flash flared in the sky and he glanced up to watch a long, thin lance of pure white fire plummet earthwards—*on this side of the barrier!*

It struck the flickering Cliff a glancing blow, perhaps three miles to the east, and hit the ground in a jarring crash. "Come on!" Savorn shouted. "We might find out whether grand-sire was right!"

It was more than three miles. Remembering that the sound of the impact had been negligible, Savorn realized he had underestimated the distance. Daylight came before they reached the site and he was surprised that no one else had been attracted.

"What is it?" Cella asked uncertainly.

He stood off and studied the huge metal object that lay like an elongated cracked egg at the base of the Cliff. "Look at the symmetry, the workmanship! We can be sure, at least, that the soaring lights are products of intelligent paws."

The ground was charred naked in a great circle around the thing.

"I'll stay and watch, Cella. You go back to the road and get to the nearest voice station. Tell Chimur what we saw."

After she left he circled the object, no sound within.

Sniffing gingerly, he went up to the thing and felt the warm metal of its outer surface, the slightly raised ridges here and there that suggested some sort of welding process.

Near one end of the crumpled ovoid, he found a rift in the metal skin almost large enough to force his head through. He stared in, then drew back, dumbfounded.

In a corner of the other side of the compartment was something—*alien!* It roughly resembled a bear, having two arms, two legs and a head. Even the facial features were similar, except that where a snout should have been was only a blunt projection of the jaw. Apprehensively, he sniffed the unursine smell that pervaded the interior of the vessel.

Clothed in material not unlike the familiar garments of bear-kind, the other creature was motionless in death. On the exposed parts of its flesh there was no fuzz. And its color was light tan, almost white.

A sense of impending peril swept over Savorn and he lurched away from the vessel. The Shimmering Cliff was advancing!

Like a menacing, boiling bubble, a huge section of the barrier was pushing out towards the thing that had once been a soaring light!

Frightened, Savorn backed off and watched the glittering protuberance sweep over the ovoid. Then, furiously, he attacked the outcropping of barrier substance, trying to force it away from his prize.

But his efforts were futile. Frustrated, he could only stumble back and watch and wait.

It was past noon when the bulge withdrew into the barrier, leaving bare the ground which it relinquished. Savorn went forward groping, as though his paws might encounter the soaring light thing that was no longer there.

Chimur paced restlessly, his great brown bulk ambling over the charred area. Three other councilors and a score of civil police, army personnel and security guards moved mechanically over the ground, searching, prodding.

The Chief Ursa halted suddenly and swung around to face Savorn and Cella.

"I don't believe there was anything here at all!" he erupted.

"But look at the ground," Savorn pleaded.

"You could have burned it."

"And that hole?" Savorn indicated the impression left by the impact and weight of the vessel.

"You could have selected just a natural configuration and centered your fire around it to give weight to your story."

Savorn thrust his arms up futilely. "Don't you believe her either?" He gestured towards Cella.

"We did—until we got here."

One of the councilors, a paw raised tentatively to the top of his snout, confronted Chimur.

"It seems to me," he said, "that such a story as a disabled out-of-this-world vessel being pulled through the Shimmering Cliff might be intended to stimulate interest in further barrier research."

Nodding his concurrence, Chimur eyed Savorn speculatively. "If you didn't plant this hoax, just what *were* you doing out here?"

Savorn tried to hide his abrupt confusion. He'd failed to foresee that he might be called on to explain his presence in the forest. "I—I—"

But Cella spoke up calmly. "Savorn and I were—We came out here last night and—Well, you see—"

She put on a thoroughly convincing display of humiliated guilt which, Savorn realized, could be dispelled only at the expense of disclosing the hydrogen bag project.

Several of the security agents were exploring the fringe area of the Cliff, pressing against the shimmering substance, forcing their way into the repelling barrier as far as it would let them.

Chimur laughed derisively. "If this alien creature is as monstrous as you say, then it's just as well that it *was* taken out of our world."

Savorn ignored the taunts of the other councilors and went over to the Cliff. Determined, he pushed into the glistening, tingling mass until he was completely engulfed and could go no farther against the fiercely repelling power.

As he relaxed finally in defeat and let the matter-that-wasn't-matter force him back, his foot caught in something firm, thin, vine-like. Straining, he reached down with an exploring paw and felt the cable pegged to the ground every few inches so that it wouldn't be repelled into the open—*a transmission cable!*

The significance of his discovery burst in on him: A line hidden in the fringe area of the Shimmering Cliff would be ideal for transmitting subversive information away from the capital area! If he traced it back to the city, would he find Murdas at its terminus?

He let the shimmering mist eject him.

"It could be more serious than a mere hoax, Chimur," one of the councilors was saying. "It might be an attempt to divert us from the war effort."

The Chief Ursa turned angrily on Savorn. "I'm not having you taken in custody at present—not until I've had time to consult the statute books. But you're going to get cuffed every way the law allows!"

He glanced caustically at Cella, then directed his outraged stare back towards Savorn. "The least you can expect is a morals charge."

The Chief Ursa turned to leave. But one of the security agents stopped him to whisper in his ear. Chimur started; stared even more indiscriminately at the couple, then stomped off.

Savorn reluctantly took time off that night to trace the transmission cable, letting the hydrogen bag project run itself.

Starting with the general assumption that the line should emerge from the barrier and go underground somewhere close to the city, he began pushing into the Cliff at random places and feeling for the cable. He selected this method rather than fight the constantly repelling force that he would face in attempting to trace the cable directly.

By dawn he had discovered the spot where the ground swallowed the line. But he drew back disappointedly. He had at least expected to find a shack or perhaps a cave that might conceal the transmitter.

There was nothing, however, but barren plain between him and the city, some two miles away. It would take weeks to uproot the cable and track it down. There was nothing to do but locate the transmission line at its origin.

At least he knew for certain now that there was a transmitter *somewhere*. And if, as he suspected, it was in Councilor Murdas's quarters, then he should be able to prove the move to discredit the research bureau was but part of the overall sabotage strategy.

It was late that afternoon, while Murdas would most likely be at his private office, that Savorn entered the building housing the government officials' dens. In the hall of Murdas's floor, he saw Chimur get out of another elevator and head for his suite. Savorn waited until the other was out of sight.

Then he went cautiously to Murdas's den, stepping swiftly into the darkened reception grotto. Groping among the massive pieces of furniture, he made his way across the room and drew out the ring of keys Thiebok had obtained from the security ministry.

He tried several before he found one that opened the door to the inner compartments of the den.

A half-hour later he stepped back into the reception grotto, thoroughly disappointed. Nowhere in the locked rooms had there been anything even resembling a transmitter.

There was the sound of pawsteps in the corridor, so he decided to wait until the hall was empty before venturing out. But the pawfalls, thumping more anxiously now, drew closer.

Savorn concealed himself behind a chair next to the inner door.

The figure that darted into the grotto was silhouetted briefly against the background of corridor illumination. It wasn't difficult to recognize the large proportions of the bronze-colored Murdas as he stepped to one side of the room, his back to Savorn's hiding place.

But there was something wrong! Savorn choked back a cry of astonishment as he watched the other's body take on a subtle luminescence—not unlike the bolder luminosity of the Shimmering Cliff!

The aura cloaking the ursine outline grew brighter. Then, slowly, the figure changed shape, going through a steady, terrifying metamorphosis.

When the process was complete, it was no longer the glimmering form of a member of the ursine race that stood across the room! Rather, it was like the creature Savorn had seen the day before in the inner compartment of the soaring light!

Overpowering in the grotto now was the scent of something alien—something only once before encountered. The glittering aura subsided and the ghastly form took more substantial shape. It reached down with two pawlike appendages and manipulated the dials on a metal box strapped to its waist.

Suddenly the aura flared brilliantly again as the creature turned back towards the wall. It went through its metamorphosis in reverse and lost its luminescence. Then it was all over and the familiar figure of the councilor strode to the entrance, was briefly outlined by the back lighting, and stepped briskly into the corridor.

Five minutes later Savorn ventured numbly from the grotto and headed for his own den, vaguely wondering what he should do about the creature masquerading as Murdas. For the moment, even the hydrogen bag project seemed insignificant in comparison with his discovery of the outer-world being.

It was late that night when he finally decided that despite his disfavor with Chimur, he had to report what he had seen to the Chief Ursa.

But the next morning, even as he prepared to visit Chimur, an armed courier came to his den and, without explanation, escorted him to the Chief Ursa office.

Inside the heavily-carpeted room, Savorn stood humbly before the brown-hued official.

"I've got to talk with you, Chimur, about—"

"The Chief Ursa banged the desk with a bludgeon-like paw. "It is I who will do the talking! And not about little white bears in tin eggs from another world! The council will meet in emergency session this morning. Do you know why?"

Savorn shook his head. "That can wait. What I have to—"

"Quiet! The council is meeting to consider an ultimatum from the Southern Nation. Either we halt our barrier research or they attack."

"But they can't dictate internal affairs!"

The other waved him silent. "Fortunately, we're spared the embarrassment of yielding, since we've already abandoned the project. I summoned you to show you the seriousness of going counter to public opinion."

Savorn should have been impressed with the ultimatum. But somehow it hardly seemed to matter now. "Last night I was in—"

"You see, Savorn," Chimur cut in, "even though I've been rough on you, I realize that basically, as a cub just starting out on a semi-public career—"

"There's an outer-world creature among us!" Savorn shouted finally.

The Chief Ursa's reaction was as though someone had fired a cannon under his snout. "What's that?"

"A being from beyond the Shimmering Cliff—Councilor Murdas! Hidden in his grotto last night, I watched him turn into a glittering monster, then into an other-world creature! I suspected Murdas was a subversive agent. But—"

An infuriated growl sounded and Savorn whirled around to see the trembling hulk of Murdas in the doorway, his vestigial fangs bared, the naked brown skin of his face flushed with rage.

But the councilor momentarily restrained himself, glancing respectfully at Chimur. "Sir?"

"I've no choice, Murdas, but to grant you the privilege of vindication under the ursine code of physical encounter, since you have been rashly accused."

Dismayed, Savorn edged away from the advancing Murdas.

"This can't be settled by the normal ursine code, Chimur!"

"Should you decide to challenge," Chimur told the councilor, "I would suggest that you do so on the basis of the more logical and damaging accusation of subversion."

Murdas spread his arms, limbered his great shoulders and advanced cautiously. "I challenge!"

Savorn faced the unursine thing uncertainly. But then a sudden determination seized him. What better way to tear away the councilor's disguise than through physical encounter?

Murdas, suppressing a growl, lunged and swung his mighty paw in a blow that might well have taken off Savorn's head if he hadn't ducked.

Pivoting, he raked the councilor's midsection, shredding three layers of clothing. But the swiping nails encountered only down-covered flesh, failing to penetrate the disguise or contact the hidden metal box.

Murdas unleashed another vicious blow that caromed off Savorn's shoulder and clouted his head with a force that sent him reeling back.

Then the councilor charged, both paws swinging furiously. Trapped in a corner, Savorn took two of the savage blows on his face before he lowered his head and barged out.

The councilor swung around though and seized him in a brutal hug. His chest crushed in the vice of thick-set arms, Savorn struggled desperately to send his paws raking through the creature's disguise.

Again, with failing strength though, his nails ripped the councilor's clothes, tore his skin. But still there was only the feel of solid flesh under his paw.

Murdas broke the hug and hurled him backwards with a barrage of bludgeoning blows. Through dazed eyes, Savorn caught glimpses of a messenger entering the room, staring at the duel, speaking with Chimur.

Suddenly the Chief Ursa stepped in and seized the councilor's arms. "Hold, Murdas!" Then, "Do you retract on the first count, Savorn?"

Wavering, Savorn stared vapidly at Murdas. The councilor's clothes were tattered. His exposed flesh was laced with crimson creases. There had been no disguise. Murdas was, somehow, only Murdas—nothing more. "I retract."

The councilor, however, was not mollified. "I challenge on the second count!"

But Chimur shoved him back. "I suspend the code of direct challenge. There are matters on which Savorn must be questioned in the interest of security."

He fixed Savorn with a stern stare. "You will return to your den and await our summons."

Savorn didn't remain available for the summons. Instead, he changed clothes and drove out to the shack, grateful for not finding Cella there and not having to answer her solicitous questions about his bruises.

The hydrogen bag was complete and was stretched across its inflation racks. The wire-net covering was being fitted on, together with the valve control device.

"How much longer?" he asked the yellow-hued supervisor.

"We'll start moving compressed cylinders into the pit tonight. Should be ready to blow her up sometime tomorrow."

Savorn cuffed the other. "Rush it. I'm expecting a committee summons that could tie me up."

On the way back to town he struggled futilely with the incident of the previous night. Convinced that Murdas was actually Murdas, he wondered persistently how he had been misled.

Then he realized abruptly that it had been quite dark in the outer grotto and the disguised creature he saw might well have been the counterfeit image of someone else.

He forced the line of thought. If it was a case of mistaken identity, he at least knew now that the camouflaged creature would have to be masquerading as some high official who substantially resembled Murdas.

But there were scores of large, brown-hued officials living in that building—dozens on Murdas's floor alone.

Savorn reconstructed the incident; pictured the out-worlder hurrying down the corridor, frantic because his disguise was failing, darting into the nearest reception grotto to make an adjustment on the metal box.

But who?

He dropped the enigma for the moment, turning instead to the incident of challenge-and-duel in Chimur's office.

The Chief Ursa had stopped the fight after receiving a message. Then he had said that he, Savorn, was to be questioned in the interest of security. What had come up? And, Savorn wondered, how was he implicated?

Shrugging hopelessly, he hurried back to his den. There was much he had to put in order before he soared over the barrier, perhaps never to return—notes to relatives, explanatory messages to officials.

Late that night he was finishing the last letter when the summons from the investigative committee arrived. He would have ignored it except for the fact that the subpoena was delivered by an armed courier who was to escort him back.

In the committee room Savorn, with the courier standing beside him, confronted Chimur and two other councilors.

The Chief Ursa leisurely thumbed through a file folder. Finally he closed the cover and motioned to the courier who opened a side door and let in a guard and a prisoner.

"Savorn," Chimur asked, "do you know this man?" Savorn stiffened. "Thiebok!"

The chief Ursa cleared his throat. "Since your association is so evidently established, we will proceed. How much restricted information have you passed on to this enemy agent?"

"Agent! That's impossible!"

"Denial will do you no good," said one of the other councilors. "Thiebok has already admitted his guilt."

"But I don't understand!" Savorn exclaimed helplessly.

"It's true," Thiebok said. "I'm an agent." He turned to the Chief Ursa. "But Savorn knew nothing about it."

Chimur waved him silent. "It's too late to avoid implicating your accomplice. You've already done that by the fact of your association and by the nature of the information you passed along the wire we traced to you."

"The wire along the Cliff!" Savorn exclaimed. "The transmitter in his den!" He remembered his fight with Murdas, realizing now that the message Chimur had received at the time must have concerned the tracing of the cable.

"So," the Chief Ursa said, smiling, "you admit knowing about the cable. Still, I can't understand why you should plant your soaring light hoax so close to it. Surely you must have known that if we investigated we might find the cable too."

"But I didn't know about it until then either!" Savorn protested.

Chimur shook his head. "You're not very convincing. It would be better to admit that you and Thiebok used your positions for subversive purposes."

"That's not true!"

"Except to avoid implicating you, Thiebok has been quite cooperative," Chimur said, rising. "Perhaps if you two discuss it you'll realize things may go easier for both of you if we get frank cooperation all the way around."

Followed by the other councilors and the armed courier, he retired to an inner chamber. The guard remained at the other end of the room.

"Is it true?" Savorn asked incredulously.

Thiebok nodded.

"Cella?"

"No. She had nothing to do with it."

Savorn felt rage surging within him.

"I know I can't expect you to trust me," Thiebok whispered suddenly. "But I'm not quite the same person who told you only a few days ago that nobody except you and me knew the Southern Nation had armored cars."

"You were aware that Murdas knew it too?"

"I *told* him. I knew he'd let it slip out. But he wouldn't tell you where he got the information since I gave it to him confidentially. I thought that was pretty smart—nursing your distrust so you'd suspect no one else."

Savorn dropped dismally into a chair.

Thiebok stood humbly beside him, his voice a contrite whisper. "But I don't see things that way now. Your Cliff project, those philosophic talks—they convinced me that everything going on inside the barrier is insignificant. That's why I didn't tell them about the bag."

Savorn stared skeptically at him.

"That bag *has* to go over the Cliff!" the other continued.

"Then everything else will be trivial—wars, unimportant. All nations will have to band together to face the outer world."

Still Savorn didn't answer him.

"That's why you're going to go soaring off over your barrier," the other enthused. "Get ready to run." Then, aloud, "Here, take it! Quick!"

He thrust something into Savorn's paw and plopped a similar object into his own mouth. They were two small bits of paper, wadded to resemble pills.

The guard, shouting, lunged forward to grapple with Thiebok. Savorn recognized the strategy: The agent, convinced his prisoners were trying to kill themselves, would forget his weapon as he tried to prevent the suicides.

Reaching Thiebok, the sentry seized him in a headlock and tried to pry his jaws apart. At the same time the prisoner's paw went out unobtrusively to the guard's holster.

There was a single report and the agent collapsed.

"Get out! Hurry!" Thiebok motioned towards the corridor, then turned to face the charge of the armed courier from the inner chamber.

Savorn dived into the hall as the room reverberated with gun-fire. He bounded down the three flights of stairs and lunged through the empty foyer. Then, fearing there might be guards outside, he left the building and started across the terrace.

"Savorn!"

It was Cella. She stood on the sidewalk beside her car. He halted and drew back suspiciously. If Thiebok hadn't lied about her not being implicated in subversion, how could Savorn accept the coincidence that she was here with transportation just when he needed it?

She caught his arm and pushed him into the car. "I was beginning to think they would never release you."

"You know about Thiebok?"

She drove towards the Shimmering Cliff. "I was at the ministry when they came for him. I tried to find you."

"How did you know I was arrested?"

"I drove up in time to watch the courier lead you off."

Outside the city Savorn turned anxiously to see whether they were being followed. But he felt reasonably safe, since barrier-ward would seem to be an illogical direction for him to take.

"Thiebok confessed," he said, watching Cella's reaction. "Then he tricked them so I could escape."

She stared puzzledly at him. "But why?"

"He said he believed in what I'm doing." He studied her expression for some indication whether she was part of Thiebok's plot.

"That sounds like Thiebok," she offered. "But it doesn't sound like an enemy agent. Are you going over the barrier after this?"

"If I get a chance to."

"What do you mean?"

He spread his paws uncertainly. "When we start blowing up that thing it'll be visible for miles. They'll come fast."

By dawn, the burgeoning bag, fed by hissing hydrogen capsules, was already poking up above the tallest trees as Savorn impatiently shouted directions at the cylinder crews. Cella came over. "It'll be two hours before it's filled. Why don't you rest?"

He smiled wearily. "I won't argue. Call me in an hour—or before, if we get a warning from the lookout."

He trudged off towards the shack but started at the sound of an automobile backfiring in the forest.

Fearing an encircling force may have escaped the eyes of the lookout he started off through the woods. Five minutes later he came upon tire tracks on the soft forest floor.

Trotting, he followed them towards the Shimmering Cliff. When he reached the edge of the forest, he found the car parked next to the barrier. Then he drew up dumbfounded. Someone was standing in front of the Cliff, his body cloaked in brilliant coruscations! Meeting no resistance, the figure stepped into the barrier.

Was it the same one who had been in Murdas's outer grotto? Or, Savorn wondered, was there more than one disguised outer-world creature who could slip through the barrier at will and circulate among bearkind?

Three shots sounded from the highway. He whirled around and sprinted back towards the shack on hearing the warning signal. As he reached the clearing, the lookout stumbled up the road from the highway.

"They're coming—three armored cars!" the guard shouted desperately. "They've seen the bag!"

Savorn turned desperately towards the hydrogen sack. It was but little more than half inflated. And there were only minutes left! Already, however, it was straining at its six mooring lines. Was there enough gas in the thing to carry him aloft?

He sprinted for the basket, half hidden in the limp lower folds of the bag. "Start cutting those ropes!"

In the gondola, he pushed the loose cloth to one side and gripped the safety rail as the crew hacked at the taut lines.

With five of the ropes severed, the great sack surged upward, tugging against its final anchor line. The winch lost traction momentarily and the bag lurched, jolting the basket.

The uninflated portion, no longer lying in pleats, now dangled inside the shroud lines like a flaccid tail, hanging curtain-like to the floor of the gondola.

Shots shattered the stillness of the forest a hundred feet below. Savorn leaned over and watched the crew cut the final line. The bag lunged skywards along the face of the Cliff.

He turned to push the dangling cloth out of the way, but his arm contacted something firm behind the material and he brushed it aside.

"I don't know why I did it," Cella said meekly. "But I had to come along."

"You fool!" he shouted. Then, more gently, "You little fool!"

As she clung to him he wondered how he could have suspected she was working with Thiebok. Then suddenly he stiffened, his face awry with alarm.

"The valve release line!" he exclaimed. "It's caught up there somewhere! We can't get down!"

With terrifying speed the bag shot skyward, skimming along the face of the great, gleaming Cliff. Savorn clung tenaciously to the safety rail while Cella held his arm in a desperate grip.

The wind howled through the shroud lines and buffeted the gondola like a cub playing with a ball of yarn. The basket swung, gently and pendulum-like at first, then more violently.

Below, miles below it seemed, tiny scurrying figures were like ants in the clearing. Shading his eyes against the glare of the barrier, he looked down on the outer-world creature's car, still parked alongside the Cliff. It was hardly larger than a gnat now.

The bag brushed against the barrier and was repelled. The motion accentuated the swing of the gondola and Savorn closed his eyes against the frightening, sickening gyrations. The wind, gathering speed to whip up over the Cliff, roared contemptuously and shook the sack as though it were a giant's plaything.

Savorn suddenly felt the numbness of fear for the unknown. He pulled frantically on the dangling material, trying to shake the valve release rope loose.

But the shrieking wind finally caught the bag up in a mighty gust and sent it rushing over the top of the shimmering ridge—away from the green hills and lush forests of his familiar world.

Hesitantly, he stared northward into the outer world. And much of his fright disappeared. The land beyond the barrier was soft and undulating, rising here and there in tall hills and mottled in the same shades of green and tan that characterized the surface of the inner world.

He called encouragingly to Cella. But she was huddled on the floor of the basket.

Swiftly now the barrier fell away and behind as the bag rose at a steep angle. Savorn suddenly discerned outer-world activity a mile below, at the base of the Cliff opposite the spot where the car was parked in the inner world.

A smoothly surfaced road ended abruptly at that point. And numerous unfamiliar vehicles jammed the end of the highway as their occupants, so remote now as to be non-descript, stood alongside and stared up.

Muffled thunder in the distant reaches of the outer world drew his attention and he turned to study a vast expanse of level ground, laid out in a square with squat buildings along one side.

The roaring sound crescendoed and three vivid splotches of light flared in the center of the rectangular area. They stretched skyward like columns of yellow-white fire, finally detaching themselves from the surface and lunging straight up. Within seconds they disappeared in the remote regions of the sky.

Savorn's stare fell earthward from the soaring lights and found another object of wonder in the distance, beyond the rectangle. A city!

But it was—huge! And it was deserted, with its tall spires half covered by deposits of soil which sprouted profuse vegetation.

Impulsively, he stared back at the Shimmering Cliff, noticing that one of the unfamiliar vehicles was moving. It was climbing skyward—towards him!

Apprehensively, he backed across the gondola as he watched the shining disc-shaped thing close in and hover alongside the bag. Through ports in its under-surface, he could see the alien creatures—scores of them, their faces pale and hairless and their eyes staring out eagerly.

From a protuberance atop the disc, a shaft of vivid light stabbed out to encompass the basket. It was a blinding, painful beam that seemed almost as tangible as the material of the Shimmering Cliff.

But it did not repel. Rather, it attracted—swiftly, like a great magnet. The basket, trapped in the cone of brilliance, swung over towards the vessel, dragging along the hydrogen bag.

Then suddenly the intensity of the beam surged mercilessly and he shouted in anguish as he collapsed.

Savorn opened his eyes and stared at the hospital room ceiling for several minutes before grim realization jarred him from his lethargy.

"The Cliff!" he shouted, hurling back the covers.

But the blue-hued paw of a nurse caught his shoulder and forced him back. "You've been under a sedative. You'll be all right."

"The barrier! I was—"

"On the other side." She smiled patiently, as though trying to help him remember. "The whole city watched you go over in your floating bag."

"But—how did I get back?"

"They found you by the Cliff last night."

He tensed, remembering Cella.

The nurse divined his question. "She's resting in the next room. They found her with you."

Savorn closed his eyes, trying to remember all.

But the nurse grasped his arm. "Beyond the Cliff—what's it like? What did you see?"

The door swung open to admit a uniformed guard and Savorn caught a glimpse of the corridor—jammed with a jostling, noisy throng.

Someone thrust a press camera in and a flash bulb's brilliance flooded the room before the guard could close the door behind him.

"You were to call me when he awoke," he reprimanded he nurse. Then, to Savorn, "You're being held in custody. The Chief Ursa is on his way over."

Savorn propped himself up in bed and stared out of the window, Chimur farthest from his mind at present. Instead, he was wrestling with the enigmas—why he had been returned through the Cliff; the nature and purpose of the barrier; its connection with the patently superior beings on the other side.

A prairie dog darted into view on the lawn and Savorn watched the animal bristle and whirl to meet an attack by another of its kind.

It dodged the snapping fangs and seized a broken branch that lay on the ground. Wielding the bough like a club, the defender held the other at bay.

Somehow the little creature seemed vitally important. But Savorn couldn't imagine why. Interested, he watched it parry and thrust and rout its adversary.

And abruptly, like a bit of puzzle fitting into place, a profound awareness of something vastly significant came over him. Somehow it all seemed interrelated—bearkind, the Shimmering Cliff, the alien creatures of the outer world, ursine culture, the intriguing and ingenious prairie dogs—

The din in the corridor welled, intruding on his thoughts, and he turned to watch the Chief Ursa enter and dismiss the nurse.

"War's started, you know," Chimur said, standing beside the bed.

Savorn stared tentatively at him.

"It's your fault," the other continued. But there was no incrimination in his voice—only a shallow indifference.

"When you went up in your bag that was the final provocation. It violated the Southern Nation's ultimatum. That's why Thiebok was so anxious for you to escape. He told us as much after the attack started this morning."

Savorn eyed him appraisingly. "You don't sound too concerned over the attack."

"Actually, I'm not," Chimur casually drew up a chair. "It's really of little consequence."

Savorn felt a sudden suspicion—a vague, nagging suggestion that the Chief Ursa was somehow part of the greater inter-relationship of the barrier and all bearkind, the prairie dog and the outer world. "Why is war of little consequence?"

"Later." The other waved his paw desultorily. Then he turned to the guard. "Let them in."

The press barged in like a torrent. They hurled impatient questions while flash bulbs flared, blinding Savorn to the eager faces behind the cameras.

A semblance of order returned when someone suggested he recount his experiences during his flight over the barrier. Through it all the Chief Ursa leaned back, smiling complacently. Savorn, glancing misgivingly at him, got the impression that he was playing the role of an amused observer.

At the point in his account where he was describing the creatures he had seen in the vessel, one of the reporters waved a pencil at Chimur. "What are your reactions? Can you guarantee it isn't a hoax?"

The Chief Ursa studied the brown fuzz on the back of his paw. "I'll stand behind this story," he said decisively. "It's no hoax."

Savorn frowned uncertainly, wondering how Chimur could back him so unquestioningly now, whereas before the Chief Ursa had skeptically rejected any mention of the outer world and its impossible creatures.

It was as though he had gone through a complete change of attitude. Now he seemed all indulgent and genial, kind and anxious to believe.

"But what does it mean?" someone asked. "If there's an outer world inhabited by intelligent creatures with scaring machines, why haven't they shown themselves?"

Savorn considered telling them about the being he had seen in Murdas's den. Indecisively he turned towards Chimur. But the Chief Ursa had gone to the window.

Then Savorn started as he noticed the other's general out-line, standing out almost as a silhouette against the outdoor light. His reaction was one of fear and indeterminacy commingled with curiosity.

He shifted to see what Chimur was staring at on the lawn.

It was the prairie dog, which was now using a piece of scrap metal to enlarge its burrow entrance.

"I think," Savorn told the reporter thoughtfully, "that their objective is to avoid us."

"Why?"

Savorn motioned through the window. "That animal on the lawn—"

Chimur turned suddenly and held up his paws. "That'll be all for now. There'll be another press conference tomorrow." Savorn had expected just that sort of interruption. Give the public—all the nations—chance to absorb just so much before going on. It would be easier in small doses.

After the others had gone, the Chief Ursa dismissed the guard and stood smiling benignly down at Savorn. There seemed to be pride and approval in his eyes.

But Savorn only squirmed apprehensively. His suspicions weren't vague any longer. He thought of the incident in the officials' residence building—how any brown-hued individual of Murdas's general proportions could have darted into the councilor's outer grotto—how he had even seen Chimur in the corridor earlier.

He had no doubt now but that Chimur was the other-world creature in disguise.

The Chief Ursa threw back his head and laughed.

"Why was I brought back?" Savorn asked finally.

"You'll be needed here. Bearkind is about to go through quite a revolution. Leaders will have to prepare them."

Evidently Chimur was making no attempt to preserve the ruse he had carried on—for how long? Nor was he hesitating to show he was aware of the other's suspicion.

Savorn sat up in bed. "The Shimmering Cliff—what does it mean? How long has it been there?"

Chimur spread his paws. "Thousands of years. It represents perhaps the most prolonged sociological project ever attempted by humanity."

"Humanity?"

"That's a new word for you. It means human—like this."

Chimur's paw flicked in front of his waist and seemed to disappear into his clothes. There was a split-second flash of shimmering substance around his body and Savorn shut his eyes instinctively. Then the odor of the alien thing that he had smelled in Murdas's grotto was back—strong. Reluctantly he opened his eyes.

The outer-world creature was standing in Chimur's place—pale-skinned, dressed in tight-fitting garments, his paws fingering the box strapped around his waist.

Savorn drew back frightened at first. But then there seemed to be nothing threatening about the figure. Instead the same geniality that Chimur had shown during the past few minutes had transferred itself to this tall, lean shape. The brilliant aura flared again and when it was gone there stood the familiar figure of the Chief Ursa once more.

"Afraid?" he asked.

Savorn only gaped.

"The Cliff, or the crude device that preceded it," Chimur resumed, "has been there ever since the first great genetic changes were observed among your predecessors—ever since mutational nakedness drove a few of your species away from hibernation and to the discovery of fire.

"We built simple barriers that were no more than fences at first. That was sufficient then, since it made no difference even if we circulated among you at that stage in your cultural development.

"But as your social groups evolved, creating the need for more complete isolation, so did human technology advance. Eventually we were able to generate the Shimmering Cliff as it exists today. But even that was before your earliest recorded history—before we had to disguise the observers and guides we placed among you."

Savorn mentally staggered before the concept of human intelligence—an intelligence that must have almost reached its fruition millennia before the first primitive bear discovered fire.

"But why?" he asked, perplexed.

"I think you know. I think you guessed it when you drew the press's attention to that prairie dog."

Savorn stared up pensively. "There's room for only one dominant species in a given environment. The race that evolves first stifles the development of all others."

The Chief Ursa nodded soberly. "We like to imagine the existence of a 'cultural corridor,' with the various candidate species trying to advance along that corridor. But once any one group makes appreciable headway, the door is closed to all others."

He drew in a philosophic breath. "It isn't that the advanced race would purposely throttle the lesser one—resentfully kill them off. Rather, it's something that happens automatically. Finding themselves surrounded by such overwhelming superiority, the rejected candidates are culturally frustrated. They face a barrier much more insurmountable than the Shimmering Cliff."

Savorn was still wrestling with the concept of observers masquerading among bearkind.

"You said you sent *guides* among us. Why?"

Chimur stared vacantly out of the window. "When we decided to isolate bearkind, we had just achieved flight between worlds." He smiled. "Not inner and outer worlds—but the true worlds of planetary proportions. We realized then that there would some day be travel between worlds of different stars and that mankind might eventually quit the world of his origin. Wouldn't it be a pity if there were no species to whom we could bequeath the heritage we enjoyed here?"

Savorn sat up stiffly. "So you tried to qualify the heirs!"

"We isolated your species to give you the privacy in which to develop your culture. And we sent observers and guides to help you along. We were working against the day when the barrier could come down and you would inherit the earth.

"We guided your technical progress and disguised representatives in all your nations. Such supervision was necessary. There were times when your research took forbidden paths and had to be discouraged—such as wireless transmission, which would have allowed you to intercept our messages and become aware of us."

"And the hydrogen bag too," Savorn reminded. "You tried to kill that, didn't you?"

"Yes, we did. You see, it was established millennia ago that when you proved yourself capable of surmounting the Shimmering Cliff, that would automatically qualify you for your heritage."

"Then fighting the project," Savorn protested, "was unfair!"

"Not quite. We had assumed that by then you would have eliminated warfare as a social characteristic. So, even though you qualified on one score, you didn't on the other."

"Why didn't you show us how to stop wars?"

The other shrugged. "That's something that can't be shown, Savorn. It has to be learned for one's self if it's going to stick.

Savorn rose and paced, ending up at the window. He turned to face the Chief Ursa. "What's the verdict? Will the barrier come down despite our propensity for war?"

Smiling, Chimur nodded. "You see, we forgot that the *human race* didn't learn to control its propensity for war until after it had opened up an unlimited number of worlds through space travel. We realized finally that it was unfair to expect more of bearkind.

"Anyway, access to the outer world will take the pressure off your cramped nations. It should be a thousand years before the necessity for war arises again. By then you may have purged it out of your system."

Overwhelmed by the conceptual avalanche, Savorn stood staring mutely at the prairie dog that was still using the piece of scrap metal as a shovel.

Chimur came over and laid a paw on his shoulder. "Beyond the barrier, in the ruins left by the human race, you'll find much to

219

advance your progress—but nothing to help you get off your new world. Such information has been carefully removed. That's something else you'll have to accomplish for yourself. By the time you achieve space travel I hope you are farther along the cultural corridor than we were at that period."

Savorn eyed him quizzically. "The human race is ready to leave now?"

Chimur laughed. "It left a thousand years ago. Those still here are only the personnel of Project Barrier. When the Cliff comes down in a few days we'll be gone too."

Savorn looked down at his paws. "About the barrier…"

"Yes?"

Hesitantly, Savorn glanced out of the window again. The prairie dog had finished enlarging its burrow entrance and was pushing several pieces of scrap metal down the hole.

"Would the secret of the barrier be too much to ask for?"

Why do you want that?"

Savorn gestured towards the animal. "That little fellow out there—he has his foot in the door of a cultural corridor too."

www.ingramcontent.com/pod-product-compliance
Lightning Source LLC
Chambersburg PA
CBHW022018170626
46808CB00001B/464